First
Love
Language

First Love Lang

破碎的心，破碎的家
Broken Hearts and Broken Homes

If home is where the heart is, then a broken home must mean that a heart is broken, too. Especially right now, since I'm supposed to be leaving for Salt Lake City. Instead of packing, I'm lying on my stomach while carpet fibers tickle that part of my waistline where my Del Rey High shirt has risen. No matter how many times I've vacuumed this floor, it still smells like cigarettes from the previous renters. My wrist cramps from holding my head up. I have boxes to take down to the car, yet I can't stop staring at the Polaroid of my chubby three-year-old self in the arms of a biological mother whose name is about the only thing I remember.

Ya-Fang and I smile for the camera in front of a pagoda. The pillars are as red as the lanterns lining the streets. The doorways are accented by a gold so vibrant that even in this outdated photograph, it reflects the sunlight of a bright Taiwan day. But where exactly was this picture taken? Was it in Taipei, the city where I was born? Or was it Keelung, the city Ya-Fang grew up in?

No matter how badly I want to ask Ya-Fang, I can't. I was five when she and Dad divorced. She stayed behind in Taipei, and we left for America. And it's not like I can ask Dad why they split either. When I was five, he told me it was so that I could experience America. But the older I've gotten, the more

I've realized that *experiencing America* is a bribe a parent tells a child. There's something more. Something so complex, I might be able to understand it only now. But I'll never be able to ask him, because he's been dead for two years. His body rests at Sunshine Cemetery—which is a bit of an oxymoron, in my opinion.

"Mavis! I don't want to keep having this conversation." My adoptive mom's voice seeps through the apartment's thin walls. "It's just for the summer. We'll be back in time for your senior year. I promise."

"If it's just for the summer, then why did we sell all the furniture?" my sister bites back.

If I've heard them fight once, I've heard them a thousand times. For now, I'd rather focus on the resemblances Ya-Fang and I share than listen to Mom and Mavis. Between our heart-shaped faces and petite noses, there's no doubt that I look more like Ya-Fang than I do my adopted family. After all, Mom and Mavis share the same blood. Even their voices sound alike—Mom with her raspy alto and Mavis with the same but just a tad more nasally.

"You know why." Mom's voice filters through my bedroom door. "I'm doing the best I can for all of us."

Mom sold our furniture to pay off our rent or else her credit score would've dropped. Besides, it's not like we can find a storage unit to keep our bed frames and couches. Those are hundreds of dollars a month. Mom has just enough money to drive us out to Utah. Assuming the car doesn't break down along the way.

Mavis doesn't say more. Instead of a response, the front door opens and slams with so much force that the entire unit rattles. My closet door even swings open.

I used to think my room was haunted. Between the slightest drafts opening the closet, the lights flickering in the bathroom, and the strange noises that turned out to be our neighbor's cats, I'd constantly tell Mom that we needed to move out. But I'd meant somewhere else in San Diego where Casper and his buddies wouldn't haunt us. Not Mormon City, Utah.

I sigh and shut my baby book. Mavis probably went out to the car, which means it's time for me to start packing again. I rise to my feet, carrying the questions I never asked Dad while he was alive: *Why did you really divorce Ya-Fang? If you'd stayed together, would I still be destined to move to Utah?* But most importantly: *Why did you have Andrea adopt me instead of giving me back to my bio mom?*

Because of the adoption, my American birth certificate doesn't even say Ya-Fang Linn anymore. Honestly, at this point, I'm not sure if her Western name is spelled with one *n* or two. If it weren't for the memories printed into this photo album, I'd have nothing tethering me to her at all. Guess I'm just lucky like that.

My door opens and Mom's voice flutters in. "Hey, Catie. How's the packing going?"

I turn my back to her so she can't see the album in my hands. It's not that I'm ashamed of looking at it. I just don't want to cause her any pain if she catches me fantasizing about a time when I'd never met her. When I never called Mavis my younger sister—if only by three months. I love Mom as if she's my biological mother because she's the only maternal figure I have. But that doesn't mean I've ever stopped thinking about Ya-Fang. Especially now that Dad's dead.

"I finished packing." I force a cheery voice as I set the baby book in my box of cherished items. Inside are Dad's old textbooks from flight school. His Bible and Book of Mormon—books I'd carry with me if I actually went to church. Even his name tag from when he served his mission in Taiwan is already packed—Elder Carlson, the young yellow-haired Mandarin-speaking kid from Idaho.

"I'll pack this in the car right now." I set my baby book on top of Dad's copy of *The Five Love Languages*. I have vague memories of him reading this book in bed and scratching out the sexist comments to write in his *own* progressive advice. He seemed to read this thing a lot during that phase after the divorce and before he met Andrea. Maybe this was the book that led him to her. I never asked when he was alive. I was just a kid—too young to realize I should take advantage of the time I *did* have with Dad. But asking Mom about it now doesn't feel like the best time.

I secure the box's lid as Mom's hand rests on my shoulder. When I turn, she's peering at me with a worried smile and an eleven folded between her brows. Mom and I are about the same height even though we look nothing alike. Her hair is thin and bright like the sun. Mine is thick and darker than midnight. Her eyes are blue like the skies Dad used to fly his planes through. Mine are soil brown. No wonder the school staff gives us weird looks when I bring her to parent-teacher conferences.

I offer Mom a dimpled smile, but it doesn't reach my eyes. "Is there anything else I should carry down with me?"

"What's wrong, Catie?" Mom asks, ignoring my question. Of course, she can see through my façade. "You've hardly said a word all day."

My gaze dips to the imprint of my body on the carpet. "I'm not looking forward to moving in with Aunt Joanna. That's all."

Ugh. Just saying her name tastes like lead. I hardly know anything about Aunt Joanna. But judging by the scripture verses and political stances she's posted on Facebook, I have a feeling that someone as biracial as *me* isn't quite *white* enough for *her*. And someone as *pansexual* as Mavis is definitely not *straight* enough for her. And considering that Mom drinks coffee and curses occasionally, she's definitely not Mormon enough for Aunt Joanna's standards.

Mom sighs. "I'm not looking forward to moving in with my sister either."

So why, then? I want to ask. But I already know the answer. We need to move in with Aunt Joanna because Mom lost her job as a personal trainer when the owners sold their gym. We need to move because the housing costs in San Diego are climbing, and Mom is unemployed. We need to move because we have no other choice.

I clear my throat and blink away tears. Now isn't the time to whine about our situation. We should've been on the road first thing this morning.

"We're already behind schedule," I say, faking a yawn so Mom won't notice my tears. "You should drop off the apartment key so we can get going."

Mom doesn't have a chance to reply because I scoop up the box and hurry out my bedroom door. I pass Mavis's room, which is unrecognizable now that her piles of laundry aren't everywhere. I pass the living area that Mom converted into her studio sleeping space. She'd set a paper screen between her twin bed and the couch. Not once did she ever ask Mavis and me to turn the TV down while she was trying to sleep. This place may have never been haunted by ghosts, but it will forever haunt my memories as one of the few places I've called home.

I carry my box down to the parking lot. The late morning sun radiates off the asphalt, sending beads of sweat rolling down my spine. Palm trees stretch into the sky but are too high up to offer any shade. It's kind of weird to see this type of sun in the middle of June Gloom. Normally, summer break starts with low clouds and heavy drizzle. But of course, today is bright and sunny. An overcast sky would've been too ironic.

Mavis sits on the curb beside Mom's Subaru, short hair pulled into a tight ponytail. Her AirPods are in, which is code for *leave me alone*. From the back, she looks exactly like Mom. From the side, her rounded jawline and thick brows are remnants from a biological father she's never met. Mom had a one-night stand in college, but Dad's been the only dad either of us has ever known.

Mavis and I have lived at this complex since freshman year. We dropped eggs with parachutes from the stairwell because we needed something for our science project. We watched the raccoons crawl through the dumpsters because we were bored on a Friday night and didn't feel like attending the football game. The rocks in the succulent garden are still misplaced from that time Mavis chased an iguana through the bushes.

I resist the urge to join Mavis on the curb and instead shovel the last box inside Mom's five-passenger Subaru. The back bench is folded down to make room for the bags of clothing, the boxes of bathroom essentials, and even my beach bag–size makeup tote. There's just enough space for me to sit behind the driver's seat while our TV rests beside me in a blanket cocoon.

Mom joins us after returning the apartment key to the front office. Mavis and I pile inside wordlessly, and Mom pulls out of the complex and heads toward the freeway. We ride past Roasters Coffee—the Gucci one, not the crusty one near Francisca's house. No, the one by her place has a busted toilet seat. Gucci Roasters has bar stools.

My phone vibrates in my pocket. I pull it out to see a text from the very friends I'm thinking about:

FRANCISCA: Are you in LA yet?

JIMMY: Man I miss you guys already. Can't believe you left me here with Fran.

MAVIS: Nah just leaving SD now

My fingers hover over the group chat. There's so much more I want to say, but writing it out won't even come close to expressing what I feel.

Mom stops at an intersection where seagulls weigh down the telephone wires. The hum of cars zooming across the freeway dulls out the sound of Adele singing over the radio. Then the light turns green, and Mom continues under the overpass.

Mavis pulls an AirPod from her ear. "I thought we were going through LA. Why are we heading to the beach?"

"I need to make one more stop," Mom answers.

Mavis doesn't ask any more questions. I keep my gaze locked on the view out the window. Shopping plazas morph into seaside mansions. The dark ocean plays peekaboo in between storefronts. Mom follows the curve of the road until the sidewalks and vegetation vanish. Now we're hugging the lip of a cliff that overlooks the Pacific. I know exactly where we're going long before Sunshine Cemetery appears.

The iron gates are opened wide like arms asking for a hug. Tombstones rise out of the ground in perfect rows as Mom drives us deeper inside. Saying goodbye to Dad should bring me comfort. It's been two years; I should've made peace with his passing by now, right? And yet my fingers fist the hem of my shirt.

Mom follows the pavement until it stops at a plot of grass and dandelions. A black fence separates the edge of the property from a sharp cliff sinking into the ocean. From here, clear skies and cold water stretch until they kiss at the horizon. Overhead, the roar of a plane vibrates the boxes inside the car. Is it a commercial jet landing at the airport? Or is it a naval aircraft flying drills? Dad always knew what model those planes were just by their silhouettes. And some part of me imagines he's the one who made the skies clear today so I can see the planes waving me goodbye.

I climb out of the car and slide my trembling fingers into my pockets. I can't stop staring at my shoelaces. I can't look at Dad's name carved in granite, knowing that although I've had two years to make good on the promise I made at his death-bed, somehow, I've done the complete opposite.

Mom and Mavis join my side silently, and I can only imagine what they're thinking. Mom is probably reminiscing about all the times Dad swept her off her feet. Mavis is probably remembering that time Dad stayed up until 3:00 a.m. to help her type a book report. And me . . .

I lift my gaze from the crunchy grass to Dad's tombstone.

"WE MUST FIRST BELIEVE IN OURSELVES
BEFORE WE CAN BECOME OUR BEST SELVES."
Captain Roderick Carlson
Beloved Husband and Father
Rest in Peace

My vision swims as I read and reread the quote on Dad's headstone—his mantra. Dad was an Idaho potato farmer who believed he could conquer the sky. If someone like him could do something impossible, then his daughters should be able to do the same. The last words he said to me before slipping into a coma were "Promise me you'll become your true self."

But when he'd whispered that with dry, chapped lips, I hadn't been thinking about me. Every thought was about *him*. Was *he* going to pull through? Was *he* in pain? Why did this have to happen to *him*?

But now that he's been gone for two years, I'm realizing that I should've taken advantage of the time *I* had with him. I should've asked him about where *I* came from. I should've asked what he thought divorcing Ya-Fang would do to *me*. I should've asked how he expects me to be my true self when I don't even know who *I am*.

Hot tears stream down my face, and I wipe them with the back of my hand. I've let two years slide by, and I'm no closer to keeping Dad's promise than I was the day I sprinkled dirt over his coffin. Moving to Utah is the wake-up call I need. And when I come back to San Diego, I'll be the version of me he always knew I could be.

全家福

Family Portraits

I've had seven hundred and fifty miles to mentally prepare for this moment, and I'm *still* not ready to meet Aunt Joanna. We've slogged through the standstill traffic of Southern California, spent the night in the barren Nevada desert, and climbed over the winding mountains of Utah. Now, Mom's parking the Subaru on Aunt Joanna's power-washed driveway, and I have no choice but to stare at her mountainside manor.

Wood pillars hold up the house's stone frame, giving it the appearance of a celebrity ski lodge. But the bees buzzing around the flower garden also give this home a cozy cottage feel. I hate it.

"Three states, two days, and a partridge in a pear tree later, we've finally made it," Mavis grumbles from the passenger seat. "Hey, Catie. Wanna make a bet to see which one of us throws ourselves off a cliff first?"

"Mavis!" Mom exclaims before I can even gasp. "Do not *ever* speak like that again."

"Oh, so I'm not allowed to say how I feel. Got it." Mavis folds her arms and sinks deeper into her seat.

"You can talk to me about anything," Mom says, her voice softer now.

Mavis snorts. "You're such a hypocrite. You literally just said—"

I stop paying attention. I've listened to them fight enough to know their arguments never go anywhere. So I unbuckle my seat belt and grab my box of treasures before stepping outside, Mom's and Mavis's voices muffled by the car door.

The Taylors' house should be inviting with its cherrywood and mosaic of glass panels carved in the middle. There's even a *Wipe Your Paws* mat welcoming me onto the patio—so, green flag, right? But the sight doesn't make it any easier to breathe.

I inhale until my lungs can't expand farther. *Act like you love this, Catie. You've gotta start somewhere.* I ring the doorbell. Chimes sound throughout the mansion, and a muffled dog bark replies to the call. It's too late to step back now.

A bob of hair shimmers behind the glass. A flash of smiling teeth. A flowing white blouse. Then the door swings open.

"Oh, Catie! It's so good to see you!" Aunt Joanna clasps her hands at her chest like she's an old-timey actress who's been gifted a string of pearls.

Now it's *my* turn to be the actress. I'll convince her that I love living in Salt Lake City. That I don't miss San Diego. That I *belong* in the Taylor household.

"Aunt Joanna! It's so nice to see you again." The lie is bitter. I swallow it like medicine.

"Goodness, look at how much you've grown. You only came up to my knees the last time I saw you."

Sheesh. When was that—at Mom and Dad's wedding? How old was I—seven? Honestly, I don't remember anything about Aunt Joanna being there. Maybe that's because all I *do* know is that Dad married Mom outside of the temple. The reception was at a Mormon church building. Dad's always been a ProgMo—the kind of Mormon who believes the church's principles are true, but is progressive enough to call out the sexism and homophobia in the doctrine, too. That's probably one of the reasons why he married Mom. She grew up in the culture even though she doesn't practice anymore.

"You haven't changed a bit," I say, feeding Aunt Joanna something she probably wants to hear.

Aunt Joanna strokes her face as if hiding a modest blush. She must know I'm lying, right? It would be impossible for her to look as young as she did a decade ago. Creases carve into her cheeks from years of smiling. Strands of golden hair cover the sunspots dotting her forehead. But her eyebrows are perfectly groomed, as if she never goes more than a week without an appointment.

"Where are your mother and sister?" Aunt Joanna asks.

I nod up the driveway to where Mavis and Mom are still arguing inside the Subaru. With the sun reflecting off the windshield, I can't see them from here.

"They'll be over in a sec. I was so excited to see you that I wanted to ring the doorbell first." *Lie.*

"Oh, that's so sweet," Aunt Joanna says, opening the door wide enough for me to step through. "You can start unpacking everything in the basement. I promise it's not as scary as it sounds."

Aunt Joanna's foyer is so grand that my footsteps echo despite wearing sneakers. Though this house is now my summer home, I get the impression that my T-shirt and pajama pants don't fit the black-tie ambience. A chandelier reflects rainbow prisms over the stark white family portraits hanging on the stark white walls. Even though my cousins' faces greet me with smiles, I swear their noses are turned up as if I smell as foul as I look.

Paws tap-dance across the wood floor, and a golden retriever appears at my hip.

"Oh, Maddie Sue," Aunt Joanna scolds when the dog licks my elbow. "Stop that!"

"It's okay. I like dogs." *Truth.* I've always preferred animals to people.

"Well, that's good. We got Maddie Sue for Rayleigh after Auburn and Tavie moved out for college. Rayleigh's been looking forward to meeting you and Mavis since I first told her you were coming."

"Oh, that's amazing." I smile and try to remember which one of my cousins Rayleigh is. Other than the fact that she's the youngest of the five Taylor kids, I know nothing about her. "I can't wait to get to know her better." *Truth . . . ish?*

Honestly, I want nothing to do with any of the Taylors. But I really shouldn't be judging my cousin so harshly before I've even met her. After all, that's the last thing I want any of *them* to do to *me*.

Maddie Sue dusts her tail back and forth as Aunt Joanna leads me to the stairwell.

"Watch your step," Aunt Joanna says, descending into the basement.

I should keep my eyes glued to the carpeted stairwell leading me down. But all I can stare at are the temples, Bible verses, and pictures of whitewashed Jesus mapping their way down the wall. It was only a matter of time before seeing all this Mormon stuff reminded me of the expectations Aunt Joanna has of us. Pray before every meal. Go to church every Sunday. No swearing. No coffee. And *no* questioning the rules.

"Ta-da!"

Aunt Joanna hits the lights once we reach the basement. This living space is twice the size of our apartment. A theater screen appears on the far wall. Shelves of books and board games tower on either side of it. A sofa the size of a trampoline sits in a semicircle in the middle of the room.

My shoulders close around my neck like a turtle shell. All this room and nowhere to hide.

"Down the hall are the bedrooms that used to belong to Auburn and Tavie," Aunt Joanna says, referring again to her eighteen-year-old twin daughters who recently moved to Brigham Young University. "Since you came down here first, I suppose you get to choose which room you want."

I nod. I'll do anything to swim out of this sea-size living room. "You're a lifesaver, Aunt Joanna. Thanks for opening your home to us."

That's supposed to be my segue to sneak away, but Aunt Joanna continues. "I'm so glad you're here, Catie. I think this will be a great opportunity for you and your family to find Heavenly Father again."

My smile flickers. Five minutes. That's how long it took for Aunt Joanna to start preaching. Since leaving the church, a part of me misses the certainty of eternal happiness offered by Mormon Sky Daddy. I understand why Aunt Joanna and Dad liked going to church. It gave them purpose, belonging, structure—and basically everything I want now. But I can't worship a god who let my father die knowing I'd be alone on this floating blue rock. And most importantly, I don't need someone else telling me how to pray, tithe, and be baptized just so I can see Dad again in the afterlife. Honestly, it's kind of messed up that Mormon God holds family members hostage like that, but whatever.

"I know you girls are less active now, but you'll love the people in our ward," Aunt Joanna says, patting my arm. "Church is going to set you on the right path, don't you worry."

"Yeah, Aunt Joanna. I'm sure it will." *Lie.* Maybe this is going to be harder than I thought.

"It's like Mosiah says in the Book of Mormon . . ."

Oh, no. I haven't even picked out a room yet and Aunt Joanna's about to recite a scripture verse. My lips hurt from the strain of faking a smile.

Aunt Joanna clears her throat. *"Yea, and as often as my people repent—"*

"There you are, Jo!" Mom leans over the railing above our heads. Flyaways poke out of her ponytail. The Coke stain on her hoodie is still there from when she spilled it during the drive. But seeing her disheveled self restores the oxygen to my lungs. Living with Aunt Joanna is going to suck. But at least with Mom's dynamic around, it'll suck less.

"Do you think you can open the garage for Mavis?" Mom asks. "It might be easier for her to haul the boxes in that way instead of going through the front door."

I swallow the lump in my throat. Ideally, the fact that Mavis is bringing boxes inside means that she and Mom have reached a truce.

"Of course!" Aunt Joanna says, bounding up the stairs.

Mom shifts her focus to me. She must notice something is wrong, because she frowns the moment we lock eyes. Instead of following Aunt Joanna to the garage, Mom marches down the stairs. "Did she already promise to write your name in the temple or something? Or was she going to make your uncle Nick give you a priesthood blessing for comfort?"

She's being funny, but I can't laugh. When I have no response, Mom sits on the bottom step. She doesn't need to speak for me to understand. I set my box down and join her. This is our thing—stair talk time.

I remember sitting on the cracked concrete steps outside our apartment when she explained what was happening the first day I got my period. When she told me about Dad's diagnosis. When she first confessed we'd be moving to Utah for the summer. She's the greatest mother I've ever known, and yet I don't know how to talk to her about Ya-Fang. How do I tell Mom that I love her, but in some illogical way, I love Ya-Fang too?

"Growing up, I used to tell Joanna that she needed to smoke with me so that she would finally get off her high horse," Mom says, breaking the silence. "And join me on my own *high* horse. She never did, though."

I chuckle against my will. "How are you even sisters?"

Mom smirks. "Believe me, Catie, I've been asking myself the same question for almost forty years. Jo's always been the 'better child.' And look at us now. I'm her homeless older sister, and she knows she's the only person I can go to for help. I'm sorry that we're stuck here. I know how much this hurts you and Mavis."

I stare down at my hands, pretending to be fascinated by the creases on my palms. If I follow one of these lines, will it carry me to a happy future far from here?

"I know you're trying your best, Mom," I say, even though these words are seven hundred and fifty miles overdue. "I love you."

Mom squeezes my arm. "I love you too. And I know I've already asked you to do so much in these past few weeks. But do you think you could do one more thing for me?"

Suddenly, I'm not as marveled by the shape of my hands. I blink up at Mom, holding her gaze and waiting for her to make another request. Though she shares the same blue eyes and thin lips as Aunt Joanna, all I see is Mom. "What is it?"

"I need you to try to be happy," Mom says with a tired smile. "I want you to have fun this summer. I want you and Mavis to find jobs that you love and make friends. But most of all, I want you to know that despite *this*"—Mom gestures to this strange house in this strange city—"you are loved. So very, very much."

Tears well in my eyes because when Mom says she loves me, it reminds me of the way Dad used to say it to her. Like it was an unchanging fact on par with plants needing sunlight. I nestle against her neck and whisper, "I promise."

鎖在鏡中

Confined to a Mirror

I'm hiding in the back seat of Mom's Subaru with my giant makeup tote and a hand mirror. Unlike the lighting in Aunt Joanna's board-game dungeon, Mom's car offers a *real* golden hour filter. Today's makeup needs to make me appear confident, competent, and like someone who is totally fit for any job—even though the only work experience I've ever had is babysitting. I'm feeling good about my job hunting prospects today. Or maybe I just know I look good in this honeydew glow.

Rays fall across my face, catching the ruby streaks in my obsidian hair. Morning sun rims my irises with molten amber. I emphasize them by gluing on a pair of winged lashes. The air-conditioning rumbles from the front seat as Harry Styles serenades me from the radio. I sing along while mapping minty lip gloss over my nude outline.

Finally. A peaceful—

The driver's-side door bursts open and Mavis throws herself into the seat. "I hate this! I hate this! *I hate this!*"

I jerk my mirror away. Mavis doesn't normally come to me with her problems. If she wants to talk, she'll go to Mom or sometimes she'll rant in our group chat.

The last time she vented to me was when Dad was still around. Back when the whites in his eyes were yellow from jaundice, but before he got bedridden. He smiled when he overheard her telling me that she had a crush on the nonbinary AMAB kid in our math class. She wasn't sure if that meant she was queer, and if she was, what did that mean for her as a Mormon? Dad gave her advice then. Gay, straight, bi—he didn't care. He just wanted her to know that life is too short to live it without ever knowing who she is truly.

"Do you see this, Catie?" Mavis whirls around and tugs at the collar of a heather jacket zipped up to her neck. "I was going to wear a crop top today, but Aunt Joanna made me throw this on. It's going to be ninety-seven degrees! But noooo. A Young Woman needs to be *modest*."

I sigh. Back when Mavis and I were active Mormons, we were shunned for wearing two-piece, high-waisted tankinis . . . despite them covering the same amount of skin as a one-piece would. But here in the Taylor home? Tank tops are to be substituted with T-shirts, because heaven forbid we should show off our provocative shoulders. And shorts? If they don't sink past our knees, then we're basically harlots. Goodbye, feeling the wind on our legs. Or in Mavis's case, feeling the wind on her elbows. Heck—on her collarbones, for that matter.

"Don't you have some T-shirts you can wear instead?" I ask, capping my lip gloss.

"Kay. Tee." Mavis barks my name in syllables. "I did *not* get voted best dressed two years in a row by wearing *T-shirts*. Look at you. Makeup is your thing. Me, on the other hand—I can't wear anything that doesn't make me feel like a mummy!"

Yikes. My morning routine may have been my "me time,"

but venting in a minivan before the birds have a chance to sing is apparently Mavis's new thing.

I return the lip gloss to my tote. "If it makes you feel better, I showed Aunt Joanna my camera roll of makeup looks last night. She told me I didn't need to work so hard to look so beautiful because of my *naturally ethnic features*."

Mavis gags. "Shut up."

I wish I were joking, but this isn't my first rodeo with microaggressions. Except this one pierced a little deeper because it came from someone who should've known better. But what am I supposed to do? Tell Aunt Joanna what she can or can't say to me in her own home?

"That's why I came out here to do my makeup. I couldn't really get in the zone, knowing that Aunt Joanna was judging me for covering up my—"

Repeating her words is already more times than enough. I sigh to quell my rising temper, because right now, this is about Mavis. She's opening up to me without Mom around—which is good, right? Big steps! Building a better relationship with Mavis shouldn't be this hard. But after Dad took his paternal advice to the grave, it's like we forgot how to be sisters.

"Look, I'm sorry this whole situation sucks," I sigh, hoping she feels my sincerity. "But maybe you just have to be sneaky about what you wear. Kind of like how I'm sneaking out here with my makeup. Take your jacket off when we go job hunting. I won't tell Aunt Joanna."

"Loopholes don't solve anything." Mavis claws at her face, pulling at her freckled cheeks as if her skin is made of rubber. "I want to be free, Catie. Free! I don't want someone else telling me what to do, or say, or wear. It's bad enough Aunt Joanna is requiring us to go to church with her every Sunday. I shouldn't have to jump through hoops just to feel like myself! I'm an eagle, Catie. I long for the sky!"

I narrow my eyes. Did she even *try* to understand what I said? Seriously. What's the point of coming to me for advice if she's not going to take it?

"Stop being so dramatic," I scoff. "You're a peacock, Mavis. All feathers, no flight."

Mavis's face sours. But there's a flicker of something else behind her gaze. Before I can make sense of her expression, she flips back around and clenches the steering wheel. I get the feeling she's going to let out an exasperated scream, but something has caught her attention.

"Oh, great," Mavis grumbles, jutting her chin out at the windshield. "Look who's here for round two."

I glance in her direction. Rayleigh waves as she hurries up the driveway. She's no longer dressed in the mismatched pajama set she wore at last night's dinner. Loose, red-blond hair flows down her back in frizzy curls. A floral sundress drapes to her ankles. The dress itself has spaghetti straps. So in typical Mormon fashion, Rayleigh wears a white T-shirt underneath to make it modest. I'd cringe if she wasn't exactly the person I wanted to see right now. Mavis isn't going to yell at me if there's someone else in the car with us.

"Goodie." Mavis shifts in her seat. "I bet Aunt Joanna sent Rayleigh to spy on us. Guess this jacket stays on. And so much for my freedom to say swear words like f—"

"Hey, guys!" Rayleigh says, opening Mavis's door.

"Sup, cuz," Mavis replies flatly.

"Can I tag along with you today?" Rayleigh smiles, revealing a set of blue-and-green braces. Between her round cheeks and rectangular glasses, she looks more like a twelve-year-old than someone who's just finished her freshman year of high school.

"Sure," I say.

Despite Mavis's accusation, Rayleigh doesn't seem like she's here to report our sins back to Aunt Joanna. Based on last night's dinner and board-game extravaganza, she seems genuinely interested in us. And a piece of me wants to learn more about her, too. Since I don't have Ya-Fang in my life, and Dad was an only child, the Taylors are the only extended family I have left, and they're not even biologically mine.

"Yeah. Join us. Come to the Dark Side," Mavis mumbles.

I kick my sister's seat. Does she really have to be like this?

Rayleigh shuts Mavis's car door and races around to ride in the passenger seat. We buckle up as Mavis begrudgingly pulls out of the driveway. Now that Rayleigh's here, we don't have any excuse to sit in a parked car, so Mavis drives us down the mountainside.

Mansions made of towering glass windows and stone chimneys roll past. Checkered patterns have been mowed into sprawling lawns, and every pine tree is trimmed into the perfect Christmas shape. Cadillacs and Teslas park on driveways large enough to fit a tennis court. Seriously, what do these people do for a living?

"Did you do your own makeup?" My cousin spins around in her seat to talk to me.

"Of course." I toss my hair over my shoulder playfully.

"That's so cool." Rayleigh beams.

I arch my brow. Aunt Joanna's daughter thinks my makeup is *cool*?

"I don't know how to do makeup," Rayleigh admits. "Mom says I'm not allowed to. She doesn't want me getting attention from boys."

Mavis stifles a response, but it comes out as a squeak. Seriously, she needs to cool it.

"Well, maybe I can show you how to do a natural look," I offer. "I could create something so subtle that your mom won't even notice."

Rayleigh perks up. "I'd like that. You can do my makeup for church this Sunday."

Mavis might think Rayleigh is going to snitch us out to Aunt Joanna, but anyone who allows me to do their makeup is an *immediate* friend of mine.

The GPS navigates us to an outdoor shopping plaza where Mavis parks beside Forever 21. I grab the résumés I printed from the Taylors' home office and take in the scene. Everyone here is tall, thin, and extremely blond. Statistically, this shouldn't be possible. And do they all shop at the same place, too? Because somehow, Rayleigh's T-shirt and spaghetti-strap combo is the staple of beauty here.

I have a printed panda poking out of the pocket of my white button-up. I thought that tucking my blouse into a pencil skirt made me look beautiful and qualified to do any job. But now I realize I can't even pull off being a . . . Utonian? Utite? Utahn? Whatever.

Rayleigh shows us around since she's the local. Thank goodness for our little tour guide because Moore Plaza is so big that apartment complexes sit atop the stores. There's even a splash pad for kids and a dog park—or is that a putt-putt course?

I don't have a chance to explore because we're so focused on job hunting. Mavis and I drop off our résumés only for stores to tell us they exclusively accept online applications. Rayleigh must notice how much it dampens our spirits, because she offers to buy us lunch. That seems to win Mavis over. Her peacock spirit is easily tamed by a turkey bacon club.

Just as we leave the restaurant, a sleek black building catches my attention. My eyes lock on the posters in the window. Gorgeous East Asian women are poised on the salon's billboard. Rivers of black hair deeper than my own roll off the models' shoulders. Their skin glows like light filtering through a dewdrop. But it's the confidence behind their eyes that I can't turn away from. That's an expression I long for, but one I can never fake.

For the first time since moving here, I've spotted another East Asian girl who isn't confined to a mirror. And if I open these doors, I'll step into a salon where people look like me—people like Ya-Fang.

I'm not sure how long I gape before finally looking up at the name of the store. Beauty by Kimi Yoon. Are they hiring? *No.* A place this fancy must be fully staffed. I bet they have a list of people wanting to work here. Besides, they'll probably tell me to apply online anyway.

But *what if*?

"Oh, that's Böhme," Rayleigh says, pointing to a store across the street. "That's actually where I got this dress. It's one of my favorite places to shop. Did you have one in San Diego?"

Mavis's response fades in the background. Or maybe I've tuned her out because my vision has tunneled around the salon's steel door handles. I should've turned around and followed Rayleigh into the neighboring store.

Instead, I say, "You guys go ahead. I'll catch up."

洋紅

Magenta

I pull open the salon's heavy doors. Gentle piano notes greet me over the whirl of blow-dryers from the salon within. Lines of hardwood stretch across the floor as if gesturing for me to venture deeper inside. A wave of air-conditioning chills the sweat rolling down my back. Ahh—sweet relief from the melting sun.

This place looks expensive. Not like an Aunt-Joanna's-mansion-on-a-hill expensive. But more like an interactive-museum expensive. Like the glass shelves holding shampoos are made to be touched. Like the marble countertops are designed to be leaned against and no one will care if you leave a smudge. I treat myself to a pump of hand sanitizer from the dispenser in the lobby. The fragrance of ylang-ylang and sweet tangerine fills the air as I rub the gel into my hands.

I step up to the front desk with my binder of résumés tucked under my arm. Touchscreen computers are there to greet me. But aside from that, no one else is behind the counter. Not even a receptionist. Maybe this is a bad omen. Maybe this place is so fancy, they don't *need* a receptionist. Besides, I doubt they'll hire a seventeen-year-old anyway.

Footsteps patter from a hallway tucked around the desk. Someone is coming my way. I peer around the corner just as a black shirt stretched over a wide chest collides with me. My binder flies out of my arms as something splatters against my shirt. By the time I realize what's happening, magenta paste is sticking to my perfect interview outfit. A glob of hair dye has even rolled into my panda pocket.

What the—?

"I'm s-sorry!" the boy carrying a bowl of dye blurts as we stand there equally petrified. His tapered eyes are wide and unblinking. Vibrant magenta splatters across his apron and specks his blue disposable mask. But it's *my* blouse that's taken the brunt of the impact.

An older gentleman enters the foyer from the side closest to the hair dryers. He holds a pair of scissors in hand as if he's investigating this commotion mid-haircut. His deep brown eyes narrow as they search the magenta dye puddled across the floor, covering my shirt, and rolling down the boy's arms.

"What did you do, Toby?" he barks.

"I-I-I—" the boy—Toby—stammers as a fever of shame washes over his face.

"I deeply apologize for this mess, ma'am. Toby will show you to our break room so we can get you cleaned up," the man says to me. Then he hurries back to the hair station, saying, "I'll get one of the stylists to wipe up the floors."

"I'm so sorry, Dad!" Toby exclaims.

Dad? Now that I've had a chance to see the resemblance, I see that they share the same lean frames and thick, flat brows. They could be about the same height except Toby's shoulders are slimmer. Or maybe they seem that way because his posture shrinks.

Toby's face is a deeper shade of magenta than the dye

staining my shirt. I'm still processing the cold paste staining my clothes. He's probably shriveling up with embarrassment. I mean, he's just destroyed someone's outfit. I could've been a customer, for all he knew.

"I'm so sorry!" he repeats as his dad storms off.

"It's okay," I say, hoping to calm him down. "Come on, let's just clean ourselves up."

Toby nods, then turns back down the hall he came from. We don't walk very far before he opens a door and ushers me inside. The room is small—just big enough to fit a collapsible table. Coats and backpacks hang along the walls. Either this is a walk-in closet or it's the break room Toby's father was talking about.

Toby pulls an entire roll of paper towels off the table and hands it to me. "Here. Wipe off your skin before the dye stains it."

I take the roll and sigh up at the ceiling lights. I'm just trying to find a job for the summer. Did I really need to lose my one and only interview outfit? And on the second day of living in Utah, too? This can't be happening. I drop my gaze down to the new design on my blouse just to make sure this is real. Yup. Still covered in hair dye. Bad omen indeed.

"I'm so, so, so sorry," Toby stammers for the trillionth time.

"You sound like a Pokémon." I wipe my arm off only for the paper towel to smear dye down to my wrist. Perfect.

Toby blinks and shakes his head as if he doesn't understand what I'm saying. "What?"

"You've literally said nothing else except 'I'm so sorry' since you bumped into me," I explain, trying to make light of the crappy situation tethering us together.

"That's because I am," he insists, ripping off his apron.

"It's fine," I lie. This is far from *fine*. But Toby seems so distraught that the last thing I want is to humiliate him further. We all make mistakes. Some are just more costly than others. "You didn't know I was standing around the corner."

Toby doesn't seem to hear me, because he's shaking like a chihuahua in a thunderstorm. "Aw, man. I think your shirt is ruined."

He's right. The color has bled so much that there's no salvaging it. This is my favorite shirt, and now it's trash.

I swallow hard and force myself not to sound bitter. After all, this is what faking it is all about. "It's just a shirt."

"Here." He lifts a backpack from the wall and rummages around before pulling out a Nike tee. "You can change into this. I'm going to get some color remover so that dye doesn't stain your skin."

Before I can object, Toby is gone. The break room door clicks behind him. I stand alone staring at the *Just Do It* slogan printed on heather-gray cotton. Seriously? *Just do it?* Just throw this T-shirt on as if wearing a stranger's clothes is a totally normal thing for my second day of Utah? Ugh, why did I listen to my gut?

Knowing that I won't have another chance to undress, I shimmy out of my shirt and drape his Nike tee over my head. The scent of coffee and citrus envelops me as I make sure the collar doesn't brush against my false lashes. The moment the shirt drops to my knees, it hits me.

This is a *boy's* shirt!

Heat floods my face. The only thing between me and his

clothing is my bra. What will Aunt Joanna think when I come home in *this*?

A knock sounds at the door, and Toby waits for me to give him the all clear before stepping inside with a bottle of stain remover and two hand towels.

"Again, I am so sorry," Toby says, pouring stain remover onto the plush terrycloth.

"Toby used *Apologize*," I say. "Critical hit. It was super effective."

"What?" Toby's brows pinch.

I wince. *Way to make an awkward situation more awkward, Catie.* "I thought you knew what Pokémon are. Never mind."

"Oh!" Toby exclaims as vermilion floods his warm amber skin. "Yeah, I collect the cards and play the games. That's clever."

"Apparently not clever enough if you didn't get the reference," I say, shaking my head playfully.

"That's because—"

"You're *so* sorry?" I say, wearing a half smile.

Toby returns my grin as he hands over the cloth of stain remover. I wipe my arms as he wets another rag for himself. Despite his awkwardness, Toby totally belongs in a salon. Not only does he know his way around, but his dark hair has been cut short along the sides. The hair atop his head is dyed pale lilac. He's styled it in a way that makes the pastel purple blend with his naturally dark new growth. I'm not sure what products he uses, but it's combed back into a trendy wave that doesn't look crunchy with gel.

"So, that was your dad?" I ask, changing the subject.

"Yeah." Toby nods while wiping his stained hands with the terrycloth. "He and my mom own this salon."

"Oh," I say, putting the pieces together. "Yoon . . . Are you Korean?"

I cringe as the question comes out. No Asian in America likes playing the where-are-you-*really*-from game. Variations include guessing someone's ethnicity as if it's a gender reveal party. But Toby and his father are the first nonwhite people I've seen since coming here. Does a local such as Toby feel like an outcast? Or is it just me?

"Yeah. My mom's Korean. My dad's Blackanese. They met in cosmetology school, and they've been together ever since."

Awesome! A full sentence without the words *I'm sorry*. And yet as Toby speaks, a tiny pang aches in my heart—like being pricked in the chest with a needle. It's the familiar jolt of jealousy that reminds me everyone has biological parents. Just not me. And no matter what, there's nothing I can do to change that.

"And you?" Toby asks, snapping me from my thoughts.

Right. It's only fair that I answer, too. "Oh, my dad's mostly Scandinavian. But he met my mom while flying for Pacific Rim Airways. He was a pilot, and she was a stewardess."

Toby furrows his brows. "But you said your dad's white. How did he land a job flying around Asia?"

"He picked up Mandarin while serving a mission in— Sorry, a *mission* is this thing Mormons do—"

"Where they spend two years away from their family knocking on doors," Toby fills in. "Yeah. Some of the stylists here are RMs."

I blink at him. Whoa, he even knows the slang term for *returned missionary*? In San Diego, Mormonism is one of those things I had to explain whenever people found out I used to practice. But Toby knows. Obviously. He lives in Utah.

"Where did you say he served?" Toby asks.

"Taipei, Taiwan," I say, cleaning the dye out from under my fingernails. "It's also where I was born."

Even beneath his mask, I can't mistake Toby dropping his jaw. "Dude! You're Taiwanese? I just got back from my first year at the University of Taipei!"

Before I can respond, Toby launches into a language I was once fluent in. I recognize the lyrical ups and downs from a time when Ya-Fang sang me lullabies—from my early years at a colorful Taiwanese school learning how to count to ten. Though now, I can't make sense of anything Toby says. I've lost my mom, and any chance of ever speaking Mandarin again died with Dad. He stopped speaking it altogether when he married Andrea.

I hold my hands up. "I don't speak Mandarin anymore."

The light in Toby's eyes extinguishes. "Oh."

I clear my throat to ease the silence. Just when our conversation had started rolling, too. "I mean, I guess it would be kind of cool to relearn it. I haven't spoken it since . . ."

Since Ya-Fang and Dad got divorced. Since Dad moved me to America. Since I was thrown into this life of not knowing who I am anymore. There are so many questions I should've asked Dad about—my culture, my biological mother, who I am . . . and now I'm two years too late.

I ponder my own words. Of all the things I've lost in my

life, my first language is probably the *only* thing I can reclaim. It's not going to bring Dad back. It's not going to make Ya-Fang magically appear at the front door. But it would be the first step to taking back the things that are truly mine.

"If you want to relearn Mandarin," Toby's voice seeps through my thoughts, "my degree is literally in Chinese language."

"It is?" I ask.

Toby nods. "Yeah. I'm already fluent in Korean, thanks to my umma. And I should've learned Chinese at home because my grandma is from Shanghai. But my dad didn't grow up speaking Mandarin. So, when I went to university, I decided to specialize in traditional Mandarin. Anyway, I'm offering lessons starting at forty-five dollars an hour. It's my summer side hustle."

I grimace. As fulfilling as it would be to remember my first language, I can't fork over forty-five dollars an hour for lessons. Not when the whole point of moving out here is to save up enough money to return home by fall. Besides, Toby and I don't even know each other. And what if I can't relearn Mandarin? It's notoriously hard to learn. What if the only thing I get from trying to remember my first language is that I'm too assimilated for it now? And yet the faintest notes of music trill in my ears.

"I'll think about it." *Truth.* But I'll also be thinking about how expensive that would be.

"Well, let me know." Toby slides his disposable mask off and tosses it into the trash.

I try not to make a show about seeing his face. With his

mask down, his deep skin radiates a natural health that none of my skin-care products could ever deliver. Cheekbones and a V-shaped jaw carve his face in a way that tells me it's been chiseled by a rigorous gua sha routine. His full lips are so hydrated that they make mine feel like the Sahara. And he doesn't have any pores. Holy crap. His skin is *perfect*. Why can't Mom open up a salon so I can look like Toby, too?

Toby catches me staring so I glance away quickly. "Hey," he snaps. I assume he's going to ask me why I'm ogling his skin. Instead, he says, "I like your makeup."

"Thanks," I reply, blushing. "I like your . . . hair." Saying I like his *pores* feels way too weird.

Toby touches his lilac locks as if noticing them for the first time. "Really? I did it myself the moment I got home from college. Colored hair in Taiwan is a bit more taboo than it is here in the US. But I'm a cosmetologist. Vivid colors run in the family. Speaking of—were you here for an appointment?"

"No, actually . . . I was job hunting," I say, which now seems ridiculous, considering that my outfit is ruined and there are magenta spots staining my arms. I rub the towel harder. Is this stain remover even working?

Toby clutches his chest in relief. "No way. We actually need a new receptionist. Do you have a résumé?"

"I do. Technically, I already dropped it off in the lobby when you—you know—dumped hair dye all over me." I keep my voice playful as I gesture to his oversize shirt.

The corner of his lip turns down. "Again, I am so—"

"Sorry," we say at the same time.

Toby laughs nervously. "Well, in that case, why don't you

come in tomorrow around nine a.m. for an interview? It's the least I can do after—well—*that*."

I can't hide my toothy smile. I thought it would take forever to find a job that I would enjoy. But if Toby can help me get a job here at the salon, that would be a *dream*.

I nod eagerly. "I'll be back tomorrow, then!"

After accepting that my fingernails are stained pink and there's nothing I can do about it, I step out of the break room and wait for the door to close. The moment it clicks, I punch my fist into the air like a Pokémon trainer who's just earned a gym badge. *Yes!* I have a job interview. Sure, I lost a shirt along the way, but it's totally worth it for a chance to work at *this* salon. And the best part is, the sooner I get a job, the sooner I have an excuse to avoid Aunt Joanna.

八零一

801

The next morning, I return to the salon so that Toby's mom can interview me. Mrs. Yoon-Hanson is kind enough to take her son's shirt back from me and to overlook my lack of experience. She even compliments my purple eye shadow and the gems I glued by my tear ducts. The interview is quick, and in less than fifteen minutes, I'm back out the door. Toby's mom still needs to discuss my position with her husband. She'll call me if I'm hired. Otherwise, no news is bad news.

I haven't stopped bouncing my foot since walking out of the interview. Even as Mavis, Rayleigh, and I huddle around the downstairs computer, I can't sit still. The ceiling creaks when Uncle Nick paces around his office overhead. The theater-size TV plays *Moana*, but no one is watching. Not even Maddie Sue, who's curled beneath Rayleigh's computer chair. My cousin answers DMs on her iPad while Mavis skims the internet for jobs. I set my phone on my lap and telepathically command it to ring.

"Maybe you should apply for other places while you wait," Rayleigh suggests as she swivels in her computer chair. "Not that I think you won't get this job. But it'll keep you occupied."

My gaze flickers to the time on the monitor. 5:52 p.m. It's so close to the evening that if Mrs. Yoon-Hanson was going to call, wouldn't she have done so by now?

"Ooh, Catie. Check this out," Mavis says, pointing at the computer screen. "They're looking for a master esthetician out in Murray, Utah. If the salon doesn't call you back, you should apply for this one."

I thunk the back of Mavis's head.

"Hey!"

"I'm not a master esthetician, dork. You need a license for that."

Mavis rubs her scalp. "Yeah, but they pay twenty an hour!"

With an income like that, we'd *definitely* raise enough money to move back to San Diego by fall. And maybe by then I'd have enough money to afford my own Mandarin tutor, too.

Rayleigh's iPad chimes as another DM rolls in.

"Who are you messaging?" I ask, shifting my attention to my cousin.

"Just my friend." Rayleigh grins. "Her name's Trinity."

"Like *The Matrix*?" Mavis asks.

"Um, more like the Holy Trinity?"

"Naturally," Mavis says flatly.

"Anyway," Rayleigh continues. "She likes to take pictures of her cat and turn them into memes. She just sent me this one."

Rayleigh flips her iPad around to reveal a fluffy Maine coon with pointed ears and a set of deep green eyes. The feline looks into the camera as its tongue flops to the side somewhere between hungry and derpy. The caption reads, "When you're waiting for Mom to finish baking cookies so you can lick the spoon."

I laugh even though I'm pretty sure I've seen a similar meme while swiping through my Instagram story. "Do you make memes of Maddie Sue, too?"

Maddie Sue thumps her tail when she recognizes her name.

"Uh, duh." Rayleigh giggles, scrolling through her camera roll before pulling up a folder filled with pics of a meme-ified golden retriever. "I've asked Mom for a professional camera, but she said no. I just thought it would be nice to take better photos of Maddie Sue on our walkies, you know?"

Maddie Sue perks her ears at the word *walkies*.

"So photography is your thing?" I ask.

Rayleigh shrugs. "More like animals are my thing. None of my siblings wanted a pet growing up, so I had to wait for them to leave before Mom finally got me a dog. They were so against having animals in the house—they wouldn't even let me keep a ladybug when I was in fourth grade."

"Monsters," Mavis deadpans.

"I know, right?" Rayleigh agrees, missing Mavis's cynicism. "I told my siblings that I wanted to be a vet and—"

"Rayleigh!" Aunt Joanna's voice rings from upstairs. "Why hasn't the trash been taken out yet?"

"Coming!" Rayleigh shouts, then rolls her eyes. "Hold on. I'll be right back. If I don't go now, Mom will get mad."

Mad? If that isn't already her "mad voice," then I *really* don't want to hear what she says next.

Rayleigh leaves her iPad on her seat as she races upstairs, Maddie Sue hot on her heels. Great. Now that Rayleigh is gone, it's just Mavis and me. Why couldn't Maddie Sue have stayed? Maybe because the word *walkies* is fresh on her mind.

"Still think she's a spy?" I ask, breaking the silence.

"Eh," Mavis answers. I wait for more, but that's all she gives me. Her attention is fixated on the computer screen as she types out her next availability for an interview: ASAP.

And with that, she's back to the old Mavis. Shut down, unwilling to talk.

I open my mouth to try to say something—anything—but Rayleigh's iPad vibrates and a message appears on the screen. I shouldn't look, but I can't help myself. There's no name, just a kissy face emoji in the place where a name should be. Wait a second—is Rayleigh really texting her friend Trinity? Or is she messaging a boy who has sparked Rayleigh's earlier interest in my makeup routine?

I'm about to lean closer when my own phone vibrates. My gaze whiplashes to the device I'd forgotten was on my lap. I scoop it up as my stomach hammers between my ribs. I don't recognize the phone number, but it starts with 801—Salt Lake City's area code.

"Answer it!" I have Mavis's full attention now.

My breath hitches. And once again, my knee bounces involuntarily. Holy crap—is this it?

I swipe a trembling thumb across my phone. "Hello?"

Pause.

What if this is just a scam caller?

And then . . .

"Catie?" Mrs. Yoon-Hanson's voice flutters in. "I adored our interview and spoke with my husband. We'd love for you to work with us! Are you able to start tomorrow?"

真正屬於我的

Truly Mine

On my first day of work, the scent of flowers and citrus welcomes me like the way Mom's perfume does when she gives me a tight hug. Lines of bamboo flooring point in the direction of the front desk, as if they know what I'm here for. Bottles of toning shampoo line the walls. They don't have arms, but I swear even they wave hello to me.

Mrs. Yoon-Hanson has me fill out paperwork in her office while she photocopies my California driver's license. After I finish the onboarding papers, I join her behind the front desk for some training. By then, clients are rolling in. For the most part, I watch as she checks them in and cashes them out. When the rush dies down, Mrs. Yoon-Hanson has me look over the services.

Since the salon doubles as a Korean spa, I have to learn everything from their body scrubs to their massages to their snail mucin facials—which I've always wanted to try. They're super popular in South Korea—or at least according to the influencers I follow. But in SLC, it's illegal to have giant snails crawl around on someone's face. So instead, Mrs. Yoon-Hanson uses a Korean skin care line that has snail mucus in it. Apparently, the facial is great for giving skin that naturally dewy look and healing it, too. It's everything my giant pores and pink blemishes need.

"It's almost noon," Mrs. Yoon-Hanson says, pointing to the clock. Like Toby, she looks like she belongs in a spa. Her short black hair is pulled back by an elegant claw clip. And like Toby, she sports all-black attire. She's even got his V-shaped face and glass skin. Now I know where he gets it from. "I have a client coming in for a body wrap. Do you think you could watch the front desk while I get my room set up? If something happens, you can come grab me."

Though I don't feel qualified to watch the front desk by myself, I nod. I mean, how long does it take to set up a room anyway?

Toby's mom disappears down the hall. I lean against the counter, reviewing the list of services. Five seconds after she vanishes, a ginger-haired guy with a fresh haircut and a Utah State alum shirt appears on the other side of the desk. *Aw, jeez. Perfect timing.*

"Men's haircut with a shampoo and scalp massage." Toby's right behind the guy. The sprinkles of orange hair on his apron tell me that he must've just finished with this client. He blinks at me as if he was expecting his mom. "Oh, hey, Cath—Kay—Car . . . ?"

Between spilling the dye and getting yelled at by his dad, I don't blame Toby for not remembering my name.

"Catie," I finish.

Toby's cheeks turn pink as he snaps his fingers. "Right! I knew that— Sorry— I'm just— I see a lot of faces. Congrats on being hired. I mean, like, I assume you're hired. Because you're at the desk so you got the . . ." Toby clears his throat. "Where's my mom?"

"She's setting up for her client," I reply, as the corner of my lip twitches with amusement.

"Do you need help?" he asks.

I nod vigorously. "Please."

Toby doesn't hesitate. It's like he's activating professional mode as he joins me behind the counter. He tucks his phone back into his pocket and apologizes to the client for the delay. Then he taps at the computer, and I watch over his shoulder.

"So when you're cashing someone out, you're gonna want to hit this tab over here," Toby explains.

But his voice fades away, because the client's eyes burn into me in that way that makes my skin prickle. I've experienced this too many times before—guys looking me up and down like they're sizing me up. Like I, in turn, owe them my attention and interest. The only thing I can do now is stay focused on Toby's explanation and—

"Are you new here?" the guy asks me, cutting Toby off.

Even Toby looks up like he wasn't expecting to be interrupted by the client. *Yup.* My gut was onto something.

"Yes," I say out of politeness. Then I turn my attention back to Toby, but the client continues.

"Cool," the client says. Silver hairs mingle with the orange of his stubble. He leans against the counter as if he wants me to notice his biceps. I know what he's doing even though he thinks I don't. *Ugh.* How old is he? And how old does he think *I* am? "I've been coming here for years—isn't that right, Toby?"

Toby finishes what he's doing, then hits Enter. "Yup. And the total is seventy-five for today."

The client hands his card to Toby even though he's still talking to me. "I'm Hank, by the way. What did you say your name was again?"

I grimace. If I was still in San Diego, I would tell him my name's Francisca, then giggle about the situation with my friends. But I'm not in Cali. I'm here, standing beside my boss's son. "Oh, um. I'm Catie."

"Nice to meet you, Catie." He flashes a set of toilet-white teeth.

I give him a courteous nod.

"By the way, I really like your makeup," Hank continues.

Normally, a comment like that would make me smile. It means that someone acknowledges the fact that I've woken up an hour before my alarm just to spend my morning working Too Faced bronzer into my cheeks and purple eye shadow over my lids. It means that my fluffy lashes are perfectly placed and that my peach lipstick hasn't bled yet. But there's a difference between the way this guy compliments my makeup and the way Toby did two days ago.

"Thanks." My voice is clipped.

"I hope this isn't too forward, but what social media platforms are you on? You seem pretty cool, and I'd love to hang out sometime."

I resist the urge to roll my eyes. Okay, this conversation has gone on long enough, and this guy needs to go. Toby's probably sensing that, too, because he's typing a little faster into the card reader.

"Oh, uh, that's so sweet, but . . . I have a boyfriend." *Lie.* This one is easy to tell. If there's one thing that gets creeps to back off, it's the threat of another man. Hooray, misogyny.

Hank blinks at me as if I've just insulted him. "Oh . . . well, I guess that makes sense. You're so pretty. Obviously, you're taken."

I glower internally. Because only *pretty girls* are taken?

"Here you go, Hank," Toby says, handing him his receipt and credit card.

"Thanks." Hank finishes signing the paper, then waves at me on his way out the door. "I'll see you around, Catie."

I say nothing as he leaves. The moment he's gone, Toby turns to me. "I'm so sorry about that. Hank hits on all the girls here. That's why I'm the only one who does his hair now."

I gag. "How old is he anyway?"

"I'd rather not think about it." Toby shudders. "Hey, why don't you take a lunch break? I think you . . ."

Toby's voice trails off as his focus zeros in on the front doors again. Oh no. Is Hank back already?

But when I follow his gaze, I don't see an older white guy. A tall East Asian girl with long brown hair strolls in. Everything from the arch of her brows to the way her hair frames her face is the perfect balance between angles and grace. Even the way she moves reminds me of a confident ballerina.

Toby tenses like a statue.

"Hey, Tobias!" The girl slides her sunglasses off, revealing a pair of blue eyes too icy to be natural. I've never met a Singaporean socialite before, but this girl carries herself like she's used to being photographed by paparazzi.

"N-N-N-Nichole," Toby sputters. "How've you been?"

I raise a brow. After accidentally dumping hair dye on me, Toby's face was pink. But now it's a shade of red that rivals a tomato.

"Oh, summer break is fine so far," Nichole says, setting her Michael Kors purse on the counter. "Finals at U of U killed me, ugh. I'm so glad the semester is over. How about you? I heard you're going to school in Taipei?"

"I was," Toby says. Maybe a little too quickly. "I mean, I am. I didn't drop out or fail or anything. And—and I'll be returning to Taiwan in the fall. Can't wait. What I'm trying to say is that I'm just not there right now. Obviously. Right now, I'm standing here talking to you. But I was in Taipei. I have been since graduation—woo-hoo! Go, Vikings!"

"Go, Vikings!" Nichole parrots.

I cross my arms. Well, this is . . . *interesting*. Toby is completely melting into a puddle for her, which is no surprise. Nichole is stunning in every way I wish I was. Judging by the way she carries herself, I would've believed she's one of the models on the posters outside the salon. Is she really just a regular college student?

"H-how's your sister liking the Mandarin homework I assigned her?" Toby asks.

My ears perk up. Wow, so Toby really *is* a language tutor.

"Oh, Lola loves it." Nichole beams. "She's labeled everything in the house in Mandarin. Everything is covered in sticky notes. She even tried to label our dog."

Toby's eyes seem to glow. "I'm glad she's enjoying her lessons. Though I'm sorry your house is a mess."

"No, no. It's great." Nichole tucks a strand of hair behind an ear decorated with three small hoops. "I'm learning things, too. I can't even go into the kitchen without knowing that the fridge is called a bing-sing."

"Bīngxiāng," Toby corrects. There's something in the way the word flows off his tongue that sounds like he's singing it.

"Imagine stretching out the last vowel sound just a little longer. Sometimes, when there are two first tone syllables back-to-back like that, it's easier to hold the pitch if you—"

Nichole holds her hands up and cuts Toby off with a sheepish smile. "I'll leave the Mandarin lessons to Lola. My brain is still fried from college. I'm going to enjoy my time *not* learning anything new, ya know?"

"Oh," Toby says. His voice is still bright, but I watch his shoulders slump. "No, you're right. I got carried away."

"It's all good." Nichole chuckles. "Anyway, I'm here to get my rhinestones replaced. Some of them fell off my fingernails while I was at the gym. Can I pay now so that I don't have to fish my card out with fresh nails?"

"Yes." Toby reaches for her card just as Nichole extends it to him. But instead of grabbing it, he punches the card out of her hand. It flies across the counter and onto the floor.

"Sorry," Toby says as he immediately crouches down and paws the tile for her card. "I've got it now."

"Great." Nichole's smile wavers.

It's so hard not to cover my eyes as Toby emerges from the floor and runs her credit card with trembling fingers. Sure, I've never had a boyfriend before. But I know how to act cool around the boys I like. Don't I?

Eventually, a receipt prints, and Toby returns everything to Nichole.

"Thank you so much," Nichole says, putting her card back in her bag. "Tell your mom I said hi!"

"Sure do!" Toby replies, but Nichole has already walked toward the nail area.

The moment she vanishes, Toby slumps against the counter and buries his head in his arms. Over the music seeping through the speakers, he whimpers to himself.

"Sure do?" I repeat.

Toby grumbles something into his arms, but I can't hear him over the plucking harp strings.

"Huh?" I ask.

He lifts himself up. "I said, I know how to talk to women. I just don't know how to talk to . . . Ni . . . Nichole."

"Ah," I note. "And apparently, you can't even say her name without stuttering."

Toby glowers at me. "You're the worst."

"I try," I tease, but Toby is too distraught to take the joke. "Okay, look. You're not that bad. I imagine you're just a little rusty with flirting. I'm sure it's difficult talking to girls since you've been overseas, and I imagine this is the first time you've seen Nichole since graduation. Besides, when was the last time you had a girlfriend?"

Toby frowns as if he doesn't want to tell me. Finally, he glances at the ground. "Never."

"Never?" I gasp before I can stop myself. How could someone who looks like a freaking purple-haired supermodel never have had a girlfriend before? Then I clear my throat. "I mean, that's not a bad thing for someone your age."

"I'm nineteen," Toby confesses.

I drop my jaw, then cover my expression with my hand. Mavis had her first kiss when she was fourteen. I *almost* had mine earlier this year with Jimmy—the only guy in our friend group chat. I guess that doesn't really count either. And

I suppose kissing someone isn't the most important thing in the world. But when someone looks like Toby *and* hasn't been kissed, I find that hard to believe.

"I know you think I'm a loser."

"You are *not* a loser," I say, but it doesn't seem to console him, so I scramble for something more. "Dating is hard— especially if you've spent your after-school hours working in a salon." *Lie?* Probably? I wouldn't know. I'm not a cosmetologist.

"Yeah, it really is," Toby huffs like I've said something that resonates with him. "That, and . . . well, growing up, everyone kind of thought I was gay because I became a cosmetologist. Plus, you know we Asian guys get called girly waaaaay too much."

"Yeah, I know a thing or two about Asian stereotypes." I bite my lip. "I'm sorry your classmates were jerks. But being a cosmetologist is awesome. Don't you like what you do?"

Toby nods. "I love it."

"Then frankly, I don't think you should care what anyone thinks. You're amazing. Your haircuts are amazing. And your clients love you—I mean, I'd know. I've been watching them leave you huge tips all day."

Toby holds my gaze as if digesting my words. Slowly, he nods. "You're right. I'm getting paid to be awesome. My classmates can suck it."

I've been so enveloped in our conversation that I don't hear footsteps coming my way until Nichole is back at the counter with glittering nails. I return to my computer as if we hadn't just been talking about her.

"That was quick, huh?" Nichole says, showing off her new

rhinestones. "Do you think I could prebook for a fill in two weeks?"

"Yes, you can," Toby says, then schedules her next appointment.

"Thanks so much, Tobias." Nichole waves as she walks away.

"My problem." As the words escape Toby's lips, I actively watch him process grief through all its five stages.

Nichole disappears out the door, and I snap my attention to Toby. "You need a date, STAT!"

Toby slumps against the counter as if he's suffering from a migraine, a stomachache, and period cramps all at the same time. "What I *really* need is a dating coach."

I giggle at his joke, except Toby doesn't laugh along with me. He perks his head up and tilts it to the side like he's taking his own words into consideration. Before I can ask him what he's thinking, Toby turns to me and says, "You've got dating experience, right? Didn't you say you have a boyfriend?"

Wait—*what*?

And then I remember. The Hank thing. I mean, yes, technically, I *said* I had a boyfriend. But I did that to a creepy dude because sometimes that's the only way to get them off my case.

Secondly—do I *actually* have a boyfriend? No. Not even a little bit. I wouldn't even count my maybe-more-than-friendship-with-Jimmy a boyfriend. But before I can explain this or say anything, Toby sucks in a big breath.

"Teach-me-how-to-talk-to-Nichole." The words rush out as one. "Please?"

I shake my head, not quite sure how to respond. I need to

back up and start from the beginning, but I can't get a word out with Toby's persistent begging.

"Pleeeeease, Catie," Toby pleads. "I've been in love with Nichole Yung since middle school. It was Valentine's Day in fifth grade. Everyone in my class had gotten cards and candies and . . . well, Nichole was the only person who gave me something."

Toby leans back as he speaks, probably because his head is so high up in the clouds that he's about to fall over. "She's sweet, she's funny, she's smart. It's just—she's so intimidating. Have you seen her?"

"Um, I think so?"

"She's everything!" Toby continues. "How do I . . . how do I take all this stuff that I feel about her and—I don't know—show it to her?"

"By . . . telling her?" This isn't astrophysics. It can't possibly be that hard.

Toby snaps his fingers before pointing at me. "See, you're already the perfect coach! Plus, you're the only girl I've spoken to since I've gotten back from Taiwan. Honestly, Catie, you're the only girl I've *ever* had a real conversation with. Pleeeeease? I just want to talk to Nichole the way I talk to you. Maybe then I'd actually have a shot at dating her."

My head spins and my tongue doesn't feel like cooperating. Toby and I don't know each other. Sure, we're coworkers, but that's where the line is drawn. This is my first full day of work and already, he's asking something impossible from me. Besides, how will I prepare him for literal courtship? It's not like there's an instruction manual I can follow.

"I'll make it worth your while," Toby says, strategizing now. "What do you want? Free makeup? A raise? Actually, I can't really do that. Umma's the one who does payroll. Um . . . how about . . . ?"

The desperation in Toby's eyes melts my heart, but I'm not this fantastical love expert that he assumes I am. The only "boyfriend" I've ever had was a severe crush back at Del Rey High. There was this one time when Jimmy gave me a really long hug at a basketball game. Our lips almost kinda sorta would've brushed if I hadn't been a weenie and pulled away.

Oh, dang. Maybe Toby is right. This *is* hard.

On the other hand, Toby has offered me free makeup—makeup that I can't afford because all my money needs to go into returning to San Diego. Or maybe if not makeup, Toby could hook me up with snail mucin facials anytime I want. Or maybe if not that . . .

"I could teach you Mandarin," Toby interjects just as the thought pops into my mind. "For free. You wouldn't have to pay a dime."

I hold his gaze and my head finally stops spinning. To speak my first language . . . for *free*. To make up for the two years I wasted never fulfilling Dad's dying wish for me to know who I truly am. Toby doesn't know how priceless that is to me. Especially now that he's offered it in a way that doesn't compromise moving back to San Diego.

"So," Toby says. "What do you say?"

不同的愛之語
A Different Love Language

We have the Taylor house to ourselves. Uncle Nick is still at his firm. Aunt Joanna and Rayleigh are at the grocery store. Technically, the only Taylor here is Maddie Sue, and she's pressed against my foot so I can scratch her with my toes.

I'm sitting at the kitchen table catching up on the seventy-five missed texts from my group chat. Jimmy tells us that the ice cream truck guy was at the skate park and he snagged one of those strawberry crunch bars that are always out of stock. Meanwhile, Francisca's already got her first sunburn of the season. She usually burns once and then is fine for the rest of the summer.

Man. Why can't we be there to slather sunscreen on each other and share rainbow pops? Why can't we be getting our knees scraped up at the skate park or digging through Jimmy's car seats for quarters?

Mavis sits across the kitchen table from me. She hasn't said a word since I sat down. Her phone is an inch from her nose, which means she's probably reading the same texts I am. My phone vibrates, and sure enough, she's added to the conversation and I see my name mentioned. I scroll all the way down to read what everyone is talking about.

MAVIS: And the air is so dry up here. My feet are all crusty

JIMMY: Dude that sucks. Doesn't Catie have some lotion you can borrow?

FRANCISCA: Is Catie even still alive? Why hasn't she texted us?

MAVIS: Catie found a job already. Today was her first day

MAVIS: Guess she's too good for us now

I set my phone down and narrow my eyes at Mavis. *Seriously?* She knows I'm literally reading her text in real time. Is she just being cheeky, or is she lashing out at me? So I haven't looked at these messages all day. That doesn't mean I'm too good for my friends. That means I've been stuck at work. Why is my sister *like this*?

I angrily drum out a response but pause when Mom waltzes back into the kitchen.

"How was work, Catie?" she asks as she stirs a pot of boiling spaghetti on the stove. At least someone notices me.

"It was . . ." I begin, then pause.

Do I really want to tell Mom about Toby's offer? I could give her a quick recap, but there's so much detail between the annoying client, the accidental lie, and Toby's deal that I don't know where to start. More than that, am I ready to tell her that I'm considering learning Mandarin?

But what if bringing up the regrets I have with Dad hurts Mom's feelings? She's already going through so much, and Mavis certainly isn't helping. Will sharing the loose ends I never tied with Dad remind her of her own? Will it remind her of dates that never happened? Of last kisses exchanged at the hospital instead of at their bench at Balboa Park?

"Busy," I say instead. "They offer so many services, and the sooner I remember them all, the smoother my day will be. How about you? Any new leads on jobs?"

"Well, you know I'm still on the hunt for something similar to what I was doing back home," Mom replies as the rising steam from the pot gives her a mini facial. "There's a coaching position at the University of Utah that I'd love. Not only would the pay be better than what I was making in San Diego, but if you girls ever want to go to college there—"

"You're not actually going to apply for that coaching job, are you?" Mavis interjects as if she's suddenly aware of our existence. "I'm not finishing high school in Utah, let alone attending college here. You can't expect me to just give up my friends like that."

Give up your friends like the way you gave me up? I almost say.

Mom's grip tightens on the handle as she stirs the pot. "I'm doing everything I can to get back home."

I focus on scratching Maddie Sue's ribs with my big toe. It's my duty as the big sister to smooth things over even though I wish Mavis would just think about someone else other than herself for once.

"What about you, sis?" I ask with forced pep. "Have you heard back from Böhme? Wouldn't it be so cool if we worked across the street from each other?"

"Meh." Mavis shrugs.

I swallow hard. Maybe Mavis is more perceptive than I thought, because she softens and says, "I might download a babysitting app. I'm sure there are tons of people here who need a sitter. Except I won't have a car unless you share Mom's Subaru."

"Isn't Aunt Joanna letting us borrow her car?" I ask.

Mavis shakes her head without looking up at me. "Aunt Joanna let *Mom* borrow it, not me."

"Oh, well, you can have Mom's Subaru if you need it," I offer. "We're supposed to be sharing it this summer anyway. Just drop me off at work and pick me up afterward—actually I might be able to get a ride home from one of my coworkers."

"Oh?" Mom arches a brow. "The same coworker who let you wear his shirt yesterday?"

I'm pretty sure Mom means it innocently. But then I catch Mavis peering at me from over her phone. She raises a brow at me. Yes, not telling them about my dating coach side hustle is the right call. Especially since I don't know if I'm ready to commit to that.

"Yeah, him," I say as casually as I can.

Mavis smirks like she's got a crackly quip on her lips. But before she speaks, the garage door opens. The whir of the crank pulling up a heavy metal door startles Maddie Sue. She jumps up and hurries to the pantry door, barking with excitement.

"I should probably shower before dinner," I say, making an excuse to leave the room before Aunt Joanna comes back from running errands. Maybe I'm just tired from the long hours at the salon, but I really don't want to deal with her.

"Okay," Mom calls as I walk away. "But dinner's almost ready."

Her voice fades behind me. I drop down the stairs and am gone before Aunt Joanna steps into the kitchen behind me. The basement is dark and I don't bother turning on the lights. The floorboards creak overhead and Rayleigh's muffled voice seeps through the ceiling. She's probably telling Mom about her day, but I don't strain my ears to listen.

I walk straight into my new bedroom. Evening light spills in from the egress window, illuminating the gray stones sitting in the window well. Tavie's name is still painted on the far wall in Pepto-Bismol pink. Her purple sheets and lime throw pillows sit in a mess on the twin mattress. Nothing in this room makes sense—from the curling iron burns left in the carpet to the stickers plastered across the headboard. And it makes even less sense now that my clothes hang in the closet while my books line the shelf over the bed.

It's such an incohesive disaster that I'm torn between organizing the unpacked boxes and flopping down in bed with the blanket over my head. I opt for the latter even though I told Mom I'd shower.

The bed frame knocks against the wall when I collapse onto it. I grab my blanket and wrap myself in a burrito. The springs in the mattress squeak as I adjust myself. I'm in a dark cocoon when someone sits at the foot of my bed. Did Mom follow me downstairs? Did Mavis? If so, I didn't even hear the door open.

I lift the blanket off my head and peer at the weight pressing down on my toes. No one is in the room. Instead, a hardcover book has joined me.

I lift my gaze up to the bookshelf drilled into the wall just over my feet. Maybe when the bed frame hit the wall, it knocked a book off the shelf. I lean over to place the book back, but the familiar cover stops me in my tracks.

The Five Love Languages by Gary Chapman.

I turn on my desk lamp and stare at the glossy cover jacket as if the book itself has cast a spell of remembrance on me. When I hold the book to my nose, I catch a whiff of minty aftershave and clean linen shirts. Of grape-flavored cough syrup drunk on feverish nights, and bowls of chocolaty cereal eaten on chilly mornings.

Of Dad.

I've never read this thing before, even though Dad gifted it to me before he passed. Well, technically one of the hospice nurses gave it to me and said that Dad left a note inside. But I've always been too scared to read it. To hear Dad's voice in my head. To potentially see another expectation he had of me—one I was sure I couldn't meet.

But now that I'm ready to make good on our promises—all of them, whatever they may be—I reach for the book and flip through the pages, searching for that letter. But instead of a loose leaf of paper falling out, my gaze skims over the blocks of text highlighted in neon yellow. Of paragraphs that've been underlined. Of inky notes in the margins smudged by time. Is this what the nurse meant when she said Dad left me a note? Like the entire thing is just one big annotation from him?

I skim from back to front, my thumb catching on the title page. Just when I'm about to give up, I find it. I recognize the boxy angles and short strokes. I saw it before, in first grade when Dad stayed up late helping me learn the alphabet. I remember the wooden table Dad and I sat at to do my homework—remember how my pencil used to catch on the grooves of wood. It made my already shaky penmanship even shakier. This was when I first came to America. When I first realized I didn't know how to talk to the kids at school, but I loved being home because that's where Dad was. For once, he was home. And for once, Ya-Fang was the one missing.

My fingers trace the dents in the paper where his fingers once were. I'm not at the kitchen table in my first American apartment—the one in LA close to the airport. I'm in Utah reading the words Dad left behind long ago.

Dearest Catie,
Wǒ ài nǐ
我愛你
I love you

The first line is in Pinyin: a Romanized spelling of the way Mandarin sounds. The second line is in traditional Hanzi. This is a written language I've never learned, though I imagine I would've become fluent in it if Dad and Ya-Fang had stayed together. And finally, the last line is written in English. My language. And the language Dad has written the rest of this letter in.

Your grandmother got me this book when I turned sixteen and was allowed to date. I'd always hoped I'd pass it on to you for your sixteenth birthday, but the nurses are saying I only have a month. Here's hoping I prove them wrong.

I wipe a tear from my cheek even though I haven't even finished the letter. I was fifteen when Dad died. Turning sixteen was the farthest thought from my mind even though it would've been a cause for celebration because I would've been old enough to date, according to Mormon standards. But as I'm reading this, I'm realizing Dad knew he'd never watch me fall in love. Never see me in a white dress. Never be a grandfather. Cancer cheated me out of *having* a father, but it also cheated him out of *being* one.

I'll never forget the first time I read this book all the way through. I'm not sure which love language inspired this idea, but I'd always imagined taking my girlfriends on five dates, each one inspired by a different love language. Of course, that never actually happened. I just thought it would've been fun!

Since then, I've read this book too many times to count. Each time, I've discovered something different about myself. It's strange how one piece of advice can mean one thing at one point in your life, then mean something completely different another time. Whenever I come back to this book, I find myself leaving new

comments in the margins. Chapman makes some very outdated
points about love, so I've fixed them for you in this edition (ha
ha ha).

Even though I won't be there to shake hands with the lucky
boy who takes you on your first date, I hope my advice will take the
place of missing out on this vital part of your self-discovery.

Be your best self, Catie. And take your time coming home
to me.

Bàba

爸爸

Dad

Another tear rolls off my chin and lands on the page, missing the ink by a millimeter. There's no way that this book falling off the shelf was an accident. I stopped believing in destiny long ago, but finding this lost letter isn't a coincidence. I may not know what I believe anymore, but I know that Dad's watching me from wherever he is. And he's still trying to be my dad no matter what.

血脉·文化

The Culture in My Veins

Maybe it's the lingering Mormon guilt within me, but not telling Toby the truth seemed like a bad idea. At *first*. But the more I think about it, the more I realize I'm sitting in a pretty position. Relearn my first language? *Check*. Reconnect with Ya-Fang and my culture? *Double check*. And the best part of it all is that I'll never have to tell Toby the truth because I'll be back in San Diego this fall. Win-win. It's not the nicest way to treat a coworker, but why do I have to be nice? Screw morality and indoctrination. I'll show Dad I found my true self no matter what.

Besides, Toby just needs someone to give him the confidence to ask Nichole out. I can help him with that. Dad basically left behind a feminist textbook in his version of *The Five Love Languages*. And he's the one who inspired me to take Toby on dates themed after each love language. I've got my lesson plan all mapped out. How hard is faking this really going to be?

"What do you remember from your first language?" Toby asks, leaning against the counter on my second day of work. His next client doesn't come in until two. So instead of scrolling through social media in the break room, he's behind the front desk helping me get the hang of things.

I bite the inside of my cheek and lean against the counter beside him. "Okay, this is going to sound weird, but I feel like the only *real* thing I remember is a nursery rhyme."

Toby raises a brow. "Yeah? Sing it."

I shake my head anxiously. "Trust me, you do *not* want to hear me sing. All the dogs within a mile radius will start howling if I do."

Toby laughs. "Well, then just say it."

I open my mouth but stop before my lips move. I haven't spoken this Mandarin rhyme since I was a child. What if I suck at it? What if I'm chasing something that will never be mine again? My gaze pans to the front doors. No one is coming in even though a part of me wishes for a distraction.

"Hey," Toby says, sensing my hesitancy. "It's okay. I know what it's like to be an outsider learning a new language. My Korean cousins made fun of me when I first went to Busan."

I like the way Toby says *Busan*. His vowels get a little rounder, and it almost sounds like he replaces the *B* sound with a *P* sound.

"You speak Korean, right?" I ask.

"Uh, have you seen me?" Toby scoffs. "Don't I look like I speak Korean?"

"Uh, have you seen me?" I mock, gesturing to myself.

"Okay, touché. And to answer your previous question, yes. I do speak Korean. I'm not perfect, but I'm bilingual enough to get by when we visit family."

"So then why study Mandarin?"

Toby tilts his head in consideration. "When I was growing up, Umma and I did a lot of traveling. We'd fly all over the Far East. Singapore, Hong Kong, Tokyo, Taipei . . . All I knew growing up was English and Korean. But it seemed like Mandarin was the language everyone else spoke. I mean, it's the most-spoken language on the planet. I think I kind of fell in love with it as a kid, and in the back of my mind, I always wanted to make up for the language my dad lost."

Something aches inside me. Is it jealousy because Toby can connect with both his parents' cultures? No. Jealousy leaves an inky taste in the back of my throat. This is something sweet, like eating a cupcake with the frosting first. Maybe I like listening to him talk about his love of language because I hear myself when he speaks.

"Wait a second." Toby smirks. "You got me monologuing. Don't think I've forgotten about your nursery rhyme."

"Did I?" I chuckle nervously. So what if I get our conversation sidetracked again? "Do you think you could give me a ride home after work today?"

"I'd be happy to," Toby says without missing a beat. "Now, about that rhyme?"

I roll my eyes. Okay, so he isn't going to let me off that easily. "Fine."

A part of me is eager to recite this—just to prove that I have some Mandarin in me even if it's a fraction of what I used to know. But like Toby said, speaking a new language is difficult—even though Mandarin *technically* isn't new to me. I just don't want to flunk out before I've even started.

Toby pats my shoulder. "Take all the time you need. You've got this."

I inhale deeply, then shut my eyes. I remember watching TV from the boxy set in our Taiwanese apartment. I was only a child then, yet this was my favorite song from my favorite cartoon at the time. I wish I could remember the name of the show. But in my head, all I see is a character with bright pink hair and lots of animal friends.

"Shǔ, Niú, Hǔ, Tù."

These are the animals in the Chinese calendar. In my mind, my four-year-old hands clap along with the characters on-screen. It's been so long since I've called upon this memory that I can't remember which word correlates to which animal. I long to put an image to the sounds. But all that come are indiscernible globs of memory distorted by time.

"Lóng, Shé, Mǎ."

I'm in the living room and Ya-Fang is somewhere in the kitchen. She's on the phone asking where her husband is. I know she's speaking in Mandarin, but losing my first language has disrupted the memory, because I hear her voice in English. She seems mad or annoyed. Maybe even scared. Is it because Dad was always in the sky when he was supposed to be home? Was this one of the *real* reasons they divorced? I'm not sure. I just liked the bright colors and pudgy animals on the TV.

"Yáng, Hóu, Jī, Gǒu, hé Zhū!"

I'm on a stage now. I'm performing this very song for a school production. The stage lights make me squint so I can't see who's in the crowd. But I know Dad and Ya-Fang are watching me. For once, they're both able to attend one of my school events. I'm screaming these words so loudly that my throat burns. Dad's here and I want him to listen to me—to make up for all the times he couldn't.

"Zhōngguó shí'èr shēngxiàooo."

I have absolutely no clue what I've just said. I was born in the Year of the Rat, but that doesn't mean I know how to say *rat* in Mandarin. To me, the words are a jumble of syllables. It's hard to believe that at one point, I understood what I was saying. But even now—even though it's been over a decade since I breathed Taiwanese air—I can't believe I still remember this.

"Good job," Toby says when I open my eyes.

I fidget with my shirt to keep the blush at bay. Despite his compliment, I know my Mandarin is terrible. He's probably saying "good job" only to keep me motivated.

"You already know the words. Now you just need to work on the proper pronunciation," Toby continues. "I suppose that's what our first lesson could be today."

Ah, yes. Tones. Mandarin is a tonal language. This means that two words can have the exact same sound, but the inflection of the sound shifts the entire word's meaning.

"Before we get to the tones, I want to dive into a little history lesson," Toby explains. "Stop me if I start rambling. I'm going to school for this so I might geek out about everything."

I nod, eager to learn more.

"The official language of both China and Taiwan is Mandarin," Toby says, rubbing his palms together like a fly diving into a picnic. "But each nation speaks and writes in their own version of it. One of the biggest differences between Chinese and Taiwanese writing systems is that in the nineteen fifties and sixties, China modified their language into something called 'Simplified.' They wanted to increase literacy rates on the mainland, so they combined characters and made them easier to read, while Taiwan kept the traditional written language."

Right. He'd mentioned something about specializing in Traditional Mandarin. "What else is different?"

Toby beams as if I've just asked him to tell me about his favorite book. "I spent all year studying this stuff and I still don't have an easy answer. But I don't want to overwhelm you, so I'll try to keep it simple."

I lean forward like I'm back in school. Except, instead of sleeping through Spanish, I savor everything Toby says.

"Basically, Taiwan's language is shaped by its history. From Austronesian islanders to Japanese imperialism to the influx of Chinese Nationalists, Taiwan even has a language called Hokkien which is pulled from the Fujian providence of China. That's where Taiwanese Mandarin comes from—a blend of Hokkien and Mandarin. But my focus is written Traditional, so I don't know a whole lot about Hokkien."

Watching Toby's eyes glisten as he talks about Taiwanese history makes the back of my eyes prick. I blink the sensation away because I'm just now realizing how much I don't know about the culture that runs through my veins.

When I'd agreed to take Mandarin lessons, I hadn't expected . . . *this*. But now that I see what makes Toby such a great teacher, I know he's worth more than forty-five dollars a session.

"The University of Taipei has an amazing program, which was one of the reasons I wanted to study abroad." Toby's wearing his biggest grin yet. He's not looking at me anymore. His gaze is distant, as if he's seeing parts of his first semester that I never will. "That, and schooling is very affordable in Taiwan. The government will even give you a living stipend just for studying there. If you qualify, of course. To get accepted, you kind of need to already know the language. Fortunately for me, I started studying back in freshman year of high school. I had to pass my qualifier exam before I could even apply."

My ears perk. To go to school in Taiwan—to walk the streets Ya-Fang walks every day. To ride her trains, to eat her food, to go back to the island where I first attended school. Going to college in Taiwan—all of it opens doors I hadn't even considered. I could locate Ya-Fang while I was there and finally ask her the question I never asked Dad. *What was the real reason for the divorce?* I could finally get the closure I never allowed myself to dream of. I could *know* my biological mother.

"Now that you understand a little bit of Mandarin history, we can work on tones," Toby says, snapping me back to reality. He doesn't know the possibilities he's just awakened in me. To him, this is just another Friday. To me, it's like the stars are aligning.

Clients roll in throughout the day. Between checking them in and out, Toby teaches me the five tones of Mandarin.

The first tone is high and flat. It sounds like I'm at a doctor's office and I have my tongue sticking out. For my convenience, Toby uses Pinyin to draw the tone out in a straight line (ā). The second tone slides upward as if I'm asking a question (á). Then we move on to the third one, which is probably the hardest for me. It's a tone that starts high, goes low, then back to high (ǎ). Toby tells me to think of it like the sound a checkmark makes—which doesn't sound like it makes sense, but it kind of does. The last two tones are simple. The fourth one is short and quick like a staccato note (à), while the fifth one is just a neutral tone (a). It's kind of like the first tone, but not as high pitched.

Though I don't need to wear a disposable mask, I slide one over my face and practice the tones under my breath. It's the perfect disguise for someone trying to relearn their first language without looking like a total dork.

I spend the rest of my day reminding my tongue where to sit in my mouth. Before I know it, seven p.m. rolls around. Mr. Yoon-Hanson comes to the front desk to count the cash register. This means it's time for Toby to take me home.

"How was your first lesson?" Toby asks, holding the door open for me as we step into the evening air.

I tear the mask off my face and tuck it into my pocket. The muscles in my mouth are tight from talking to myself all afternoon, but still, I grin.

"I had a lot of fun," I say. It's too hard to explain how much this all means to me. And Toby's just my coworker. He doesn't need to know that now I am itching to attend college in Taiwan. He doesn't need to hear about Ya-Fang. "I'm already looking forward to my next lesson."

Toby smiles as if he understands the reward of learning something new. "I'm excited too. But do you think you could teach me how to talk to Nichole now? To keep this exchange fair, we should probably take turns."

I practically trip on the sidewalk. *Crap.* I'd been so enveloped in Mandarin tones that I'd completely forgotten about *my* end of our bargain. A language lesson for a love lesson. It's my turn to play teacher.

不言而喻
Without Actually Saying It

Moore Plaza's empty parking lot shines under the evening sky. Even though it's only seven p.m., it feels a lot later than it should be. A thin golden haze rises above the jagged mountain peaks in the west. If I were in San Diego, there would still be several hours of sunlight left in the day. Not whatever this weird evening limbo is.

"Ha ha! Yes, I do have a lesson planned for you. And it's a great one. So great. Like pewssshhhh . . ." I do my best to imitate an explosion sound. "Mind-blowingly good. You're gonna be like 'Whoa, Catie came up with this?' and I'm gonna be like, 'Ain't nothing but a chicken wing.'"

Am I having a stroke?

Toby's making the exact face Nichole gave him when he punched her credit card out of her hand. And on top of that, his brows are pinched like he's asking himself why he recruited me to be his dating coach—*me*, of all people. And without keeping my end of the bargain, I don't get free Mandarin lessons. And without those, I won't have what it takes to go to Taiwan and find Ya-Fang. I won't even be able to keep my promise to Dad.

"I'm going to help you figure out your love language," I blurt out before Toby can change his mind about me.

"Love language?" Toby's flawless forehead scrunches into wrinkles.

Oh, no. Is he on to me? Can he sniff out my inexperience? Ugh. This thing is over before it begins, isn't it?

"Sounds cool!" Toby's smooth forehead returns. "What's the love language?"

"You've seriously never heard of them before?" I shouldn't be too surprised. If I hadn't skimmed through Dad's notes last night, it probably would've taken me a while to remember what each of them are.

Toby scratches his chin as we head to the parking lot. Most of the stores have already locked up. Streetlamps light our way under the setting sun. Mannequins stand on display in the windows of empty stores. They're the only people watching us. Them, and a lady walking her goldendoodle past a soda shop.

"I mean, I saw a love language quiz pop up on my social media years ago," Toby says, looking up at the crescent moon as if that's where his memories are.

Huh. It hadn't crossed my mind to have Toby take an online love language test. Those are all over the internet. But an exam won't help Toby learn how to hold a conversation with Nichole. Besides, if I'm going to match his professionalism, I'm going to have to provide him with real-world experiences. Which I can totally pretend I have.

"What's the love language?" Toby asks. "I bet it's French."

"It's not *the* love language. There are five of them in total," I clarify.

Toby drops his jaw. "Five whole languages? Crap. That's a lot. Is English one of them? Wait—what about Mandarin?"

I shake my head to myself. He really has no clue what I'm talking about, does he? This is great for me, I suppose. There's nothing for him to compare my lessons with.

"The love languages aren't *spoken*. They're more like nonverbal ways to communicate affection. So there's Acts of Service, Gift Giving, Quality Time, Words of Affirmation, and . . ."

I rack my brain trying to remember the last one. Crap. I should've done a better job of reading the book last night. But between my exhaustion, tears, and the fact that my thoughts kept slipping away to Dad, I can't remember what the fifth love language is. But before I can recall what I read, Toby interjects.

"I'm not going to lie. All of that went over my head. What does it mean? How do you . . . speak something like—what was it—acts of gift giving?"

"Acts of *Service*," I correct. "And you don't *speak* a love language. At least, not necessarily. Like I said, a love language is a way to communicate the affection of love. Think of it this way: Verbal communication isn't the only way we can express ourselves, right?"

Toby jingles his car keys as he nods to himself. There's a distant focus in his eyes as if he's taking time to digest what I'm saying.

"We can also use body language, facial expressions, and I'd even argue that sliding into someone's DMs is a modern form of nonverbal communication. These love languages can help you tell someone you love them without actually saying, 'Hey, I love you.'" I smile to myself. *Look at me, sounding like I actually know what I'm talking about.*

Toby nods with slightly more surety now. "Interesting. So what are you going to do?"

My answer rises up my throat, but I swallow it back down. I know what I can offer him in exchange for Mandarin lessons. Dad gave me the idea. But once it's out in the air, I can't take it back. I'm committing to this persona Toby thinks is me. But in the end, it'll be worth it. Right?

"I'll take you out on five practice dates," I say, exhaling the taut balloon in my lungs. "Each one will be centered on helping you figure out what your love language is. Once you know, this will help you better express your feelings to Nichole. Plus, you won't have any first-date jitters because you will have already gone on so many practice dates with me."

I can't look at Toby. I'm rubbing my sweaty palms against my skirt and grateful we're required to wear black, so he can't see the wet imprints staining my clothes.

"I don't know how I feel about that." Toby grimaces. "Don't you have a boyfriend? And wouldn't going on practice dates be kind of awkward?"

Oh right. The ol' *boyfriend* thing. I can feel Toby slipping away again—like he's about to reevaluate our agreement. But I'm not losing my first language when I've just gotten it back.

"Jimmy says it's cool," I blurt. Where the heck did that come from? Probably from thinking on my toes at Aunt Joanna's house. *Lie. Truth. Lie.* It's all a blur now.

Toby cocks a brow. "Jimmy?"

"Yeah, he's . . . my boyfriend," I lie, unable to make eye contact.

Okay, this wasn't expected, but I shouldn't panic. Toby needs to think I'm a love expert, because this whole agreement is riding on that. I pull out my phone and flip through my camera roll until I find a picture of Jimmy and me at a basketball game. It's the most couple-y snapshot I have of us. He's taking a bite of a chamoy pickle that he got at the concession stand while I'm trying to snap a picture of our matching *Go, Del Rey Chaparrals!* shirts.

"We're doing long distance," I say. "I told Jimmy about us swapping services, and he thinks it's a great idea. He even joked about how he wishes he'd gone on a practice date before taking me out. Trust me. You have his blessing."

I almost want to laugh at myself. If Jimmy could hear me now, he'd never let me live this one down. Either that, or he'd be freaked out by how flawlessly this lie sounds coming out of my mouth. Especially now that I know for sure there's no lingering romance between us. He'd just broken up with his ex and I thought he was cute. In hindsight, I'm glad we never *actually* kissed. But judging by the way Toby's rubbing the back of his neck, I imagine he's not entirely on board. I need to convince him that this exchange will be worth it.

"Either way, dating is going to be awkward at first." Where did that come from? The book. Dad wrote those exact notes somewhere in the margins of the first chapter. My fingers had traced the sentence a million times over. "The biggest fear of dating is always the whole 'what if they don't like me?' thing. And trust me, I like you, Toby. I wouldn't be doing this if I didn't. So, no matter how awkward you feel or how bad you think the date is going, just know that I'm here for you. And like I said, if you can take me on five practice dates, then you'll definitely be able to take Nichole out on one real one."

Toby swallows hard. He's probably picturing it—him and Nichole hand in hand. Him and Nichole sitting in a rowboat. Him and Nichole doing that *Lady and the Tramp* thing.

"Okay." Toby says. "This sounds . . . kind of fun, actually. So, what love language is our first practice date going to be centered on?"

Finally, a question that I have a thought-out answer for. Mostly because I came up with it five seconds ago. Actually, I have Toby to thank for this. He mixed up acts of service with gift giving, and I've been thinking about it ever since.

"Acts of service," I declare.

Toby scrunches his brows. "And how exactly are we going to have a date centered on acts of service?"

I nibble on my lip as we finally reach the parking lot. Across the sea of asphalt, a Cheesecake Factory appears like a beacon of brilliant ideas. Service. As in waiters. Service like . . . cooking a meal for someone.

I *am* having a stroke. A stroke of genius.

"You'll see what I'm talking about," I say, tossing my hair over my shoulder playfully. "But first, we need to go to the Asian market. Wait—do they even have one in SLC?"

Toby stops in front of a sporty gray Mitsubishi. He clicks his car key fob, and the LED headlights flash. This is his car? Even in the dusk, the sleek charcoal paint job reflects all the light the city has to offer. It must be one of the newest models. How much does this thing cost anyway?

"Yup! Believe it or not, the whitest place in America has a couple of Asian markets," Toby says, unlocking my side of the car. "Hop in. I'll show you."

驚喜

Surprise

Toby's Mitsubishi smells like a gym bag that's been masked with the ylang-ylang and patchouli shampoos from the salon. His passenger seat is littered with gym clothes, shaker bottles, and even a backpack full of Chinese textbooks. Ha. We're both using textbooks as our source material. Sort of.

"S-sorry," Toby stammers, tossing everything into the back seat for me. He's already in the driver's seat and the air-conditioning is on full blast. It doesn't budge his perfect hair at all. "I haven't cleaned my car since I've been back."

"No worries," I say as he finishes clearing off the passenger seat. I climb in and buckle up even though there's still a shaker bottle at my foot. "Thanks for giving me a ride anyway."

As Toby reverses out of his parking spot, I send Mom a text so that she knows I'll be staying out late. And since it's officially the weekend, I don't have work tomorrow. Wow. One week into living in Utah and I'm already staying out late with a coworker?

Toby cuts through the parking lot until we reach the back of Moore Plaza. A pair of stray cats watch us from the dumpsters as Toby zooms off the lot. Soon enough, a wall of fir trees and maples surrounds us. Toby slows his car over the railroad tracks, and I find myself in a neighborhood I've never seen before.

It reminds me of the streets Mavis and I used to walk to get to Del Rey High. Potholes litter the road, and the sidewalks are cracked and uneven. Piles of junk lie on the curb as if the city is a month late on their brush pickup. It's almost like San Diego except there's one big difference between this neighborhood and the one in Cali. Fumigation tarps are draped over every other house we pass.

"Termites," Toby explains as if he's reading my mind. "There's a heat wave this summer, and apparently it has killed off the termite's predators or something like that. Anyway, we're seeing a surge in pests this year because of it. Welcome to Salt Lake City."

I nod. Jimmy had to fumigate his house once. But back in San Diego, the issue seemed to be cockroaches. His family had to live in a hotel for a week. I shudder at the thought of that happening to Aunt Joanna's house. Her neighborhood is up the mountain, not down here in the valley where Uncle Nick would say the *low-income scum live.*

Toby accelerates onto the highway. From here, the mountains are an ominous backdrop against the sky while the rest of the Salt Lake Valley is an ocean of glittering lights. It isn't long before he exits the highway and turns into another parking lot. Tucked between a karaoke bar and a ramen shop is the Asian market.

I climb out of the car and peer up at the sign above the market doors: *Seoul Superstore and More.* A lucky golden cat waves us inside. Red and gold streamers dangle over the shelves lining this warehouse-size market. It reminds me of Chinese New Year, shrines for my ancestors, and sparklers that look like incense.

Toby grabs a cart and waves at the cashier. "Annyeonghaseyo!"

The cashier is an old man with a full gray beard and equally bushy brows. He glances up from the newspaper he's reading and does a double take before waving Toby over. "Oh, Toby! Come in! Come in!"

The two launch into a conversation I don't know how to participate in. Mostly because they aren't speaking English or Mandarin. This is Korean. Toby stretches the words out by bouncing through syllables. To an untrained ear, all East Asian languages probably sound the same. But I can tell the difference even though I can't speak any of them. Sometimes it feels like people prefer to make narrow-minded excuses about the diversity of Asian languages even though appreciating them takes minimum effort. All anyone has to do is listen.

Then the cashier points at me. Toby glances back with flushed cheeks before quickly returning to the conversation and shaking his head. I've seen that shade of tomato red before—back when Nichole made him stutter. Did the cashier ask if we're together? Like, romantically? I haven't been oblivious to the fact that we look like an actual couple. Toby with his lilac hair and me with my glittering eye shadow. I shift away from him so that the cashier knows we're just coworkers.

Finally, Toby bows to the cashier and gestures for me to follow him. "Sorry about that. Mr. Lee is an old family friend. We've been coming here since as far back as I can remember. He was just asking how Umma is doing and wanted to know . . ." Toby's voice lulls, and then he shakes his head as if deciding not to continue with that train of thought. "So, what are we getting?"

Right! We're here for our first practice date. And . . . what exactly is my plan, again? I skim the aisles as my stomach grumbles.

"Okay, so here's what we're going to do. The whole point of this date is to serve each other. And what better way to do that than to cook? You're going to make me one surprise dish, and I'm going to cook one for you, too. And—just for some spirited competition—we're going to judge each other's cooking by the end of the night." Maybe it's the fact that Mavis and I are always competing, but everything absolutely needs to be a contest.

Toby's smile is the widest I've ever seen. "Cook each other food? Now you're talking!"

Toby doesn't need more encouragement to start dumping food into the cart. He walks down the first aisle and plucks a jumbo packet of rice noodles straight from the shelves. Like the kind of jumbo packet of rice noodles that makes me wonder how two teens are supposed to eat this much food in one night. Then he adds oyster sauce, garlic paste, sesame seeds . . .

Okay, so maybe I haven't thought this entire thing through. I assumed I was nailing this whole dating-coach thing when really, I haven't considered the most important part of this evening. Who's paying for all this? Because *I* can't. Toby turns down the next aisle, and the cart squeaks as he adds all the best snacks—rice crackers, sesame sticks, *squid legs*. I should be thrilled he picked up my personal favorite. But with every item he adds, my throat tightens.

"Hey, Toby." My voice is such a whisper that he can't hear me over the crinkle of pineapple cakes landing atop the growing grocery mountain.

I swallow and try to speak louder. "Uh, Toby?"

"What's up?" he asks, dropping a jar of lychee jellies into the cart. They're in a plastic panda, and suddenly, I remember that these were the treats my Taiwanese schoolteachers used to keep behind their desks.

"Um . . ." How do I tell him that I'm broke without also embarrassing myself? *"I'm* taking you out on this date, remember?"

Toby holds my gaze. "Yeah?"

I'm not sure why it's so hard to push the words out. Finally, I squeak, "That means *I'm* supposed to pay."

Toby stops in his tracks and looks down at the mountain of food. All the warmth in his face fades. "Oh, crap. I'm such a dick. I wasn't even thinking about that."

I twist the hem of my shirt. "This is just a practice date, remember? It's okay to make mistakes." Am I saying this for him or for me?

Toby nods as if he really is my student.

"As a rule of thumb: If you're the one suggesting the date, then you're the one who pays. But that rule is flexible if you and your partner agree on something else. Like, you could offer to pay for the dinner, and I'd offer to pay for the movie. When in doubt, communicate."

This isn't a rule I read from Dad's margins. This is one I saw him practice. Dad was never one of those I'm-a-man-so-I-have-to-pay kind of guys. He was never threatened by feminine energy like some of the older men in our church were. He'd wear pink jammies with Mavis and me on the weekends he wasn't flying out. He'd quote *Mean Girls* back to us and actually tried to make *fetch* happen. He learned how to do a Dutch braid so that Mavis could sleep with wet hair, then take it out for school. Now that I think about it, Toby's kind of like Dad in that way. He thrives around women in the way a father of daughters does.

Toby looks up at me through his lashes. "Is it too late to offer to pay now?"

I glance down at the pile, then back up at him. "Yeah. I think that works."

"Cool." Toby beams as the warmth in his skin returns. "Because I was picking some stuff up for my umma, too. Come on. Let me show you the video department."

Videos? That must've been what *more* meant in *Seoul Superstore and More.*

Toby pushes the cart to the back of the market where the shelves of food have morphed into rows of videos. "This is where my umma gets all of her K-dramas. I've been trying to get her on a streaming service, but she's obsessed with collecting VHS tapes and DVDs."

Film cases line the shelves. Posters of actresses wearing traditional hanbok sit next to posters of modern-day Koreans slurping bowls of ramen. Intermingled with the K-dramas are kung fu films. Jet Li graces a banner mounted to the wall. There's even a poster advertising *Shang-Chi and the Legend of the Ten Rings.*

"Tell me when to stop," Toby says, snapping me from my thoughts.

"Huh?"

Toby marches down the aisle without hesitation.

"Uh, stop?"

Toby freezes, closes his eyes, and knocks a random film into his cart. "There. That's how I pick K-dramas out for Umma. I found her favorite rom-com doing this. I swear it works."

I grin as we snake our way back up to the cash register. Toby has picked out more than enough food for both of us. I'm sure that between everything in the cart and a quick Pinterest search, I'll be able to whip up a recipe. I've winged everything so far. Might as well keep it going.

As promised, Toby pays for the food. He racks up a bill and then hands over a platinum credit card. Dang. Maybe one of these days, I'll have a platinum card, too.

"Are you ready to lose this cooking contest, Miss Catie?" Toby asks, pushing the bagged items out the door.

"Excuse me?" I snap. I'm holding the door open for him, but I'm tempted to close it on his face. *Miss Catie?* What am I—some grandma?"

Toby's ears burn and he shifts his gaze away. He's not very good at hiding his expressions, is he? "Sorry. Force of habit. I call all my clients Miss, Mr., and Mx."

"I'm not your client," I snort, following him out to his car. The grocery cart rattles over the asphalt as Toby leads the way.

Toby cocks his head. "Well, I mean, you kind of are. Not for hair but for language lessons. You're my Mandarin client."

"Well, then I guess that makes you my love client." I don't realize what I've said until it's already out in the air. *Love client?* What the heck is that? Also—Toby's my boss's son! I can't call him my love—*anything*! We're supposed to be professionals.

There's a chance Toby isn't even paying attention—thank

goodness. He's already popped his trunk open and is loading groceries into the back. And sure enough, his trunk is just as messy as his front seat. His spare tire is sitting out with a winter coat that I'm sure he hasn't used in months.

"We're going to my place, right?" Toby offers, slamming the trunk lid down. "I have a kitchen in the basement. We renovated it back when my friend Alex lived with me. But they've moved out, so now it just kinda sits empty. Besides, I'm supposed to serve you, right?"

I blink at him. Oh. I hadn't thought about *where* we'd cook until now. *Sheesh, Catie. Get it together!* "Yup. You figured it out. You're learning so much already."

"Only because I have the best teacher." Toby smiles.

My breath hitches. I'm not expecting him to say that about me. I mean, we've just started and I'm making everything up as we go. But maybe if we keep things at this pace, this summer will be over and Toby won't suspect a thing. But before the thought festers, Toby climbs into his car and I take the seat beside him.

"All right," Toby says, gripping the steering wheel. "If we're going back to my place, I should warn you."

"About what?" I ask, the hair on the back of my neck prickling.

Toby gives me a lopsided smirk. "I have a Munch."

"A—what?" I sputter. "What's a Munch?"

Toby starts the engine with a mischievous quirk of his brows. "Oh, you'll see."

雨雲

Rain Clouds

I assumed Toby's family is wealthy enough to have a mountainside mansion. But I don't realize he's the kind of rich person who has a gate surrounding his house until he turns up a driveway that doubles as red carpet. In the center of his property is a modern home constructed of glass walls, white brick, and black accents. Floor-to-ceiling windows create the illusion that there isn't anything separating the sprawling lawn from the museum-chic interior of the living room. Paintings inspired by the four seasons hang over a couch the size of a school bus. And that's about all I glimpse before he clicks his garage door opener.

Toby parks his Mitsubishi beside a Porsche. Of course his parents own a Porsche. At this point, why doesn't he just park next to the yacht?

I help Toby carry the groceries inside while simultaneously wondering how a garage could be big enough to play racquetball in. Toby instructs me to kick my shoes off outside the basement door before he opens it. And when I walk inside, I fight my facial expressions because—*wow.*

A kitchen with a black wood floor stretches across the room until it morphs into the carpeted living area. White cupboards with gold handles wrap around the walls. At first, I think the countertops are made of white stone until I catch the gray veining of marble. Even the island is marble. And there's a sink built into it, too. Golden pots and pans hang over the island like a chandelier. Do they use those things, or are they there for decoration? The colors pull from the accents along the cupboards and tie everything together. This isn't a home. This is the set of a cooking show.

"You can set the groceries on the island," Toby instructs. "I'll put everything away."

I do as I'm told even though my fingers itch to sift through these cupboards. What sort of high-end, organic spices are inside his pantry? I flatten my hands against the kitchen island to keep from exploring. If I start snooping, will it be obvious that we come from different tax brackets? Sure, Dad made good money as a commercial pilot. But after the cancer treatments, we were left with nothing.

I'm so focused on not touching anything that I don't notice a tangerine-striped cat until it brushes against my legs. The sensation of soft fur against my bare shins sends me leaping backward with a yelp.

"There you are, Mr. Munchkin!" Toby stops what he's doing to pick up his cat.

Mr. Munchkin is absolutely *not* a munchkin. Thick tuffs of orange fur curve around his hind quarters. A well-fed belly pudges out as Toby cuddles the cat like a baby.

"Oh, so *that's* Munch," I realize, relieved as I let the adorable tiger cub smell my fingers. Mr. Munchkin sniffs while staring into the depths of my soul with his electric green eyes. "Since you call him Mr. Munchkin, does that make him one of your clients, too?"

"It sure does. He's my best client." Toby kisses Munch between the ears, then sets him back down. Munch lands on the floor with the gracefulness of . . . well, a cat. "He was the runt of the litter when we got him. But now he's kinda chonky, huh, Monchers?"

Mr. Munchkin? Monchers? Munch? Toby's got nicknames for his nicknames.

Munch isn't paying attention to us. The moment all four paws hit the ground, he's already trying to get onto the island. In no time at all, he leaps onto the bar stool and crawls across the marble counter.

"He's going to want to eat our food, by the way." Toby laughs to himself as he swings open a cabinet door. It's packed with spices. Of course it is. "I can put Munch upstairs if you want."

"Are you kidding me?" I shake my head. In San Diego, we were never allowed to have animals in our apartment. Living with Maddie Sue and now meeting Munch are kind of like dreams come true. "Munch needs to stay. Who else is going to be our food critic? He can tell us which one smells better."

Munch pauses his prowl as if he knows I'm talking about him.

"I don't see why we need a judge, because I'm going to crush your dish anyway." Toby grins, stuffing the snacks into the pantry. "Just wait, Miss Catie Carlson. You don't even know what's coming."

I slam my fists together like I'm ready to brawl. "Oh, yeah? Game on, Mr. Tobias Yoon-Hanson. Game on."

Toby immediately gets to work. Not once do I see him reach for a cookbook or check his phone. He flows through the kitchen like a dancer who's already memorized intricate choreography.

Meanwhile, I'm skimming through Pinterest trying to find something, *anything*. Eventually, I discover an easy ramen recipe. This one doesn't require stewing bones for hours. I plop a set of chicken drumsticks and herbs into a pot of water. Toby peeks over my shoulder and quickly realizes what I'm making. Well, there goes that secret.

But try as I might, I can't figure out what Toby is cooking. He pulls some marinated beef from the refrigerator, then chops up onions, carrots, and peppers into toothpick slices. He dumps them all into the skillet, and the air thickens with garlic and toasted sesame oil.

"Okay, I *need* to know what you're making."

Toby fries noodles in another skillet but pantomimes locking his lips and throwing away the key. "Can't. I got this recipe from my aunties in Busan. The marinated beef is a family secret passed down from generation to generation."

Toby's words punch me right in the stomach. Maybe it's our competing smells. Or maybe it's the fact that no one ever taught me anything about Taiwanese food. That's the thing about living with rain clouds over my head. I can be in the middle of something so fun and then—*snap*. I remember that no matter what, part of me is somewhere else.

"What's wrong?" Toby stops stirring his concoction. Apparently, I'm easier to read than I thought.

Should I tell him what's really on my mind? Would Toby even understand? He has money and I don't. He has parents and I don't. He belongs and I have to force myself to believe that I do, too.

"I wish I was like you," I finally say, not sure why I open up. Maybe it's because he's the closest thing I have to Taiwan. And he's not even Taiwanese. "It's just . . . do you ever miss something you've never had?"

I dare myself to look at him—to see if this rich boy with a home and parents and secret recipes could ever understand someone like me. And to my surprise, the answer is yes. I see it in his eyes—in the way they go distant. I see it in the way his shoulders slump as if there's an invisible force pulling them down and he's tired of holding himself up. I see it in the way he twirls a finger around a loose curl, and I hear it in the way he says, "Every day of my life."

The air is thick with steam. I feel like I should ask Toby what he means. But I know he doesn't want to talk about it. Because everything about him, from the tilt of his head down to the way his toes are pointed away from me—it all speaks a language of pain I didn't realize I was fluent in.

Toby turns the heat down before crossing into the living room. DVDs line the walls. I assume this is where Mrs. Yoon-Hanson keeps her K-drama collection. Toby sifts through the shelves before picking up an old DVD and sliding it into the player. The entire back wall fades to black. It takes me a moment to realize he doesn't have a TV. He has a projector and a theater screen. Naturally.

The film starts and the opening title screen appears. Though the script isn't in English, I recognize the boxy angles and the swooping strokes of Hanzi. In subtitles, the words *Far from Home* appear.

"One of the best ways to learn a new language is to immerse yourself in it," Toby explains, returning to the cutting board beside me.

The air is still heavy, but it doesn't smell like tears anymore.

"This is a Taiwanese movie about a girl who's trapped in San Francisco and can't get back home to Taipei. I have the subtitles on, but I feel like the best way to learn Mandarin is to listen to the words and watch the actors' body language. Even though I understood Mandarin, people knew I was American because of how much louder and animated I was. They do a really good job of showing Americans through a Taiwanese lens."

The film starts, and Toby doesn't share any more stories about his freshman year in Taipei. At first, I think it's because he feels bad for me. But as I slice my over-boiled egg, I realize he's gone back into teacher mode so I can focus on the film.

I plate my ramen long before Toby finishes his dish, and make my way to the living room. The fibers from the plush carpet tickle my toes as I patter over to the couch, making sure my broth doesn't spill. I plop down and sink into the heavenly cushions. Munch takes that as his cue to curl up at my feet. I slurp the noodles as I watch the film—eyes dancing back and forth between subtitles and actors. Every now and then, Munch looks back as if double-checking that I'm paying attention. Or maybe he's waiting for me to let him lick my broth.

Sitting here with a bowl of homemade ramen and a T-drama on-screen feels so simple, but so important. It makes me think of when I first came to America. Ya-Fang called me every Friday, but it felt like she wasn't just on another continent, she was in another universe. With each passing week, my words became more and more jumbled until my Mandarin was completely gone. By then, Dad had a new wife, and the phone stopped ringing.

What I wouldn't give to go back and tell my younger self to savor my moments with Ya-Fang. To ask for family recipes. To practice my Mandarin with her. Good food and good conversations. So meaningless when you have it, then meaningful when it's gone.

I finish slurping the broth when Toby sits beside me with a plate of fresh noodles. "Do you mind if I pause the movie for a bit? I want to see what you think of my japchae."

"What's that?" I ask, taking his plate and setting my bowl on the coffee table.

Toby reaches for the remote and pauses the movie. The scene is frozen on a shot of the Golden Gate Bridge. Fog rolls in from across the water, but that deep blue ocean is similar to San Diego—so close to home.

"Japchae is the life force of all positive energy on Earth," Toby explains solemnly. "The noodles aren't made of just sweet potato. They're made from threads of music. And the vegetable medley is actually a vegetable *melody* that harmonizes with music. Whatever. There's a pun in there somewhere. I'm not as clever as you are."

I chuckle. With Toby, I don't have to over-annunciate and gesticulate for him to understand me. We can sit in silence and we'll still speak the same language.

"But—" Toby says before I can take a bite, "since this is a family recipe, I didn't add the last ingredient. That's confidential. It should still beat your dish out of the water. I just want you to know that even without the secret ingredient, this competition was no contest."

I kick Toby's shins playfully. "Yeah, yeah. You're an amazing cook. I know."

Then I scoop up the japchae with some chopsticks and plop it into my mouth. Before I even bite into the veggies, the sweet beef marinade rolls over every corner of my tongue. When I finally sink my teeth into it, the crunch of carrots and peppers pops against the contrast of soft noodles and steamed spinach. Toby's dish is still warm, too, unlike my room-temperature ramen broth. Yup. He wins.

"I can taste the music." I groan.

"It's like that scene from *Ratatouille*, right?" Toby asks, leaning back in the seat beside me to eat his own plate.

I jab the butt of my chopstick at him. "Where Remy sees fireworks when he eats food? It totally is!"

Toby and I inhale our japchae as if it's the very oxygen we need to live. We slurp, we crunch, and I'm pretty sure Toby burps, or was that me? Whatever. My chopsticks clank against the plate. Then before I know it, my dish is empty and my stomach is bloated.

"Okay, final question," I say, smoothing out my skirt. "How do you feel about serving me?"

Toby sets his plate on the coffee table beside my bowl. He wipes his mouth with the back of his hand before answering. "I loved it, actually. More than I thought I would."

"Yeah?" I ask, realizing that I've used the second Mandarin tone.

"I do. I mean, I'm a cosmetologist. I kind of service people every day. I also really enjoy teaching you Mandarin and cooking for you. I felt like I was in my own element, you know? Like it's not a chore for me to do all this. I did it because . . . well, it's fun, I guess."

I hadn't considered that acts of service would resonate so well with Toby. But the most important thing is that he enjoyed doing it. What a total win! My first trial run as a dating coach is a success, and Toby has no clue that I made the whole thing up.

"Maybe one day I'll work up the courage to do this exact same date night with Nichole." Toby sighs. "Tell your boyfriend I said thanks for okaying this. He's a pretty chill guy."

The smile plastered across my face begins to waver. But before I can reply, he's already moving on.

"If anything, this exercise taught me that . . . practice dating isn't as terrifying as I thought it would be. At least, not with a pro like you."

When I'd first agreed to this, I hadn't really thought about what it meant to lie to him. Honestly, I never really saw it as a *lie*-lie. Just a little . . . withholding information. But now that I'm sitting here gazing into his warm eyes, I'm realizing—

This is messed up.

I'm messed up.

I need to come clean. I need to—

"I'll let him know," I hear myself say.

Come on, Catie, why did you do that? I'm *lying* to this guy who's putting his trust in me. Toby has already inspired me to find Ya-Fang in person, and I'm treating him like this. He deserves better.

Chill. Another part of me bites back. *Why do you even care what he thinks about you? He's just a coworker you'll forget when you're back in Cali.*

I swallow, the taste of japchae still lingering on my lips. Toby is just a moment. And like everything else in my life, he'll be gone, too. And I won't miss him the way that I miss Dad or Ya-Fang.

Toby glances at his watch and comments about the time. But before we leave, he pulls the DVD from the player and hands it to me. "Take this with you, so you can finish it."

I hold the case in my hands and peer down at the cover of *Far from Home.* The main character, Ting, stares up at the camera with a shocked expression. Behind her is the Golden Gate Bridge and the iconic Taipei 101. I clutch the DVD to my chest. In so many ways, Ting and I are the same.

"Feel free to rewatch it as many times as you want," Toby says, leading me back to the garage.

"When do you want it back?" I ask.

Toby clicks his car key fob, and the bright angel lights illuminate the garage. "Keep it. But I will expect a thorough review of the film the next time we have a language lesson. You have homework."

紅唇

Red Lips

When I return to the Taylors' foyer, the lights in the hallway are off, which means that everyone must've already gone to bed. I kick off my Vans and carry them to the basement so that my footsteps won't wake anyone up. Just as I reach the stairwell, a voice calls from behind.

"Catie?"

My soul leaps out of my skin. Then my brain catches up and I recognize that voice. "Yeah, Mom?"

My mother pokes her head out from the living room. Judging by her PJs and the sudoku puzzle in hand, she stayed up waiting for me. "How did it go? What did you and your coworker do?"

Right. Mom knows I was with Toby. But I haven't quite told her about the whole lesson-for-a-lesson thing yet.

"So. I'm not really sure how to tell you this," I begin, toes curling in my socks.

Mom's face turns sheet white. I can only imagine what it sounds like I'm about to say. I mean, I was just out with a boy, and I have some news for Mom? She probably thinks I'm pregnant.

"Toby is teaching me Mandarin," I blurt before I can go back on my words.

Mom presses a hand to her chest and sighs with relief. Sheesh! She really *did* think I was pregnant.

"Sweetheart, that's amazing," Mom sings. "I'm so happy you're reconnecting with your heritage."

"Thanks, Mom."

I want to feel relieved, too, knowing that she isn't disappointed in me or mad that I'm returning to a place and a culture I knew before her. But then I think about all the other questions scratching at the surface: What will she say when I eventually tell her that Dad's death made me realize how little I know about myself? That while Mom's been my mother for most of my life, I haven't stopped longing for my biological mom? She's done the hard work—raised me, cared for me, guided me. How will she feel when she knows how often I think about Ya-Fang?

Mom wraps her arms around her rib cage. "How did your language lesson go?"

"It went really well," I whisper, not sure if the Taylors can hear us from their rooms. "Better than what I was expecting." *Truth.* Wow. For once I'm not lying about something.

"Well, I'm happy you're making friends. And it seems like you're adjusting to Salt Lake City. I wish I could say the same for Mavis." The crinkles around Mom's eyes fade as her gaze sinks to the floor. "I know she's having trouble feeling at home here. And all the rejections on her job applications are making it that much harder. But I think if she made some friends, that would help her feel welcomed here, too."

The corners of my lips pinch together. I hadn't thought about the weight of rejection pushing Mavis down. It's one thing to put yourself out there. It's another to be told no while you're doing it, too.

"Do you think you could help her . . . find some community here?" Mom asks, her voice pleading.

"Of course," I say, though even to my own ears, I don't sound convinced. "I mean, Toby's kind of the only friend I've made so far. I'll introduce them sometime. And if I make any more friends, I can share them with Mavis."

Mom nods eagerly at the idea. "That would be great. I've been wanting to show her some of my favorite places from when I grew up here. I think that would help her feel a sense of community, too. But when I brought up the idea, Mavis didn't seem very interested."

"Yeah, that sounds like her." I sigh. "She probably just needs a little more time to adjust before she'll be open to something like that."

"I hope so . . ." Mom's voice falters as if her thoughts are far away. "What about you? Are you happy here?"

A small smile grows on my face. "I think I can learn to be." *Truth.*

♥

On Sunday morning, Aunt Joanna, Uncle Nick, and Cousin Rayleigh drag us all to church. I wish I worked today so that I had an excuse not to go. Though even if I *did* work on Sundays, the Taylors would insist I ask for the Sabbath Day off. Ugh. Whatever. If I'm being forced to go to church, I'll at least look good while sitting in the pews.

I haul my makeup tote up the basement stairs, because doing my makeup in Mom's Subaru has become a ritual. I'm about to open the front door when Rayleigh meets me in the foyer.

"Hey," she says, nodding down to my bag of Rare Beauty, ColourPop, and Urban Decay.

I stop in my tracks. I still haven't forgotten about Rayleigh's request. "Makeup?"

My cousin grins. Apparently, she hasn't forgotten about it either.

Rayleigh ushers me into her room. It's way bigger than mine and Mavis's. Along the far wall is a giant window that peers into the backyard. Maddie Sue sunbathes on the patio while the neighbor's pool shimmers from behind a maple tree. But most importantly, this sun-drenched window offers the lighting I need for a flawless makeup application.

I eagerly dump out my collection onto her carpeted floor. Lashes, eye shadows, and contour palettes mingle with samples I've accumulated from Ulta and Sephora rewards points. The makeup's powdery smell tingles with creative possibilities.

"Whoa." Rayleigh's eyes bulge as I organize my makeup. "That's a lot of stuff. I literally don't know anything about it. Mom doesn't want me wearing it since . . . well, she says she doesn't want me looking like the W-word."

Her version of the W-word must not be Maddie Sue's version—*walkies*. "You mean *whore*?"

Rayleigh winces. "Yeah, I'm not allowed to say that. But I'm glad Mom's not breathing down your neck like she does mine. I think she knows Aunt Andrea wouldn't be very happy with her controlling you and Mavis the way she controls me."

Oof. Rayleigh said the C-word, not me. But I don't blame her. We've all been thinking it. Who would Rayleigh be if she were allowed to be herself rather than have to fit into the Mormon mold?

"Maybe after we move back to San Diego, you can come out with us for a summer," I say, meeting Rayleigh's eyes. "You can wear all the makeup you want and say all the bad words, too. Maybe even kiss a boy . . . ?"

I don't want to bring up the DM I saw on Rayleigh's iPad. But the idea hasn't left my mind. Who was she messaging? And is she comfortable enough to tell me about it?

"Oh, man. Mom would kill me if I ever kissed some guy." Rayleigh laughs awkwardly to herself, then shifts the conversation. "Do you know how to do nineteen fifties Old Hollywood makeup? I've always thought it looks so classy. I feel like it's light enough to not make Mom mad. But I don't know how to do the wing-y eyeliner thing."

Ohhhh, pinup? If anything can make me forget what I was talking about, it's my hottest shade of red lipstick. I know Aunt Joanna won't approve, but my hand is already climbing over the mound of makeup, hunting down everything I'll need. "That's one of my favorite looks."

Rayleigh takes her glasses off, and I dust translucent powder on her eyelids. I layer on a natural eye shadow base before carving out a symmetrical winged liner. It might look too dramatic for Aunt Joanna's liking. But against my cousin's pale blue eyes, it looks fantastic.

"Are you planning to sit with us for sacrament meeting?" Rayleigh asks while I coat her lashes with mascara, trying to keep it light. She wears glasses, after all.

I cap the wand. "What do you mean?"

"I overheard Mavis telling Aunt Andrea that she's planning to sneak out to the nursery during sacrament meeting." Rayleigh blinks slowly as if she's scared moving will ruin her fresh face. "She says she's planning to kick-start her babysitting gigs, but I know she's really just ditching sacrament."

I carefully place my mascara wand back in the pile. "Oh. I—um . . ." I'm not about to out my sister, no matter how rude she is to me sometimes.

"I don't blame her. Really." Rayleigh's expression is stiff. "But if Mavis *really* wants to ditch church, she should go to the genealogy office."

I forgot about things like genealogy offices. It's been years since I've thought about the importance of family history to Mormons. As an adoptee, I've always hated how the church put such an emphasis on tracing bloodlines. Probably because you can't do sacred Mormon temple work for your non-consenting dead relatives if you don't know your family's history. Besides, every time I've done genealogy work, I've reached a dead end, starting with Ya-Fang.

But what if things have changed? What if there *is* a way to trace my family back to Taiwan? Maybe I won't have to go to college in Taiwan just to find her. Maybe there's an easier way.

I'm doubtful. So many doors have been slammed in my face that I'm scared to knock again. But there's a candle inside that's always burning—always giving off just enough light for hope to find it.

"Oh, well, I don't know about Mavis, but if Mom can't find me after sacrament meeting, that's where I'll be," I say, using a steady hand to trace Rayleigh's cupid's bow.

Rayleigh doesn't nod. She doesn't say anything. She doesn't even hum through her nose. She's as still as a statue while I paint her lips, and yet I know she's saying, *okay!*

When I'm done, I cap my lipstick and press a hand to my chest. "Rayleigh, you look—"

A knock sounds at the door. Rayleigh and I both whirl around as Aunt Joanna pops her head inside.

"Rayleigh, we're going to be late for—"

She freezes, her gaze zeroing in on Rayleigh's lipstick. Centuries seem to pass by as she stares. And stares. And *stares*.

I wait, unsure if I should say anything.

"Whose attention are you trying to get?" Aunt Joanna finally snipes, shaking her head. "You're going to be in Young Women's all day. You don't want to look like a whore, do you?"

I grit my teeth. Is this the real reason Aunt Joanna doesn't want me wearing makeup? It's not about showing off my *naturally ethnic features*, it's about not looking like a harlot.

"Take that off," she snaps. "And hurry up. We're already late for church."

Then she shuts the door.

"Sorry." Rayleigh sighs, swiveling around to admire her reflection for the first and last time. "It looks really pretty though. How long do you think it will take to remove it?"

I could take off Rayleigh's makeup with some micellar water. But then she'd look like a clown with raccoon eyes. The best thing to do is wash her face off in a steamy shower. But I doubt Rayleigh has enough time for that. So, I reach for something else instead. A nude matte lipstick.

Rayleigh lets me paint the neutral color over the fire engine red. By the time I'm done, a slight pink shimmer bleeds through her lips. Something that Joanna will notice only if she stares hard enough.

"Better?" I ask, capping the lipstick.

Rayleigh turns to the mirror once more. Between her glasses covering her eyeliner, and the nude lip color painted over the red, Rayleigh looks beautiful in a way that only she knows.

"Better." Rayleigh nods.

"Rayleigh! Catie! We are leaving!" Uncle Nick's booming voice carries from the foyer through Rayleigh's closed doors. He sounds mad, but when doesn't he?

I climb to my feet. I haven't even done *my* makeup yet. But the sooner I get this day over with, the sooner I can rewatch *Far from Home.*

足以吞噬星系

Large Enough to Swallow Galaxies

Mom and the Taylors enter the chapel. As the doors open, the honk of an organ barrels into the lobby. There's a massive congregation inside making small talk, shaking hands, and being Utah-white. I twirl my locks, knowing I'll stand out like coal on snow.

Mavis darts down the hall before anyone notices her missing. She's probably already found the nursery before I even tell Mom I'm going to use the bathroom. Mom tells me to hurry back, and I respond with a grimace. I don't plan to return. I'd rather spend sacrament meeting at the genealogy office.

The layout of this church building is just like the one we went to back when Dad was home for Sundays. We used to go to church only when he wasn't in the air. It was too weird going without him. And just like our old building, these halls are lined with that weird hemp material that serves no purpose other than to look like a cat scratching board. Other than it being an absolute staple in Mormonism, I have no clue what its purpose is.

I loop around the singular corridor, following it to the back of the building. The classroom doors have windows, so I peer inside, hoping to spot the genealogy office. Most of the rooms have the lights turned off. The only thing I can see from the windows are foldable chairs shaped in semicircles and half-erased chalkboards.

Finally, I reach a door by the building's rear exit. I peep inside, expecting the same chair ensemble. But instead, I spy a room full of computers. Curiosity takes over. This is new. But I must be staring for too long, because moments later, the door opens.

"Can I help you?"

An elderly woman stands in the entryway, white curls like clouds atop her head. Her dress is cut in a pattern that reminds me of Mrs. Claus and sugar cookies. Even though thick glasses magnify her pale blue eyes, she still squints at me as if she can't see me well. Or she's trying to guess my race.

"Oh," I say, startled. "I'm sorry, I was just . . . Um, do you know where I can find the genealogy office?"

The woman grins. Her teeth are gummy and the wrinkles around her lips pull in every direction. "Well, you've found it. Come on in."

She takes a seat at one of the computers and starts clicking away. How do her fingers move so quickly? I can't even type that fast, and I was practically born with a cell phone in my hand. I follow hesitantly as the door swings shut behind me.

"What's your name, honey?" she asks.

"Uh . . . Catie," I say, creeping closer.

"Is that a nickname or your given name?"

"Um, that's what's on my birth certificate," I say hesitantly. It's my name but I'll never know *why* Dad chose it for me. Unless I find Ya-Fang.

"Last name?"

"What?"

"Last name?" she repeats.

I scratch my arm like I'm sprouting a rash. "Wait. Are you looking up my family history right now?"

The lady stops typing. I'm not sure what her name is, but she looks like she could be my granny. At least, on Dad's side. "Well, normally, this place is for members who are trying to find names to take to the temple. But if you want, we can look up your genealogy just for fun. Or you can keep me company while I do some librarian work."

I swallow hard and take a step back. This is all happening so quickly. "I'd like to . . . look up my genealogy," I tell her, "but, um, here's the thing. I'm adopted, so you won't find anything on the Taiwanese side of my family. I was wondering—"

"You're adopted?" Granny's bushy brows shoot to the ceiling.

I freeze as if I've just outed myself as an alien wearing a human skin suit.

Granny's lips pull into a weak smile. One that I know I wear. One that I've seen on Toby's face, too. Then she says in that tone I know all too well, "Me too."

I hear it like an accent on her voice. She's lonely—like me. And yet, how can people like us be lonely when we're surrounded by others? Mom never neglects me. Mavis has been at my side for years. But still, I walk around every day feeling like my heart is a black hole. Given that it's something large enough to swallow galaxies, how can no one else see what's inside me?

"I've never met another adoptee before," I confess. There

must've been other adopted kids at Del Rey High. But it never seemed like I could share my experience without becoming an outsider.

"I hadn't either," Granny says, "until I discovered genealogy. I'll admit, recordkeepers could do a better job of—well, keeping records. Including adoption papers. But I have a trick up my sleeve to help you find the Taiwanese side of your family. Despite being adopted."

I recoil and can't stop my lips from pursing. This lady doesn't know me. How can she be so sure that she'll find loopholes? And yet something tugs at my chest. I need to know where Ya-Fang is—if she thinks about me. If she misses me. If she knows what happened to Dad, and if she's willing to share why he got custody of me in the first place. And now Granny is saying that there's a way I can find out?

What if . . . ?

"Take a seat and I'll show you," Granny says.

I scoop up a chair from one of the computers and sit down beside her. *Don't get your hopes too high, Catie. Let's just see what she can do first.* I'm so used to seeing the dead ends on my family trees that even now, it's hard to *wish*.

"The church uses FamilySearch for their genealogy software," Granny explains, closing her window and clicking on a widget that's already been installed on this computer. "But there are many other software programs available. When it comes to finding ancestors from overseas, I like to use PanGenea. It's different because some ancestry sites collect only American obituaries, newspapers, and birth certificates—all that. PanGenea is a bigger site with even more records and global librarians—like myself—who fact-check universal records. It's a great resource for you to get started, if you know the general location of your ancestors."

I play piano on my kneecaps in an effort to air out my clammy palms. I've been down this road before, back when Mavis and I did a church activity centered on finding our ancestors. Except she'd run into the issue of not knowing who her bio dad is.

But what if things have changed since the last time I bothered to dig into my Taiwanese family? Has technology really advanced that much? Could it really be true—that people from around the world volunteer to read records and bookkeep bloodlines? If that's true—will I find Ya-Fang's birth certificate? Will I find evidence of Dad's first marriage?

I'm letting my wildest daydreams spiral. Water pricks my tear ducts as if asking permission to fall again. I suck them back inside. I'm not sobbing. Not until I know for sure.

Granny asks for some information about Dad and Ya-Fang—like where they were from and where they were married. But it isn't until I reveal I was born in Taipei that we finally have a breakthrough. With all that information combined, PanGenea is able to sift through millions of documents relating to the keywords and dates Granny has inputted.

A spinning image of the planet appears along with the words *We're searching through 150,000,000 records for you*. Then that number drops to 50,000. Then 500. I wait, stomach rolling. Palms sweating. Ears ringing. *Stop, Catie. It's not going to find anything*.

And then it stops.

We've found 1 record relating to your search.

"Are you going to take a look?" Granny asks, leaning back and offering me the mouse.

I take it with hot hands and guide the cursor to the underlined 1. My finger quivers when I click on it. And then the page loads and I'm looking at the results. There on the screen are three images. A picture of Ya-Fang in her early twenties with a graduation cap on her head and a scroll in her hands. A picture of Dad graduating from flight school. And a blank square in between them with my name on it. Catie Carlson.

I blink.

This isn't real.

This *can't* be real.

I've wanted this so badly, and now my mother's digital face has arrived in minutes. I haven't seen my biological parents in the same room since I was a child. But I rub my eyes and there they are, frozen in time—smiling at me from these pixelated photographs as two lines connect them to my name.

"Would you look at this." Granny points a bony finger to a drop-down menu under Dad's image. "This gold *T* icon means someone's translating your genealogy."

"T-Translating?" I stammer. "Does that mean my dad has records in Mandarin? Like a marriage license? Pay stubs from working in Taiwan? Visas?"

I'm a beehive of thoughts. Dad didn't tell me many stories about his life before I was born. There was always this unspoken rule that it was better to not talk about that stuff—the *hard* stuff. If I dig deeper into PanGenea, I might find the answers to some of my questions. Maybe there will be flight logs of all the places he visited while working around the Pacific Rim. What if this site has pictures of Dad petting elephants in Thailand, or of him standing on the top of Marina Bay Sands in Singapore? What if Ya-Fang is in those pictures, too?

Granny nods. "That seems to be the case. There are genealogists who sift through documents and input the material into the computer all the time. This icon just means that your documents were originally in Taiwanese but someone translated them into English. Sometimes, relatives are the ones putting this together—"

I suck in a sharp breath. *Ya-Fang? Is she the one doing this? Is she trying to find me, too?*

"But most of the time, it's a genealogist who loves doing this kind of historical research," Granny concludes. "Like me."

I swallow as a new thought crosses my mind. Could Ya-Fang be a genealogy librarian? Is that even possible?

I'm spiraling again—willing things to be true even though I have nothing to prove it. For now, I remind myself to be grateful for this new starting point.

"Can I see what's been translated?" I ask.

"Of course!" Granny says. "Have fun."

I click on Dad's gold *T*. The site refreshes and takes me to a new screen. It kind of looks like a résumé except there's a picture of Dad's official pilot headshot in the upper left corner. The one where he's wearing a blue uniform with a buttoned collar and a captain's cap.

To the right of his image, bullet points mark the milestones in my father's life. *Birth. Marriage. Education. Death.* My dry tongue scrapes the roof of my mouth as my gaze instinctively hovers over *Death*. And yet, seeing him on the computer al-most brings him back to life. He looks so healthy in that photo. I'd almost forgotten about the pinkness around his nose and the way his gray eyes twinkled like there was always a joke on the tip of his tongue.

"You can hold the mouse over the milestones to peek at what's been added," Granny encourages.

I guide the little arrow down the list. *Birth*—a small thumbnail of a blurry birth certificate appears beside my cur-sor. I imagine that if I click on it, it will take me to a clear, digitized version of the paper document.

Marriage—another small fuzzy image. But this one catches my eye. I can make out the blob of a white dress and the blur of a black suit. And there's something else, too. But this thumbnail is too small.

I double-click on it. The image expands to reveal a fuzzy photo as if it were taken with a disposable camera. Despite the blurred edges and bleeding colors, I can't mistake the image of Ya-Fang in a fluffy white dress and Dad in a suit. It would look like an ordinary Christian wedding if not for the Buddha statue behind them.

Oh. My. God.

Memories of sitting and chanting resurface in my mind. For a moment, I'm transported back to a shrine in Taipei. I'm seated beside Ya-Fang with the smell of waxy candles in the air. Men with large ears and shaved heads sit around me. I remember their ears because the Buddha statue at the front of the temple had big ears, too. How had I forgotten that while Dad was off flying planes, Ya-Fang was raising me Buddhist?

Was marrying someone outside of their religion one of the reasons that ultimately led to their divorce?

"Is the information wrong?" Granny asks, oblivious to the memories swimming through my brain. "Sometimes the librarians put in the wrong information. We are volunteers, after all."

I shake my head. How do I even begin to explain everything? Granny has unlocked a door—one that I was too scared to open because I'd always imagined the only thing behind that door was a vacant room. But my past isn't empty—it was just blurry, distorted, and drenched in cringy 2000s fashion. But most importantly, it's all real. And it's all truly mine.

A knock sounds at the door, cutting through my thoughts like thunder.

"Catie?" Aunt Joanna's familiar voice tears me away from the screen. She stands in the doorway as her attention slides from me, to Granny, to all the computers in the room, and then back to me. "What are you doing in here?"

My temple bubbles with sweat like I've just been caught looking at porn or something. Aunt Joanna can't see the computer screen from where she stands. Thank goodness, because I don't particularly feel like sharing this moment with her. But at least she's caught me doing something as productive as genealogy. If I'm going to skip out on sacrament meeting, this really is the second-best place to be. Okay, third, but Mavis already claimed the nursery.

"We've been looking all over for you," Aunt Joanna continues, hand on her hip. "Come on. Rayleigh and Mavis are in the car waiting for you."

What? How long have I been in the genealogy office?

When I don't move, Aunt Joanna taps her shoe. "Let's go, Catie."

I groan to myself as I climb from my seat. Granny and I have just started diving into Dad's past. Will I find pictures of him in college? In high school? What if he wore braces or wore those thick dorky glasses as a kid? He told me that he played the French horn in his college marching band. But in all the years I knew him, I never actually saw a French horn in his hands. When I went to church today, the last thing I imagined was that I'd want to come back.

Aunt Joanna ducks back into the hallway. But before I join her, there's something I need to ask.

"What's your name?"

Granny smiles at me with a full set of teeth. "You can call me Eloise."

I return her smile. Granny Eloise it is. "Will you be here next Sunday?"

"I'm here every weekend," Granny Eloise chirps.

I resist the urge to wrap her in a hug and settle for a friendly wave instead. I've only just learned her name, and yet she's made a greater impact on my life than any sermon could ever. Maybe today is a sign that I need to be right here, right now.

Dad dropped *The Five Love Languages* at my feet so that I'd take Toby on practice dates and start learning my first language. Ya-Fang's image showed up today to remind me to reconnect with my spirituality. And considering how my life is finally starting to come together in the ways I least expected, I know what I have to do next.

一刹那的過去
A Flicker of the Past

I burst into Mavis's bedroom without knocking.

"What the—?" she screeches, sitting up in bed with a Sunday nap in her eyes. Mavis hasn't changed out of her church clothes. It's a white blouse with an old maxi skirt she must've dug up from her clothing graveyard. At one time, I think it was solid black, but now it's a weird off-gray color that's been washed so many times, it needs a lint roller to get the fuzzies out. She's thrown on an oversize Del Rey High hoodie, making her former church outfit perfectly *Mavis*.

"Where's your candle collection?" I ask.

Mavis scrunches her face but doesn't ask me to repeat myself. Instead, she juts her chin to the corner of the room where boxes remain unpacked. I don't blame her. I still haven't put away all my stuff either. "The candles are somewhere in there. Why do you need them?"

"I'm doing stuff," I reply.

"Ladies and gentlemen, we've got a storyteller over here."

I cross the room and roll my eyes so she can't see. "If you really want to know . . . I'm, uh, going to meditate."

Mavis narrows her eyes. "With a candle?"

I wince because I know how ridiculous this sounds. What am I thinking? I don't remember anything about Buddhism other than lighting candles and watching them flicker. Wait—am I mixing up my memories of Buddhism with the ones of Ya-Fang praying at ancestral shrines? What if I'm going about this all wrong? Or what if it's appropriative of me to attempt practicing now? A part of me wants to Google this stuff for clarity. But what if seeing pictures that aren't mine only contaminates my faded memories?

"Yes, a candle. It's kind of the only thing I remember about Buddhism, and I want to reconnect with that side of my spirituality."

My gaze dips to the floor. I haven't had a genuine conversation with Mavis in months, and I'm not exactly ready to share this moment with her. She doesn't know about everything I've been feeling about Dad, about Ya-Fang, about my language lessons with Toby. I don't think I'm San Diego Catie anymore. Maybe it *is* time to unpack all my boxes.

"Never mind. You wouldn't understand," I grumble, popping open a cardboard lid. This one has mostly shampoo bottles and packages of period products. She's been hoarding these this whole time?

Mavis shifts in bed. I half expect her to flop over and fall back to sleep. Instead, she asks, "Can I meditate with you?"

I whirl around. *"What?"*

Since when has Mavis wanted to do *anything* with me? I meet my sister's hopeful gaze. There's a silent plea in her eyes like she's tired of being told she's not good enough to work a job, or she's not good enough to be a nanny. She's trying. She really is putting herself out there—searching for her own home, too. But unlike me, everything and everyone keeps telling her no.

"Okay," I say hesitantly. Meditating is something I want to do for myself. But I'd rather have her company than be another rejection on her list.

Mavis kicks the blankets off her legs and reaches for something under the nightstand beside her. "Cool. I actually have Mahogany Teakwood over here. Is that okay?" Sure enough, she's holding up a Bath & Body Works candle.

"Uh, I guess?" It's not like I have any idea what I'm doing. I'm just going for it.

Moments later, Mavis and I are seated cross-legged on the floor of my room. My back is to the wall while Mavis leans against the corner of my bed. The room would be totally dark if not for the afternoon sun casting a golden beam on the carpet. That, and the orange sparks of the lighter in Mavis's hand. She's trying to ignite the candle, but the lighter she packed must've been damaged by a leaky perfume bottle.

"So how do you meditate?" Mavis asks, holding the candle to her face as if that will help.

I want to remember so badly—but digging into my past is like watching a blurry movie with scenes missing. Without Dad here to fill in the details, all I can assume is that Dad and Ya-Fang were content with an interfaith marriage—at least for a little while. Judging by Ya-Fang's white dress, I imagine there must have been some Christian influences in the ceremony, too. Dad probably still held on to his Mormon teachings even though he got married in a Buddhist temple instead of a Mormon one. Maybe there was a lot of compromising at the ceremony, but not so much after. Not that any of this information helps me answer Mavis's question.

"We could just kind of sit here silently and stare at the candle," I finally suggest. "And . . . try to think about what we're missing in life?"

Mavis scoffs. "San Diego. Friends. Roller skating at the beach. Freedom. A home. What am I *not* missing?"

I tug at the carpet's loose threads to avoid Mavis's gaze. "It's not like Mom had a choice."

Mavis stops clicking her lighter. "Are you kidding me? Mom had options. She could've gone to Fresno with Grandma. She could've gone to LA with Dad's side of the family. But Utah? With these people who can't even understand a lifestyle other than their own?"

I continue twisting the carpet threads around my finger. I should've known better than to get Mavis riled up. She still hasn't accepted the fact that we're stuck here. And I'm wondering if she ever will.

Mavis exhales and her voice softens. "Remember that time during Young Women's?"

She doesn't need to say more. I know where this conversation is going. "The marriage activity?"

When we were fifteen, Mavis and I attended a youth event where we were instructed to bring in magazines and create collages of the celebrities we wanted at our wedding. The whole point of the activity was to romanticize marriage—*gag*. But when Mavis said that she wanted to marry a female K-pop idol, the activity was shut down so that the leaders could lecture us about the sin of homosexuality. That was the day Mavis realized that she no longer wanted to live by anyone else's rules, and Dad supported her. He never wanted Mavis to be anything but herself. And now that I'm in Utah, I'm starting to understand why he was so adamant about that.

"I've spent the last two years undoing the trauma church gave me." Mavis's voice dips into a whisper. "I finally feel like I can accept who I am. But now I'm back to living like I'm someone I'm not. And I don't think y—Mom—gets that."

I don't look up from the carpet, but I do catch Mavis slipping on her words. *You.* She wasn't talking about Mom not understanding. She was talking about *me.*

Even though Mom and I both want Mavis to be happy, I've never stopped to consider *why* she's been unhappy in the first place. From the beginning, I assumed it was because she didn't want to lose the life we built in San Diego—which is partly true. But deeper still is the fact that she didn't leave just her friends behind, she left herself back there, too. The version of Mavis we know and love is standing like a ghost over Dad's grave. And I never noticed.

"What's your ideal community?" I ask. This is what I should've done in the first place—listen before I speak. Understand where the conversation needs to go *before* I attempt to steer it.

Mavis's lip twitches. She's snapping at the lighter again even though only sparks come out. "I know it's kind of impossible, but I want a Utah community that's just really *gay.* Unapologetically, proudly, California-style gay."

I can't stop the laugh that rises out of me. *Whoa.* Did Mavis make me do that? Without a third person in the room? "You know Mom's been wanting to show you around Utah."

Mavis groans and her expression drops once more.

"Hear me out: What if instead of her taking you to her favorite places, you go with her to a queer community center or you volunteer with her at a Pride Center or something?"

Mavis stops clicking the lighter for a moment. She sits there like a statue before nodding slowly. "That . . . sounds kind of fun, actually. But what about Aunt Joanna?"

I wave my hand. "Aunt Joanna doesn't have to know. Unless you come home covered in glitter or something."

Mavis snorts out a laugh. She opens her mouth to say something just as a flame catches on the wick. It sizzles, and wax dribbles down the glass. "Okay, I'm not a coincidence person, but how cool is it that the candle lit when you said that?"

I smirk because I don't believe in fate either. But it does feel *right*.

Mavis sets the candle on the carpet between us. The scent of mahogany and teakwood mingles with ash. I shut my eyes and focus on the toasty amber light bleeding through my eyelids and the warmth of the small flame between us.

I hope that closing my eyes will take me back in time once more. Maybe I'll recall another lost memory or see the face of a former Taiwanese schoolteacher. But as I sit there . . . I realize just how awkward this whole thing is. Why do I suddenly hear the water running through the pipes in the walls? And does my left nostril really whistle every time I exhale?

What are we having for dinner?

Focus, Catie.

I hope it's funeral potatoes. I mean, no one has died. But man, can Mormons bake—

Focus, Catie.

Inhale.

Exhale.

The door creaks beside me. *Okay, this house is really old for looking so new.*

Inhale.

"What are you doing?"

A reflexive shriek explodes from my mouth as I throw my eyes open. Rayleigh stands in the doorway, still in her church dress. Her hand rests on the doorknob while her unblinking eyes widen behind her glasses.

"Ummmm . . ." My hands quiver. I should've hung up a Do Not Disturb sign or something.

Before I can focus my breathing, the door is pushed open wider. Rayleigh isn't alone. Uncle Nick stands behind her with his church tie loosened around his neck. His dark brown eyes catch the light in the candle flame as he takes in the scene. Two girls sitting cross-legged in a dark room. He probably thinks we're witches.

"What's going on?" Uncle Nick's voice is craggy and booming. And when he directs his question at me, it feels as if he's roaring.

Of course. I should've realized I can't connect with an Eastern spirituality in a Western home.

"I'll ask again." Uncle Nick's voice crackles like a falling tree. "What are you two doing in here?"

"We were just meditating," Mavis says. Thank goodness she finds her voice. I'm still trying to make my body move.

"Meditating?" Uncle Nick repeats. "You look like you're holding a seance. What's wrong with you?"

What's wrong with you?

The phrase pierces like a hot arrow and stings my skin. What *is* wrong with me? Why did I think this would be a good idea?

"Blow that candle out." Uncle Nick jabs a finger at the flame. "I never want to see either of you playing with candles again. You're going to set the whole house on fire. Now get upstairs. We're having dinner."

And with that, Uncle Nick is gone.

I'm still shaking. My bones rattle like instruments as I gape up at Rayleigh. She's still in the doorway, her mouth opening and closing like she wants to say something. But when no one moves, Rayleigh disappears just like her father.

"I told you she's a snitch." Mavis pulls her knees to her chest as I sit there petrified. The girl I did makeup on, the one who encouraged me to go to the genealogy office—*she* turned me in? And to think I trusted her.

"Are you okay?" Mavis asks, shifting her attention to me.

My appetite is gone. I don't want to go upstairs to eat. I don't even want to show my face to Uncle Nick. And the last thing I want to do is sit across the table from the backstabbing cousin who's still wearing my eyeliner.

"Catie?" Mavis presses when I don't say anything.

I force my stiff neck to turn her way. "I'm fine."

Lie. But I'm good at it these days.

漂亮

Beautiful

I'm seated in the salon break room. I have an hour for lunch so I'm scrolling through Beauty by Kimi Yoon's Instagram. While some of the pictures are of nail art or glassy skin, the photos that I focus on are of hair. I study images of silver curls and summer blonds. If I looked more like the Taylors, would they accept me like I was one of their own?

The break-room door opens, but I don't look up from my phone. Instead, I shovel pizza into my mouth. The Yoon-Hansons have ordered food for the staff today because everyone has back-to-back clients.

"Hey."

I jump at Toby's voice. Ever since the Uncle Nick thing, I can't shake the feeling that I'm perpetually in trouble for existing. Unfortunately, it means that Toby has caught me so off guard that my phone leaps out of my hands and clatters to the floor.

"Sorry!" I stammer as my face burns. Wait, why am *I* apologizing? *He's* the one who scared *me*.

I want to slide out of my seat to retrieve my phone, but Toby is already bending over and scooping it up. "Are you thinking about lightening your hair?"

I peer down at my screen to see that the Instagram page is still up and wish I could make it disappear in front of Toby's eyes.

"I can give you a quick consultation if you'd like," Toby offers, returning my phone.

I nod, still too embarrassed to speak.

Toby stands behind me as if I'm a client in his chair. His fingers slide through my hair, combing through the strands until he reaches the base of my neck. A chill spreads from my scalp to the hairs on my arm.

I didn't realize this is what he meant by *consultation*. I thought he was talking about a discussion on pricing. This is a total misunderstanding, and I should pull away. But I don't move. I don't speak. I just let Toby play with my hair, because when his pinkie brushes my ear, it feels like I'm being told everything will be okay.

Toby straightens the part down my middle, then rubs my scalp. He's probably checking for buildup, but I sit there like Maddie Sue getting belly rubs. I've always liked having my hair played with. But I didn't realize how much until Toby tugs at my face-framing layers to see if they're symmetrical.

Toby tucks the strands behind my ears. He cups my jaw with both hands and tilts my face from side to side. This is probably how he matches haircuts to people's face shapes. But why is embarrassment melting into something else? Something I'm not sure how to name.

"Your hair is really healthy." He searches my face for a moment before letting go and taking a seat beside me. My cheeks are cold at the absence of his touch. "Your roots are strong, but if you want to lighten to a level eight or nine, I recommend cutting at least two inches off first just to get rid of the damage and split ends. But overall, your hair is beautiful as it is."

Beautiful. Who says things like that? Toby. Obviously. He's a cosmetologist. It's his job to make his clients feel seen. But then again, I'm not his client.

I curl a strand of hair around my finger. He's right. I need to get rid of all the damage and split ends. "Thanks. But maybe I'll wait until the salon dies down a bit. You've been so busy with your regulars. I don't want to take away your time."

"Hey, you're part of the salon family now. I will always make time for you," Toby says, reaching for the hand sanitizer bottle on the break room table. And yet something about the sincerity in his voice reminds me of his fingers in my hair all over again. Maybe after the whole Uncle Nick situation, I just really need a hug. And maybe Toby's hands in my hair are close enough.

Toby rubs the hand sanitizer into his hands before nabbing a slice of pepperoni. "What did you think of *Far from Home*? You finished it, right? I told you I'd quiz you the next time I saw you."

I unravel the lock of *beautiful* hair. "It was such a great movie. I mean, the storytelling and the acting were both so authentic . . ."

I hesitate. I want to launch into a lengthy exploration of the hopelessness Ting feels when she can't return to Taiwan. But Toby probably doesn't want to hear about the sentiment. He's just my language tutor, after all. That movie is supposed to help me learn Mandarin. Not be therapy.

"I had a feeling you'd like it," Toby says, his eyes crinkling. "So, what words did you learn from the film?"

I press my finger to my chin as I think. "Well, there was that one scene where Ting finds a rat in the kitchen, so she climbed on top of the stove and shouted, 'Shǔ! Shǔ!' Now I know how to say my zodiac animal."

"Nice." Toby smiles so brightly that crescents form under his eyes. "And what a great segue into today's lesson: nouns. Well, specifically, pronouns."

I blink at Toby. Oh, we're doing this? On my lunch break? Well, anything to stop dwelling on blond highlights and Uncle Nick.

"In simple conversations, you'll almost always start a sentence with some type of pronoun." Toby goes straight into teacher mode. "For instance, *I* am hungry. Or *she* needs sleep. Or *your* hair is beautiful."

I don't expect him to say that last part, and yet that feeling bubbles in my tummy. I liked it when he said it before. And I'm enjoying it all over again. *Stop it, Catie.*

"Think back on *Far from Home*." Toby rests his elbows on the table. "What's the Mandarin word for *me* or *I*?"

I've known this answer since before watching *Far from Home*. Dad wrote it in his copy of *The Five Love Languages*. And every time I heard an actor in the movie say that word, I thought of him.

"Wǒ."

Toby presses a finger to his nose. "Correct. And very good pronunciation. So when you're talking about yourself, you'd say . . . ?"

"I'm Catie!" I smirk.

"Okay, you're technically not wrong. But that wasn't the answer I was looking for."

I giggle. "Wǒ."

Toby chuckles. "Awesome. Next question. If you want to use the word *you*—for instance, *you over there*"—Toby points to an invisible person in the room—"how would you say that in Mandarin?"

"Nǐ." I knew he'd ask this. In preparation, I recalled the scene where Ting curses her ex out on the phone. Nǐ shìgè húndàn. I figured out that *nǐ* means "you," *shìgè* means "are a," and *húndàn* means . . . okay, so I'm not exactly sure what *húndàn* translates to. The subtitles said "jerk," but the reactions from the other actors implied that it was a bit more crude than that.

"Nǐ is correct!" Toby says it with the enthusiasm of a game show host. "And last question. How do you say *him* or *her* in Mandarin? I'll give you a hint: These pronouns are identical when spoken."

I rack my brain and take a wild guess. "Is it nǐde?"

"So close. Nǐde means 'your.' In fact, if you add the *de* to any of these pronouns, it makes them possessive. Wǒde takes the 'me' and turns it into 'my.' The Mandarin word for *him-her-them* is tā. So tāde becomes 'his, hers, theirs-singular.' Does that make sense?"

I nod. Honestly, this lesson is so simple, it makes me feel silly about ever being nervous to relearn Mandarin. "You're a good teacher."

Toby's face brightens as if my compliment meant more to

him than just a compliment. "Well, you're not so bad yourself. Speaking of *your* language lessons—can I ask you something?"

I blink so fast that my lashes tickle my cheeks. Right. I'm also a language teacher—a *love language* teacher. But there's an anxious tug in Toby's lips that makes me wonder if he's going to ask me about something else.

I gulp. "Sure."

"I was working out with my friends the other day, and somehow we got on to this conversation about whether friends can fall in love. I don't have any dating experience, so I wanted to ask you. Can two friends ever become more than friends?"

Wait a minute. Is he talking about *us*? No, no way. I'm not sure if Toby and I even count as friends. We're *friendly* coworkers. But then I realize: He's talking about Nichole. *Obviously.*

"Well, anything is possible with love, isn't it?" I retort. Mostly because that's the answer I would want to hear if I were Toby. "If enemies can become lovers, I'm pretty sure friends can, too."

Toby nods to himself as if digesting my words. "Okay, so then I have a follow-up question."

Oh, goodie.

"What's the difference between like and love?" Toby rubs his lip in contemplation. "Was there a moment when you realized you didn't *like* your boyfriend, but you were actually *in love* with him?"

A wave of heat shoots up my chest and burns the crown of my head. I don't need to look down to know that even my hands are red. How do I answer this? Am I supposed to make up a story about how Jimmy and I kissed at the base of the Eiffel Tower and that's how I knew we were in love? Or maybe I can pull from a Hallmark holiday special.

But then another thought comes to mind—a story Dad left behind for me in the margins of his book. One about Mom.

"I was getting gas one day, but the machine wasn't reading my card, so I had to go inside to pay with cash." I recite the story as if I'm my father. And tweak a few minor details. "While I was there, I saw that they had a two-for-one sale on Monster energy drinks. They're Jimmy's favorite, so I bought some for him. When I got back to the car, his whole face lit up. Seeing him so happy over something so simple—that was the moment I knew I was in love with him."

I give Toby a weak smile, hoping it sells the story more. But in truth, answering his question feels like reading from a script I've just been handed. I'm holding his gaze and that smile on my face is growing heavier. He's staring at me like I've told only half the story. Like I'm supposed to explain how it *felt* to realize I was in love. But even Dad didn't leave behind something that intimate. So I recite another line from his book instead.

"When you love someone, you do more for them."

That seems to satisfy Toby. He takes the words in, then finally swallows. "Thanks. I think I'm starting to get it now."

I exhale a sigh of relief. Crisis averted. "So, does answering your questions count as my lesson plan?"

Toby reaches for another slice of pizza between us. "No,

I'm expecting a full-on lesson with textbooks and a thesis. Besides, you've only shown me one of those love languages. What are the other ones?"

I open my mouth to answer, then stop to wag my finger at him. "Hey, what kind of teacher would I be if I just gave you all the answers? Why don't you tell me?"

Toby chuckles. "Fine. There's acts of service . . ."

"I'm glad you haven't forgotten that one yet."

Toby's cheeks dimple. "And then there's—"

A phone chirps.

At first, I assume someone is calling one of the phones left behind in the break room. But Toby leaps up and digs through his apron pockets to find his own device. "I've gotta check on my client's hair." He silences the alarm. "Make sure the bleach hasn't fried it all off. But . . . what are you doing Friday night?"

My head jerks back reflexively. "What?"

"It's the weekend," Toby says, sliding out of his chair. "You taught your first lesson last weekend. Why don't you have your second one this weekend?"

"Oh," I say blankly. "Right. Yeah. Love language lesson number two. And you better come prepared, Toby. I've got my syllabus planned."

I absolutely do *not* have a syllabus, and yet those words pour from my lips as effortlessly as tea into a cup. My lies used to be hard. But now they're so easy. *Too* easy.

"Sweet," Toby says. "I'm looking forward to it."

你所需要的

Just What You Need

On Friday, Toby asks me if I'm ready to go as his last client walks out the door. I nod *yes* even though I *still* haven't thought of a good date.

"Awesome. I just need to clean up my station and then we can head out."

I give Toby a pathetic smile, but he's already hurrying back to his chair. My fingers fumble over the computer as I input the final sale of the evening. Any minute now, Mr. Yoon-Hanson will come close out the register. Seriously, what am I going to teach Toby for today's lesson?

Toby bounces back up to the front desk. His apron is stripped, his loose curls have been touched up. He flashes a set of pearly teeth. "Ready?"

I force a smile to match his enthusiasm. Why does Toby have to be so . . . Toby? This would be a lot easier if he was a jerk. But he's just *kind*. And my guilty conscience is working overtime to forget that.

Toby holds the front door open for me, and the wash of a Utah evening envelops me. Gray clouds hang low enough to scrape the peaks of the neighboring mountains. The setting sun bleeds through the haze, creating heavy molten clouds.

"What's today's lesson going to be about?" Toby asks, guiding me back to his car.

I clear my throat. Toby is in a great mood, which means that I need to be in a great mood, too. I won't be much of a dating coach if Toby ends up teaching me how to have fun on this date. Besides, what if my bad attitude gives away my lack of dating experience?

I shake away the dread. *One problem at a time, Catie.*

"Today's lesson is gift giving." That's the easiest one, right? All I have to do is buy something with the small paycheck I got earlier today.

Toby pumps a fist in the air. "All right. So, what are we going to do? Find a mall Santa and help him wrap gifts?"

His suggestion pulls a genuine giggle from me. "In the middle of summer?"

"Santa makes gifts all year-round." Toby shrugs. "As a kid, I used to wonder why they don't have mall elves wrapping gifts in the middle of summer. But then I grew up and realized Santa's not real and—"

"He's not?" I quip.

Toby shoves my shoulder playfully. "Don't even."

I'm smiling even though my stomach is still in knots. At the very least, his suggestion did give me an idea I can pull from. "Well, you got half of that right. Since this date is all about giving gifts, there's no better place to go than the mall."

Except—we're kind of already at the mall? Moore Plaza is shutting down, but there must be an indoor mall that stays open later. Especially on weekends.

Toby loops his car keys around his finger. "Awesome. I know just the place."

Leave it to the local.

We reach Toby's Mitsubishi, and once more I climb into the passenger seat. I'm buckling my seat belt when the scent of cedar and cherry wafts up my nose. Is Toby wearing cologne? No, wait—

"You cleaned your car!" I gasp, whirling around to peer at his back seat. Gone are the shaker bottles and dirty gym clothes. He's even got one of those dangly pine tree things.

Toby starts his engine. "Yeah, well—I mean, I'm implementing your lessons."

It takes me a moment to remember what he's talking about.

"I needed to clean my car anyway," Toby continues, pulling out of his spot and cruising out of the parking lot. He must be too focused on driving to see my puzzled expression. "Nichole can't think I'm a slob."

Of course. Nichole definitely *can't* think he's a slob.

Toby merges onto the highway and keeps his blinker on until we've reached the toll lane. We head south. The setting sun is to my right. It's golden hour but soon this night won't be golden anymore.

"Are you okay, Catie? You've been kind of quiet."

Right. I'm the teacher. I'm supposed to be talking. But Toby's expecting a lesson with a syllabus, not me rambling about how I've been staying up late to read Dad's book. Not about how I'm looking forward to church this Sunday. And especially not about how the last lie I told him about my fake boyfriend has been eating me up more than the other ones have.

"I know you said this date wouldn't be about helping Santa Claus," Toby says, keeping his gaze out the window.

"But the anticipation is making me feel like I'm waiting for Christmas morning. Come on—spill! What are we doing?"

I force another smile and rack my brain for a quick date night idea. Ugh. My hamster wheels are running on empty. The only thing I can think of is a trend that popped up on my social media. Fine. I'll resort to stealing ideas from viral internet couples.

"Here's the plan: We are only buying each other *one* gift and that gift cannot cost more than twenty-five dollars. But I'm not going to tell you what I want. We're going window-shopping and hinting about the gifts that catch our interest. The person who purchases the correct item first wins."

Toby drums on the steering wheel. "That sounds like fun. You have such great ideas. Your boyfriend is one lucky guy."

There it is again. The very fake boyfriend that I absolutely do not have. But it's too late to come clean now. I've told Toby so much about Jimmy. And I can't pretend we broke up just so that I can save face. The only reason Toby wants me to coach him is that he thinks I'm an expert. And what expert would I be if I can't handle a little long distance?

A looming building appears off the highway, which must be the mall. Toby exits the ramp, then parks outside JCPenney. Though I'm excited to look at summer fashion and fantasize about having a giant wardrobe, I still can't bring myself up to the level of energy Toby has.

We walk inside. Floral perfumes mingle with woody colognes much like the smell of Toby's car. Mannequins stand in the doorway like guards wondering why I'm not taller and thinner. Racks of summertime swimwear, beach day blouses, and Fourth of July fashion spread across the store like an ocean of cotton and linen.

"If I were Catie Carlson, I'd probably want an eye shadow palette with vivid colors," Toby mutters to himself.

He's so committed to this assignment. And he isn't wrong. If I really were a love expert—and I'd really come up with this dating plan—I would want another makeup palette. It's not like one paycheck is enough to treat myself to anything super special.

Toby leads me toward the makeup and skin-care section of JCPenney but stops midstep. "Wait a second. You don't want makeup. I know exactly what you need."

What I *need*? How can Toby be so sure? I'm pretty sure I do want makeup. But what's on display here is probably more than the twenty-five-dollar limit.

Toby grabs my wrist and drags me out of JCPenney. I have to take two steps for each one of his. I'm just about to ask him where he's taking me when Toby and I emerge in the food court.

A sea of people are sprawled across tables eating burgers and sipping milkshakes. But that isn't what makes my stomach rumble. It's the smell of fried chicken and baked bread. It's the sizzle of oil falling into a wok, and the plumes of steam rising off beds of fried rice. Neon lights loop the walls while checkered tiles line the floors as if this place used to be a roller rink. But there's something about those retro vibes that make me extra excited to be here.

I slap a hand over my face and laugh. "Is there a problem food can't solve?"

Toby bounces on his feet. "So, does this mean I win?"

I rub my hollow belly. "Yes, Toby. Winner, winner, chicken dinner."

Toby's eyes dimple in that way they do when he's *really* smiling. Then he glances away, and I find myself wishing I had a moment longer to examine his expression. There's something else in his face that I haven't seen before. But right now, he's busy deciding which one of these lines he wants to stand in.

I scan the room with him. There's Chick-fil-A, In-N-Out, Café Rio, Sarku Japan . . . Those are some of the longer lines. Then it seems that Toby and I look at the same eatery at the same time: Bubble Boba.

"Tea?" Toby asks.

"Tea!" I echo. Now I'm bouncing on my feet, too. We'll probably get something more sustaining later. But for now, I can't resist the sweetness of brown sugar and the squish of tapioca pearls.

Toby and I weave through the food court. We pass laughing patrons and hungry babies until we become the last people in a short line.

The Bubble Boba menu hangs over the counter in a shade of green that says, *Everything here is good to go!* Employees bustle in the background frothing foam, blending smoothies, and sealing cups with a plastic film. A girl with dark hair tucked into a cap takes orders at the front of the line.

I'm so focused on the menu that Toby has to tap my shoulder to get my attention.

"The cashier just said she's from Taiwan," he tells me. "So I'm going to teach you how to order boba in Mandarin."

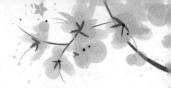

紅燈，綠燈

Red Light, Green Light

So far, the only Mandarin lessons we've had were about tones and pronouns. We haven't even learned any verbs yet—like, I don't know, *order*? And now he wants me to speak a full sentence? My underarms prickle with sweat. It's like doing my job interview all over again.

"This is how you say, 'I would like to order two cups of boba tea' in Mandarin." Then Toby moves into translating something I can't focus on.

My ears experience some auditory version of tunnel vision. Toby's lips move, but my focus turns to the cashier and the five spaces separating us from the front of the line. My memories spin back in time. Suddenly, I'm transported to an elementary school playground, and I'm surrounded by children playing Red Light, Green Light.

"You cheated!" a girl in pigtails says, jabbing her finger at me.

How old am I? Four? Five? Either way, I'm fresh off the boat, because I can understand what this girl is saying. I just don't know how to respond.

"You moved when I said *red light*!"

I stand there frozen. *No, I didn't. The girl next to me moved. You were looking at her and not at me.* In my mind, I scream those words in perfect English. But externally, I say nothing. I don't know how to move my tongue to mimic those sounds. I can't even remember the names of my classmates, because they all sound so foreign to me. How am I supposed to communicate with someone who can't speak my language?

"You're a cheater!" the girl says. "We don't want to play with you!"

I look to the rest of my classmates, begging someone to interject. Even the girl who moved instead of me should say something. But no one comes to my defense.

"I . . . sorry." It's a simple phrase—one I learned early on. But that doesn't communicate all the extra words I'm shouting in my mind.

The girl shoves me in the shoulder. Hard. But that isn't what hurts. What pains me most—even to this day—is the fact that I learned English later than everyone else. And as a result, I hated school. Classes were terrible because I couldn't focus on the words my teachers spoke. So instead of learning, I daydreamed.

I hated reading. Spelling was impossible and words jumped around on pages. I had to focus just to keep them in place. People thought I had dyslexia.

I hated speaking. Even though I was fluent in English by middle school, public speaking assignments terrified me. People thought I was an introvert. I kept my head down and hoped that no one would talk to me. All this because of one language barrier.

"Catie?"

My name brings me to my present. I'm no longer at the

playground, and yet my shoulder aches as if I've just been shoved.

"Are you okay?" Toby asks.

The group at the front of the line has finished placing their order. We're fourth now.

"I-I-I don't think I can order," I finally stammer.

Toby sets a hand on my arm. The warmth of his palm cancels out the chill running through me. His touch invites me to take a deep breath. Toby's brows furrow in concern, and his dark eyes search mine as if he's trying to see the memories inside my head.

"I think I get it now," Toby finally says, pulling away and massaging his forehead. "I'm literally going to school for this. How did I not see it?"

I cross my arms, my joints slowly thawing. "See what?"

Toby slides his hand down his face and parts his fingers to look at me through the gap. "You have PTSD from learning your second language, don't you?"

I wince in surprise and can't fight the way my face scrunches. "PTSD?"

Toby nods. "I learned this in my psych class. You're probably still dealing with culture shock. It can happen to immigrants both old and young. But when children experience it at an early age, they can be triggered by it for the rest of their lives. I think you have some sort of PTSD from learning your second language. I noticed it at the salon when you said that nursery rhyme, but I didn't put the two together until just now."

I glance down at the checkered cafeteria-style linoleum as I digest his words. It makes sense. A part of me panicked when he wanted me to say the rhyme out loud. And I'd panicked *again* when he said I'd be ordering in Mandarin. I'd been told so many times to *speak English* that even as I try to reclaim my lost language, I can't forget the first lesson I learned: English—good. Mandarin—bad.

I suppose I've always known I had some form of culture shock. I just hadn't put a name to it until Toby did.

"I still want to learn Mandarin, though," I insist, shaking my shoulders as if I'm dusting off the girl at the playground and her hard push. Uncovering past traumas wasn't what I signed up for when I challenged myself to relearn my first language. I didn't realize I'd be facing my early years in America once more. But this time, I refuse to apologize.

"I want to order in Mandarin," I say. Now that I understand where my anxiety comes from, I feel a little better about tackling it.

Toby holds my gaze. "Are you sure?"

I exhale until my teeth stop chattering. "Yeah, I'm sure."

We spend the rest of our time in line learning that one sentence. Toby breaks it down phrase by phrase until I'm able to combine everything into something cohesive.

> I would like = *Wǒ xiǎng*
> To order = *Diǎn*
> Two cups of = *Liǎng bēi*
> Boba tea = *Bōbà chá*
> *Wǒ xiǎng diǎn liǎng bēi bō bā chá.*

I recognize some of the words from *Far from Home*. Liǎng is the unit value for the number two. Normally, the number two translates to *Èr*. But this scenario requires the unit term instead of the numerical one. Then, of course, Toby taught me the proper pronunciation of *bōbà*. Thank goodness it means using some of the easiest Mandarin tones.

Toby and I finally reach the front of the line. My hands tremble and I ball them against my shirt. I scream the words in my head like I did when I was a kid. But this time, I'm going to say them out loud, too.

"Nǐ hǎo! Wǒde . . ." And that's all I can follow as Toby greets our cashier. I imagine he's explaining that I'm relearning Mandarin and I want to practice.

The cashier's body language shifts. Her eyes light up, and she claps her hands under her chin. This isn't the reaction I'd expected. Especially since my experience with learning English was met by eye rolls and people walking away from me midsentence. Finally, she nods when Toby finishes speaking and replies in such fluent Mandarin that it makes Toby's speech look elementary. Then she turns to me.

"I'm so happy you're speaking Chinese. I'm learning English now, too!" She beams at me with the radiance of the moon. "I'll take your order now."

I suck in a calming breath. This is about to become the first time I've spoken a cohesive sentence in Mandarin since I was a child. My self-doubt tells me that I'm going to get the pronunciation wrong. My words will likely be inaudible. But that's okay. I'm a work in progress and I'm proud of myself for even trying.

"Wǒ xiǎng diǎn liǎng bēi bōbā chá."

My nausea tells me that I've butchered it, but the cashier's reaction to my sentence could've fooled me. She cheers. Her smile is so wide, I can practically count all her teeth. She even gives me a thumbs-up. It's just about every expression of praise I can think of. All spoken but no words said.

"Hěnhǎo! Hěnhǎo!" she exclaims. "You speak very good!"

I bite my lip to keep from smiling too brightly.

"Keep working hard," the cashier continues. "My English is not so good. We learn to speak new words together."

"It *is* good, though," I say, with my biggest smile. I realize I'm hopping in place because I can't contain my excitement.

The cashier grins. "Xièxie!"

Toby completes the order by filling in the flavors of tea we want. Minutes later, our cups of boba and chunky straws are delivered to us. A layer of fluffy milk foam sits atop a lake of black tea and brown sugar. At the bottom of the lake is a rock bed of boba thickened with syrup.

Toby and I find a table. I sit down across from him as he holds his cup of tea out. "Cheers to learning a new sentence in Mandarin."

I giggle and clink my cup against his. "Cheers to learning so much more."

Then we drink and I'm slurping down some of the best bōbā chá I've ever tasted—here in Utah, of all places! It's not like the watered-down stuff I used to get at the mall with Jimmy and Francisca. This stuff is actually made with *milk*! Cold, refreshing tea mingles with the brown-sugar-infused tapioca pearls. I chew on the boba, letting the sweetness tango with the bitter black tea.

I'm one step closer to reconnecting with Ya-Fang, and in the end, sharing a cup of boba with her someday is all that really matters. I'll find her on PanGenea. We'll meet in real life. My Mandarin will become so good that I can ask her all the questions I never asked Dad. I'll fulfill his promise *and* so much more.

For a moment, everything really does feel okay. Until I catch sight of the person standing behind Toby.

紅茶和廣藿香

Black Tea and Patchouli

I take her in all at once: wispy blond hair, designer clothing, and a posture of entitlement. *Aunt Joanna.* She stands in the Chick-fil-A line with her platinum credit card already out. But that also means she's only five feet away. If she turns, she'll inevitably see me. She'll inevitably see Toby—purple-haired, cosmetologist, and works-with-women-all-day Toby.

I shoot up in my seat as if I've been stung by a bee.

"We gotta go." I don't wait for Toby's response. I just grab my boba and run.

I've never been to this mall before, so I have no clue where to go. Before I can make it farther than the food court, Toby catches up to me.

"Why are we running?" he asks, panting, the ice in his boba rattling with every step.

My thoughts spin like the tapioca pearls in my cup. I tell Toby the truth before I can stop myself. "I'm hiding from my aunt."

"Um, why?"

This time, I *do* stop myself. I can't tell Toby that I don't want to be spotted with him. He looks . . . like someone Aunt Joanna has a lot to say about. And that's putting it delicately.

"In here." Toby grabs my wrist and tugs me backward. A wall of curtains falls around me, and then my butt hits a hard bench. Toby has pulled me inside a photo booth—one that must be made for little kids, because it's tiny.

My bewildered expression is reflected at me from the camera screen. It's as big as a bathroom mirror, and this bench is no larger than a toilet seat. It should be impossible for Aunt Joanna to spot us now, right? But there's no way I'm risking it by poking my head outside the curtains, even if my leg keeps slipping out.

"Why were we running from your aunt?" Toby asks again.

My chest heaves, and my breath echoes around the booth. Toby's long legs are practically glued to mine, and our shoulders are pressed together like magnets. The heat of his skin radiates onto mine. I take a quick sip of my iced tea to cool off.

"I don't like my aunt," I answer halfheartedly, trying to get comfortable, but I'm pinned by his long limbs and the booth walls.

"Well, obviously." Toby speaks to my reflection because we're too cramped to face each other. "Why don't you like her?"

"She's a control freak!" I blurt, surprised at how easy it is to let go of everything I've been holding in. "She wouldn't let us live with her unless we agreed to go to church again. Oh, and you should see how she treats her actual daughter. You know she won't let my cousin wear makeup? So the fact that I come home every night looking like the *W-word* is probably driving her up the wall. And don't even get me started on my uncle Nick."

Toby rubs his lips together. It looks like he's about to ask a question, but I press on. Once I've opened my mouth, there's no closing it.

"And you know what the worst part is? I'm stuck living with her. My mom lost her job, and our landlord back in San Diego decided to raise the rent. We had no choice but to move here. My bigot aunt is the only one willing to take us in. But honestly, a part of me thinks she's just doing it because she's a *holy woman* and *we are her charity case* and *look at how Christ-like Joanna is for saving us*. I'm just an accessory to her, not a person."

Toby's expression hasn't changed. He waits a moment as if making sure I'm done venting before he adds, "Wow. I'm so sorry, Catie. That sucks."

I sigh. Yeah, it *does* suck. And maybe I just need someone to validate that for me. "My back is against the wall with her. I have no choice but to comply or else she could kick us out of her house."

"Do you not have any other family to go to for help? Your boyfriend? Or any friends?"

My gaze sinks to the cup of boba in my hands.

"Not really. Ever since my dad died, I have my mom and Mavis, but they're always fighting. And my um . . . *boyfriend* and friends . . . well, they're back in San Diego. Without Dad, it's like a part of me is always missing no matter how hard I try to fill in that void."

Toby takes a slow sip of his tea as if he's contemplating a response. Finally, he whispers, "I can relate."

I hardly hear him over the bustle of shoppers on the other side of the curtain.

"I lost my younger brother when I was fourteen," Toby says, staring blankly ahead. "I know it's not exactly like losing your dad. But I know what it's like to have a part of you missing.

And to always wonder where you'd be if you'd never lost someone you love."

Even if I could move my lips, I wouldn't know what to say. This is Toby speaking. Perfect, wealthy, knows-who-he-is-and-where-he's-going Toby. I've envied him for all his stories about family recipes and trips to South Korea. But now I know that the moment we had in his kitchen wasn't a figment of my imagination.

"Ezra and I wanted to go bouldering one weekend." Toby's quiet voice fills in the space between us. "We'd watched one of those survival shows, and he'd become obsessed. So, we got a group together, and one of our friends' parents drove us deep into the mountains. We thought we were in good hands. We had the proper equipment and did the safety checks and everything, but I guess . . ."

Toby shuts his eyes. Through his thick lashes, I recognize the swell of tears. He doesn't continue until they subside.

"Ezra always had too much energy for his own good. He was just being a kid. He just wanted to have fun. And . . . well, when he fell . . . I mean, we didn't know where we were. We didn't have any signal. They had to drive all the way back to the highway just to call for help. But even then . . . I don't think that would've changed . . ."

Toby takes another sip of boba and looks down at his sneakers. But I can tell he's on the verge of tears.

I don't realize my hand is on his arm until I'm squeezing it. We may not have lost the same people, but we both know what it means to grieve. To leave someone behind. To have a family that will never be whole.

Toby looks at my hand before his gaze traces up my arm. For the first time since squeezing into this cramped photo booth, our eyes meet. His face is so close to mine, I can smell the tea on his breath and the products in his hair.

"I'm sorry, Toby," I whisper, leaning in as if the gravity of his pain is orbiting around mine.

The tenderness of his voice matches mine when he speaks. "It's not your fault."

I remember thinking those exact words at Dad's funeral. People kept telling me how sorry they were, and I kept thinking, *Stop saying that. How can you be sorry for something that you didn't do?* I should've known better than to say that to Toby. So instead, I do what I wished those mourners had done for me.

My arms wrap around Toby. He doesn't hesitate to squeeze me back. Toby's head slides over my shoulder while my ear presses against his chest. I can hear his heartbeat like it's telling me something.

Lub-dub. Thank-you.

Lub-dub. For-listening.

♥

That night, I'm tucked in my cousin Tavie's bed, but I can't sleep. Toby's smell is in my hair, and my skin can't stop wondering what happened to his touch. He's not just a coworker. He's someone who *understands* me.

Our second practice date wasn't supposed to be for me. It was supposed to be for him—so that he'd learn about the power of gift giving. And yet Toby has given me something more than just boba. Meanwhile, here I am, taking advantage of his generosity and returning it with deceit. How can I possibly come clean about my lack of dating experience after he bared his soul to me like that?

Thunk!

Something heavy falls from upstairs. Mavis has made me watch enough horror movies to know not to go toward the noise. And yet, against my better judgment, I sit up in bed and listen.

Footsteps.

Someone is walking around up there. If it's an intruder, surely Maddie Sue would be barking by now. So who's really up there?

I pull my sheets off and slide out of bed. Mavis is dead asleep—her snores confirm that. The rest of the basement is completely dark, since the living room windows have blackout curtains.

I creep over to the stairwell and listen. Not only are there footsteps, but I can also hear the tip-tap of Maddie Sue's paws against the hardwood floor. Has someone come to the kitchen for a midnight snack? Is it Mom?

"Hello?" I whisper, tiptoeing up the stairs.

"Oh, jeez!" someone yelps.

"Rayleigh?" I gape.

My cousin freezes in the hallway with her hand on her chest. There's one dusty shoe on her foot and another kicked off to the side. Maddie Sue's right beside her, wagging her tail and looking up at us with her trademark floppy tongue.

"What are you doing?" I ask, jutting my head at her shoes.

"Please don't tell my parents," she pleads, her eyes bulging in the darkness.

"You snuck out of the house," I realize aloud, putting the pieces together.

"Shhhh," Rayleigh hisses. "If you tell them, you're going to get me in trouble."

"Oh, like how I got in trouble for meditating in my own room?" The remark springs from my lips before I can think about what I'm saying. I haven't talked to Rayleigh about it. Since then, Mavis and I have been keeping our distance from our not-so-favorite cousin.

When Rayleigh doesn't respond, I turn back to the basement stairs. Tomorrow morning, I'll let Aunt Joanna know that her daughter snuck out of the house. Maybe that will take the heat off Mavis and me for lighting a candle.

"Wait!" Rayleigh snatches my arm and tugs me back. "I'm sorry about what happened last Sunday. I went downstairs to tell you it was time for dinner. I didn't realize you were meditating. If I'd known, I would've made up some lie to keep Dad from noticing."

I purse my lips. Was Rayleigh really willing to lie for me? Or is this just another lie so I won't rat *her* out?

"I wasn't really sure what you guys were doing in there," Rayleigh whisper-shouts. "But it kinda looked like you needed your privacy. I'm sorry. Really. You can use my room to meditate. I have a lock on my bedroom door."

I sigh as my gaze dips to the floor. Apparently, I've been lying long enough to recognize sincerity when it bleeds from her voice. Or at least give her the benefit of the doubt. Everyone deserves a second chance, right? "I'm trying to practice Buddhism again. I wasn't really sure where to start, so I figured I'd meditate."

"Oh," Rayleigh says, blinking fast. "Wow. I feel like such a jerk for walking in on you then. Everyone deserves a safe space to develop their spirituality. I really am sorry."

I scuff the hardwood floor with my bare feet. "Thanks. But since I told you what I was up to, you have to tell me what you were doing."

I meet Rayleigh's gaze, but she glances away quickly. "Oh. Well. Um. I was just . . . going for a walk. I needed to think."

"It's, like, one in the morning." I peer into the kitchen around Rayleigh's shoulders. Actually, according to the microwave, it's closer to two.

"Mom can't know about this. Promise me." Rayleigh's voice turns serious—dark, even. She knows I'm not buying her fib but she's not going to volunteer information like I did.

I've never heard that tone before. I can't say I know what Rayleigh's big secret is, even though I'm pretty sure it has something to do with the hidden boy she's been messaging. But who is it—the bishop's son? *Scandalous!*

"Promise me," Rayleigh repeats.

I'm not sure how to trust her when she can't even trust me. But Rayleigh knows I have more ammunition to use against her if I need to.

Slowly, I nod and extend my pinkie finger. Rayleigh reaches for it, but I pull back at the last second. "Are you serious about letting me use your room?"

"As a heart attack," Rayleigh insists.

Hesitantly, I let Rayleigh's cold finger wrap around mine as we shake. "Good. Because I want to meditate after church again."

I'm planning to do more genealogy work at church on Sunday. There's so much more to explore on Dad's side, and I haven't even tapped into Ya-Fang's genealogy. If I'm going to believe in myself truly, then I need to rediscover more of what's truly mine—starting with my past.

Rayleigh smiles. "Cool. Because I think I can help you there."

悲傷之樓

Mansion of Sorrow

I go to church with the Taylors and don't fuss about it. This time, I make sure I'm not the last one in the car. I plop down in the back of the Taylors' SUV. Rayleigh and Mom climb into the middle, and then Mavis finally takes a seat beside me. Just like last Sunday, Mavis wears a hoodie over her church dress. But unlike last Sunday, her hood isn't up.

I nudge Mavis's shoulder as Uncle Nick drives us down the street. "You seem like you're in a better mood."

Mavis's eyes shine. Her focus shifts to Aunt Joanna and Uncle Nick before she leans into me and lowers her voice. "I took your advice. Mom and I went to the Pride Center and—"

A gasp escapes from me before I realize just how loud it is. I know Mavis wants this to be a secret, but come on! How do I *not* contain my thrill?

Mavis slaps my arm and shushes me. "One of the workers there gave me a schedule of all the activities they are planning this summer. Did you know they're planning a—"

"What are you guys whispering about?" Rayleigh spins around in her seat. Her eyes sparkle like she wants to join in on our fun.

"Nothing," Mavis snaps, folding her arms and sinking into her seat.

Rayleigh's gaze shifts over to me. I want to say something,

but this isn't my news to share. I give her a smile instead. Though the strain in my cheeks must mean it looks more like a grimace.

"Are you going to help out in the nursery again, Mavis?" Mom's voice cuts through the bubble of silence locking us in the back of the car.

Mavis clears her throat like nothing is wrong. "Yeah. I met Sister Hammer. She mentioned she might need a sitter during her work hours."

I bite my lip as Rayleigh flips back around and stares out the window. I can tell by her pinched profile that she's annoyed we gave her the cold shoulder. Especially after what we talked about at 2 a.m. But doesn't she know that Mavis isn't ready to trust her? And honestly, I'm not entirely convinced either.

Uncle Nick parks the SUV. Rayleigh says she's going to sit with her friend during this sacrament meeting. Mavis heads to the nursery. Meanwhile, I know exactly how I'm spending my next two hours.

"Catie?" Mom calls from behind. She's opening the door to the sacrament hall while I'm rounding the corner of the foyer. "Aren't you going to sit with me today?"

I twirl a hair around my finger until it's so tight, it might cut off my circulation. Is now the time to tell Mom what I'm up to? How do I even have this conversation with her? A wave of guilt washes over me like I'm cheating on my mom with another mother. She wouldn't get it. And I don't want to hurt her feelings. Not when she's already got so much going on right now.

I take a step back. No. It's not the right time or place. I'll tell Mom when I have more information. *If* I even find more information. "If you're okay with it, I feel like I've made friends with Granny Eloise. I'm going to keep her company at the genealogy office today."

I watch a flash of betrayal race across her eyes. Like maybe she doesn't want to be alone at church either. But then she smiles and says, "I'm glad you're making friends."

Mom moves into the sacrament hall while I find the genealogy office. I've never really thought about how Mom needs friends, too. Maybe I could introduce her to Granny Eloise. That might be a good way to finally let her know what I've been up to. Eventually. But for now, I need today to be about me and PanGenea.

I push the office door open and find her sitting at the same computer she was at last week. Her cloud of white hair catches in the draft from the fan that's been set on her desk. It rotates around, cooling off the room.

"Can you leave that door open?" Granny Eloise asks before tapping on the chair she's already pulled up beside her. "Then we can get to work."

I use a rubber stopper to prop the door open and take my seat next to Granny Eloise. I'm not sure if it's doing anything to cool the room down, because my skin is already sticky by the time I sit beside her. Between the summer heat and all the computer exhaust, this office is practically a sauna.

Once more, she opens the PanGenea window. My knee bounces as I wait for the software to load. The collar of my shirt feels like it's choking me, but I'm not sure if it's because of the heat or because I'm eager to see what's listed under Dad's profile. If Ya-Fang is the one who's been translating his genealogy, she'll have more information on him than I could ever imagine. Either way, I'm ready to see who my dad was before I was even born.

In a few short clicks, Granny Eloise reopens my profile, and then she slides the mouse to me. With anxious fingers, I take it and click on Dad's profile. I scroll through moments in Dad's life until I find a carousel of photos. There's a grainy image of Dad on his mission. He's in an alleyway with his companion—another missionary also wearing a white shirt and bike helmet, and holding up the peace sign. There are only five images on this carousel, but all of them are of Dad on his mission in Taiwan. Dad at the same apartment complex. Dad with the same mission companion.

I've never seen these images before. Whoever took them must have access to things I don't—things in Taiwan that someone like Ya-Fang could have. And considering that there isn't much information on Dad, maybe now's the time to look at Ya-Fang's profile. Because *what if* she learned English and is translating this?

With Granny's encouragement, I move over to Ya-Fang's profile. Just like Dad's information, a list of bullet points drops down her page. *Birth, Marriage, Education, Death.*

My heart stops at the last word. Hold on. What if I've been wrong about my hunch? What if it's not Ya-Fang who's been putting this together? After all, why would *Death* be listed if she isn't on the same plane as Dad?

Granny Eloise seems to sense my worriedness. "All profiles

have a default drop-down box. The *Death* option is just one of them. But you won't know if there's anything there until you click on it."

Do I want to know if my biological mom is even alive? Because what if she isn't? Every Mandarin word I've learned has been for her. For us. For the conversations we never had and the questions I've never asked. But I never even considered she might not be alive. That all these conversations I want to have might never occur.

"Catie?" Granny Eloise nudges when I still haven't decided on what to click next. "You don't have to start at the end of her journey."

I know I don't, but I *need* to know.

I take a deep breath. If Ya-Fang is dead, well, then maybe that's a good thing. It means I don't need to keep taking Mandarin lessons anymore and I can stop lying to Toby. It means I don't need to have that awkward conversation with Mom about finding my bio mom. I hold on to these thoughts to make my heart hurt less.

Then, I click on the *Death* icon.

The page loads. It's the moment during the coin flip when all of my deepest desires rush to the surface. *Please be alive*, I find myself silently begging. *I have so much to ask you.*

Words appear on the screen—mostly in Hanzi. My brain scrambles to make sense of what I'm seeing, but I can't read any of this. Then my eyes latch on to the only thing in English. I'm reading the words before I can stop myself: *Ya-Fang Linn. Deceased: February 18, 2021. Keelung, Taiwan.*

I read the words. Over and over and over and over again.

My biological mom is *dead*. Both my biological parents are gone. I don't have anyone connecting me to either side of my family. I'll never know why she let me go to America, if she ever thought of me, if she loved me. And she'll never know just how much I have missed her and will continue to miss her.

I search the page for more: How did she die? Why did she die? Was I on her mind when she took her last breath? But her death date are the only words I can read. Once again, a language barrier stops me from being what I've only ever wanted to be. Whole.

I wait for the tears to run down my cheeks, but they don't come. I'm not sad. I'm not relieved either—despite my futile attempt to convince myself that being free from Toby's lessons would be a good side effect. No, I'm none of those things. I am red.

I ball my fists in my lap and resist the urge to push the computer off the table. To tear these doors down. To hurt someone—like Rayleigh, or Aunt Joanna. Because it isn't fair that they get to have families. They get to have a place of belonging—a place to call home no matter where they go. What have *they* done to deserve *that*? And what have *I* done to deserve *this*?

I'm the laughingstock of destiny, because it doesn't matter how desperately I want something—it doesn't matter how much I've worked for it, how much I've suffered—this is my fate. And what's worse is that I'm so vividly *aware* of just how never in control I will be.

If the faintest part of my fury didn't realize that lashing out won't solve anything, I would throw that computer mouse across the room. But instead, I stand up and walk to the door. There's no point to anything anymore.

"Wait." Granny Eloise's voice cuts through the crackle of flames burning down my mansion of sorrow. "Did you know your mother had brothers?"

I stop with one foot halfway out the open door. The roar of fire stops screaming in my ears for just a moment. Even if my rage could demolish this room, I'd still be left with a foundation of longing.

I spin around. "How do you know?"

Granny Eloise gestures for me to return to her side. "Someone's uploaded a picture of them. It could've been another librarian. But when I see personal details like this, it tends to be from some living relative. Would you like to look at it?"

I've already lived a lifetime in the span of an hour. And I'm tired. Tired of wanting and never having. Tired of pretending that I haven't been cheated out of things that are truly mine like a mom, a dad, and an entire culture. But more than anything, I'm tired of hoping. I'm done. And maybe I should never have tried searching for Ya-Fang to begin with.

If Dad knew this was the result of me keeping his promise, would he have given me a promise to keep at all?

"No," I reply, maybe a little too sharply. "I don't care if I have uncles." *All I want is my mom and dad.*

Granny Eloise looks taken aback. She blinks at me as if waiting for an explanation. But I don't have one, because if I open my mouth again, I'll scream.

"I understand," Granny Eloise says softly. And a part of

me feels that she really means it. "You can always come back when you're ready to learn more."

I nod and slip out to the hallway. Instead of going back to the sacrament hall, I find the restrooms and sit in a stall until my rage turns to tears.

親情

Connections

That afternoon, I burst into Mavis's room without knocking.

"Again?" Mavis explodes. She's shirtless while her church dress sits atop one of the many laundry piles mounded around her room. "Are you allergic to knocking? Some of us are trying to get into our PJs!"

Mavis wraps her arms around her torso as I flop down onto her bed. I hug one of her pillows and sigh. "Can I tell you something?"

Mavis tosses on an oversize tee. Her head pops out of the collar, and wisps of hair frizz around her like a lion's mane. "What happened?"

Now that I've had a chance to process everything in the genealogy office today, I find myself telling my sister everything. About how keeping Dad's promise led me to take language lessons with Toby, and how those lessons led me to search for Ya-Fang. I *don't* tell her about becoming his dating coach. One thing at a time. And right now, I just need someone else to understand what I feel. And since Mavis has never met her biological dad, she must know what I'm going through.

Mavis sits at the foot of her bed, listening. By the time I'm done talking, she looks comfortable in her jammies while my throat is dry from talking so much.

"It just sucks," I conclude, leaning against the wall from

my seat atop her pillows. I press the back of my hand against my forehead to check for a fever. Even though I feel like I'm cooking from the inside out, my hand comes away room temperature.

Finally, Mavis speaks. "Dang, dude. That sucks. It's like finding out Dad died all over again but also, not like that at all, you know?"

I sniff, blotting my eyes with my thumb. Yeah. In some weird way, it kind of *is* like that. But it's more like a combination of remembering Dad's funeral and the guilt of never getting to know my biological mom as a person. There's something else stirring in my gut, too. Disloyalty. Because missing Ya-Fang also feels like I'm turning my back on Mom.

Mavis picks a piece of lint off her sweatshirt when I don't say anything. "Are you telling me this because Mom helped me find my bio dad?"

I sit up slowly. Mavis knows her bio dad was a one-night stand and that he only showed up to her birth to sign away his rights. But it never dawned on me that she tried to search for him.

"I didn't even know you did that," I admit. I've sat up all the way now, but that pillow is still in my arms. "Wait, how did Mom help you? How did she even know where he was?"

"She still has his email address." Mavis shrugs. "It was easier to track him down than I'm sure it's been for you and your Taiwanese family. At first, Mom didn't want to give me his email. I had to ask about him. A lot—actually. I basically begged for it after Dad died."

I stare at my sister, because she looks exactly like the girl I know. Her shoulder-length hair is the same as always. Her brown eyes are round enough to make people think she's sweet, until they see just how dark they really are. She's the same person here as she was in California. And yet, I've always been too scared to talk about this with her. Too scared to open the wounds that I can't see on her. Too scared to even acknowledge my own emotions. But this conversation is yet another one we should've had while Dad was here. Something tells me if the cancer hadn't happened, we would've eventually circled back to this sooner rather than later.

"When I first started asking about my bio dad, Mom didn't want me to dig into it because she was worried I'd get hurt," Mavis explains, fidgeting with the waist strings of her pajama pants. "She thought I'd learn about the kind of man he really is and it would reflect poorly on the way I see myself. But after a while, she came to the realization that I have a right to know. She gave me his name and his email address. I sent him a ten-page letter. He never responded."

I put Mavis's words together like puzzle pieces. My sister laid out her heart and her biological father didn't bother to reply? What kind of man does something like that to a child? My knuckles pop as my fists clench reflexively. Slowly, I loosen my hands. "Are you okay?"

Mavis is staring at the wall across the room, but I'm not sure if she's actually seeing anything. "I genuinely just . . . don't care. I think I'm in that phase of my life where I'm not going out of my way for someone who never went out of their way for me. If he decides to reach out later in life, I'd be open to a second discussion. But for now, I'm good."

Mavis is okay with just being *okay*? There was a time when I tried to convince myself that I was content with never knowing what happened in Taiwan. It was easier to just throw those unanswered questions out of sight, because if they weren't there, I wouldn't have to deal with them. But just because I could trick myself into not caring, it didn't mean that I *stopped* caring.

"I think you should tell Mom what you're going through," Mavis declares. "You might be surprised. She can be receptive. *Sometimes*."

I stroke the pillow like it's an emotional support animal. Saying all this stuff out loud should've made me feel better. And it does, sort of. It's comforting to know that Mavis and I are on good terms like this again. That we don't need Dad to be our mediator. We're growing up little by little, I guess. But at the same time, I can't shake this sick feeling. I don't have that sour taste in the back of my throat, and I don't have that mental haze that comes with the flu. But there's more I need to get off my chest even if I'm not sure what exactly that is yet.

A knock sounds at the door. Mavis and I both snap our attention to it. Gently, the door opens, and even more cautiously, a head of curly red-blond hair peeks in. Rayleigh. She pushes the glasses up her nose as she searches the room for me. "Hey. Are you ready?"

Mavis tenses on the bed. She doesn't know what Rayleigh is doing down here, and I don't blame her. Especially after everything.

"I told you that you can use my room today, remember?" Rayleigh says, gesturing for me to follow.

Right. She promised I could use her room to meditate. But that was before I learned Ya-Fang is dead.

"Uh, Rayleigh," I call after my cousin just as she starts heading upstairs.

Rayleigh freezes and stares at me, blue eyes magnified by her rectangular glasses. I find myself wanting to tell her that my biological mom is dead and that maybe now isn't the time to dig into spiritual connections. But I can't. Maybe I *do* still want to learn more about Ya-Fang's religion, about *my* first religion, even if she's dead.

My cousin doesn't wait for me to find my words. "Come on. Before my dad finds out what we're up to."

Reluctantly, I swing my legs out of Mavis's bed and head toward the door.

"What are you using Rayleigh's room for?" Mavis asks as our cousin vanishes from the doorway.

I open my mouth to answer, then shift gears and say, "Come see for yourself."

Mavis scrunches her face, but she slides out of bed anyway. She's got too much FOMO to let this go. Mavis follows me out into the basement living room while wringing her hands.

"Rayleigh says I can use her room to study Buddhism," I say, thinking this will calm my sister.

Mavis climbs the stairs beside me. "Are you sure you can trust her?"

I understand Mavis's hesitancy. Church is long over, but what happened on the way there is still fresh on her mind.

"She said last Sunday was an accident," I reply. "Besides,

I've got dirt on her. If she tells Aunt Joanna what I'm really up to, then I'll just tell her I caught Rayleigh sneaking out at night."

"Rayleigh—what? Ugh. No fair," Mavis wails. "I miss midnight Taco Bell runs. That's what she was doing, right?"

Though Rayleigh never admitted what she was up to, I still haven't dropped my sneaking suspicion that she's secretly dating a boy she definitely shouldn't be.

To my sister, I shrug. "No clue."

We patter across the foyer to Rayleigh's bedroom. Uncle Nick is in the living area with college football playing on the TV screen. He doesn't seem to notice us opening his daughter's door. Maybe it's because he's like all the other adults in the house right now—fast asleep for a Sunday nap.

Mavis and I step inside Rayleigh's room. Immediately, we're enveloped in darkness. As my eyes adjust to the low lighting, I understand why. Rayleigh has closed the curtains to her giant window and lit candles all around the room. A warm amber glow bounces off the walls and shimmers as if we're under a flaming ocean. It's like I'm not even in the Taylor home anymore.

Mavis whistles. "Wow. You did all this for Catie?"

"It's the least I can do." Rayleigh gives a sheepish shrug, then turns to Mavis. "Are you studying Buddhism, too?"

It takes Mavis a moment to respond as she weighs her options. Finally, she nods. "Apparently, I am."

Rayleigh pushes her glasses up her nose. "Okay. Well, I have plenty of books for everyone. Check this out."

Books? When Rayleigh said I could use her room, I wasn't

expecting so many candles—and I especially wasn't expecting books. But when she said she could help me with my spirituality, this must've been what she meant.

Rayleigh pulls a giant tote out from under her vanity. She drags the bag into the middle of the room before scooping the books out one by one and spreading them across the carpet.

"Trinity's mom is a military chaplain. It's her job to understand all religious practices so she can help veteran families grieve," Rayleigh explains. "I asked her to bring me books on Buddhism, and this is her supply. Here's *The Art of Happiness* by His Holiness the Dalai Lama. And *Mindfulness in Plain English* by . . . I'm not sure how to say this guy's name. And then there's . . . *The Subtle Art of Not Giving an F-word*. It's not necessarily a Buddhist book, but it applies Buddha's teachings about letting go of attachments."

"Sweet. Dibs," Mavis says, snatching up the book. Though the lighting is low, she lies on her stomach by the window and squints to read.

"Which one do you want, Catie?" Rayleigh asks. "Or you can just focus on meditation. I found a Spotify playlist with meditative chants if you'd rather listen to that."

For the first time all day, my lips tug into a smile. Maybe it was a good thing Rayleigh brought me up here after all. After learning about Ya-Fang, I just needed someone to tell me that they care about me. And Rayleigh did. "Thank you. For all of this."

Rayleigh adjusts her glasses, peering up at me. "Of course. My faith is a part of my identity. I know Mormonism isn't for everyone, but everybody deserves a safe space to find what their spirit resonates with most. I get to have that. It's only fair that my cousin does, too."

My cousin. That's the first time Rayleigh has referred to me as her family. And after knowing that she's capable of all this, I'm happy to call her the same thing.

"Thanks," I say. "What book should I start with?"

Rayleigh peers down at the floor of hardcovers and paperbacks. "Um. Honestly, I wouldn't know what to tell you. But since this is your spiritual journey, why don't you go with what feels right to you?"

Of course. It's *my* decision. So I sit down on the floor and skim the books. Some of them are worn. Some of them look brand-new. Eventually, one catches my eye.

The cover is a picture of a gold Buddha statue with big ears. The statue's hands are folded on his lap as if he's deep in meditation. I'm not sure why, but it feels like I've seen a figure like that before. Maybe the statue in our Taiwanese apartment had the same hand placement. I pull the book closer and flip to the first page.

I'm not sure how long the three of us spend reading. Rayleigh eventually turns on a lamp for better lighting. One of the candles burns itself out, leaving the room smelling like soot. Mavis falls asleep on her book. But my attention is glued to these pages.

Reading about Buddhism is unlike my memories of it, but it does help me understand some of Ya-Fang's beliefs. Though there are many sects of Buddhism, they all follow the same foundational philosophy: Life is suffering but happiness can still be obtained. Even before learning this—well, relearning this—I knew that my existence was adversity. No matter where I go, no matter what I do, the pain of not having biological ties carves out a black hole in my stomach. Reading about the Four Noble Truths brings at least a little validation to that pain.

Even though I'm reading this for me, I can't stop picturing Ya-Fang. Not just her features—with her wispy bangs and thin-rimmed glasses—but her life. She searched for Nirvana, which means she sought enlightenment by letting go of earthly attachments. Was she a selfless person? I imagine her at a grocery store picking up extra eggs to give her elderly neighbor. I imagine her with humble clothing and minimal decor on her bedroom walls. My biological mother—a mindful woman.

I shut the book to keep my thoughts from spiraling. She's gone, and seeing her in this new light won't bring her back. I'm too late to know her. Too late to ask Dad about her. The last time I felt this way, I ignored my pain for two years until moving to Utah made me *do* something about it. And even though I know I shouldn't let another two years slide by, I find myself falling into the same habit.

A yawn catches me, and I stretch my arms above my head. "I'm done reading for today."

But I say those words to no one, because Mavis and Rayleigh are fast asleep.

A glance at the clock tells me we'll be having dinner in about thirty minutes. Anxious to not be caught with these books, I tuck them back into Rayleigh's tote and blow out her candles. I drape Mavis with one of Maddie Sue's blankets before leaving my sister and cousin to nap.

The moment Rayleigh's door clicks behind me, my phone vibrates. I pull it out thinking it's my San Diego group chat. But another name appears on my screen.

TOBY: Hey what are you doing right now?

I'm reading his name on my phone, but I'm seeing his face in my mind and feeling the warmth of his touch. This is the first time Toby has texted me outside of work, and my mind races with all the reasons why he's thinking about me off the clock.

ME: Getting ready for dinner. Why?

Ugh. I sound so boring. But maybe that's a good thing. If he's texting me on a Sunday, it probably means he wants to meet up. Or he needs relationship advice. Either way, his presence is a welcome distraction from today. And it becomes even more so when his next text rolls in.

TOBY: You want to go to a party with me?

美人的標準
Conventionally Attractive

I blink at my phone. No way—a *party*? This is perfect! It's an excuse to get out of Aunt Joanna's house *and* a reason to stop thinking about Ya-Fang. And actually—this scenario couldn't be better, because I promised Mom I'd help Mavis make friends this summer. Now I *finally* have a way to introduce her to people.

My thumbs hover over the screen, ready to hammer out an enthusiastic reply. But then another text rolls in like he can hear me asking for details about this event.

> **TOBY:** Some of my old high school classmates are throwing a back from college party.

> **TOBY:** My friends were asking about you so I thought it would be cool if you met!

Oh no. College means alcohol. And alcohol has never been my thing. It tastes like spicy acid-water, and I've never liked the spinny headache that comes with being drunk anyway. I don't see the appeal, but Mavis would do anything to be there. She loved the ragers Francisca's older sisters used to throw.

Especially since I was always the designated driver by default.

> **ME:** Yeah sounds like fun!

> **ME:** Is it ok if I bring my sister?

> **TOBY:** Sure! Can't wait to meet her.

Great. I push open Rayleigh's bedroom door and hurry to Mavis's side. She's still asleep, but I shake her shoulders until she wakes.

"Whaaaa?" she drawls, eyelashes fluttering.

"Go to a party with me," I say, beaming.

That gets Mavis's attention. She sits up, blinking away sleep. Her blanket pools on her lap. "When?"

"Tonight."

Mavis's sleepy eyes suddenly glisten. But just as quickly as her smile appears, it fades. "I can't."

"What do you mean *you can't*?" I scowl.

"I already made plans with Jimmy and Francisca." Mavis's voice is groggy with sleep. "We're playing some online game Jimmy hasn't shut up about."

I think back on my friend group chat. Since when has Jimmy talked about a game? Actually, since when have any of them even texted me? I've been so busy, I haven't thought about how quiet my phone's been until now.

I lower my voice. "What game?"

Mavis finishes rubbing her eyes and sighs. "So we actually started a new group chat. One, um, without you."

I can't deny the sting in my chest. My own friends cut me out? I know it's partly my fault. I should've made a better effort to keep in touch. After all, I'll see them again this fall. But maybe my life in Utah has pulled me in so deeply, I've lost part of my San Diego self.

"Oh," I say, swallowing the lump rising up my throat.

"Do you want to play with us?" Mavis gently asks.

I want to say yes. But do I really want to invite myself to a game night with my friends when they've intentionally left me out? It would be like wearing purple on the Wednesday that everyone else wears pink.

"No, that's okay. I already told Toby I'd go," I say, trying not to sound more bitter than I feel.

"Who all is he going with?"

I shrug. "Friends."

Mavis pats me on the shoulder. "Vet them for me. If they're cool, you can introduce me later."

Mavis and Mom are the only ones who know I'm going to a party. Mom can trust me not to drink because she knows I don't even like alcohol. She's smelled beer off Mavis enough times to know that partying is a habit she picked up only after Dad died. Meanwhile, Aunt Joanna and Uncle Nick think that the reason I'm leaving after dinner is so that I can squeeze in a language lesson. They were understanding until they realized my Mandarin tutor is a *guy*. That combined with the fact that I'm meeting him so late made them give me disapproving pouts. But whatever. I'll be too gone to care.

After I've dusted on black and gold eye shadow, Toby sends me an address and I head out around ten o'clock. I follow my GPS up one of Salt Lake's mountains. Mom's Subaru strains to climb the steep slopes. As it turns out, this party is closer to the Taylors' home than it is to Toby's.

Finally, I reach the end of a cul-de-sac. Towering pine trees and shimmering aspens stand like curtains, casting the illusion that I've arrived at an exclusive party. I round a bend and find myself on a cliff with an overview of the Salt Lake Valley. Twinkling lights and rivers of roadways glow from the basin below. At the end of the street is a mansion even larger than Toby's house. Four floors of balconies hang over the mountainside.

I park a block away and carefully walk up to the house. Already, people are dancing and laughing with drinks in their hands. Heavy bass shakes the mansion. It's like being on the set of a music video. If the Taylors saw this, they'd probably call the cops and hose this place down with baptismal water.

Toby's recent text tells me to meet him in the kitchen. But where the heck is that? I wander around, noticing that everyone who went to Toby's high school must've been as wealthy as he is. Maybe this is the rich side of SLC. Well, *richer*. Either way, hunting him down and waiting for him to text back is a goal that obstructs thoughts of my living Taiwanese relatives.

I find a kitchen—but is it *the* kitchen? Considering how

many rooms are in this place, I wouldn't be surprised if there was another one somewhere else. A plastic bin of red juice sits on the island. People walk by, dipping their cups inside like ladles. They carry their drinks into the living room, leaving trails of splattered juice along the wooden floor. Yeah, I'm not about to drink from a bin that other people have been dunking their nasty hands into.

I lean against the kitchen wall and check my phone. No response. Seriously, where the heck is Toby?

"Whose house is this?" someone asks from beside me.

I turn. Nichole stands by the fridge with a red cup in her hand. Her long brown hair is pulled back by a claw clip while she sports a trendy crop top and high-waisted jeans. Though she still holds herself with the familiar poise I saw at the salon, I can tell by the hunch in her shoulders she's a little tipsy.

Next to her is a short Southeast Asian girl with long dark hair. A baggy U of U sweater hangs off her shoulder while her skirt stops midthigh. It's a comfy party look—one that says *I go to college* while also saying *I know how to let loose.* Judging by how close she's leaning into Nichole, I imagine this shorter friend is her roommate or maybe even a bestie from high school.

"I think this is Lawrence Hebert's house," the other girl says over the thumping music. "His mom's running for senator or something."

"No way," Nichole exclaims, voice drawled. "His place is incredible."

"He's single," her friend says, wiggling her brows. "Just broke up with his college girlfriend."

Nichole giggles and slaps her friend's shoulder. "Shut up! I'm gonna go talk to him. Where is he?"

Nichole spins around, searching the crowd. But when her eyes meet mine, my lungs switch places with my stomach. She's just caught me eavesdropping.

"Can I help you?" Nichole asks, a sharpness in her voice.

"H-hi!" I stammer, thinking fast. And then it strikes me—the only thing I know about Nichole is that Toby is in love with her. So what if I play matchmaker? That's what a dating coach does, right?

"I don't think you remember me. My name's Catie," I say with my biggest, most confident smile.

Nichole furrows her brows.

"I work at the salon with Toby Yoon-Hanson."

Nichole's eyes widen with recognition. "Oh, that's where I've seen you! You looked familiar. I remember that when I saw you at the salon, I kind of thought you were Toby's girlfriend. You were wearing purple eye shadow, and it matched his purple hair. Total couple's fit, if you ask me."

I force a laugh even though my thoughts spin—Nichole thought we were *together*?

"No." I swat the air, trying to look as carefree as possible. "We aren't dating. I don't even have a boyfriend—"

I wince the moment the words leave my lips. Did I seriously just say that? Utah Catie is supposed to have a long-distance boyfriend. California Catie needs to sit down and shut up.

"And Toby's single, too," I circle back. "Honestly, how does he *not* have a girlfriend? He's such a catch."

"Aw, well, you two look so cute together!" Nichole says, gesturing to my makeup with her red cup. "Why aren't you two dating?"

I shake my head before the picture can settle into my brain. "Nah. Toby and I aren't like that. We're just coworkers. But you've been friends with him for a while now, haven't you?" My heart's thundering. Is it because of the music? Or is it because I'm kind of sucking at being a wingwoman?

"We went to school with him." Nichole gestures to herself and to her friend. "This is Ginny, by the way. The three of us were always in math class together. We were such nerds back then."

"Well, Toby's definitely not a nerd anymore," I say, steering the conversation toward a direction that paints Toby in a better light. Maybe a good starting point is to highlight things about him that are conventionally attractive.

"He's pretty cool now, though, right?" I say, coaxing them into agreeing with me. "I mean, he's super kind, and his clients always say he's the sweetest person they know."

Ginny scoffs at my remark. "Yeah, well, they must not have grown up with him."

Nichole giggles. "Seriously, remember those playing cards he used to bring to lunch?"

I laugh along even though I have no clue what they're talking about. Toby brought card games to lunch? Man—who was he in high school? A part of me wants to let my imagination run wild. But the other part of me knows how chaotic my life will get if I don't start reining everything in.

"Well, I haven't seen him play card games lately," I say.

"He's usually at the gym nowadays. I don't know how he finds time to do it all—work full-time and get jacked."

Ginny nods along thoughtfully. "That's a good point. Talk about ugly duckling syndrome. Toby had a major glow-up senior year. I think that was when he started working out."

"Yeah, but I feel like I can't unsee him from middle school," Nichole adds. "He was always so scrawny. I felt bad for him. He'd sit on the sidewalk and collect rocks during recess. He needed a friend, so I gave him a stick of gum for Valentine's Day. I feel like that's been our thing ever since."

Toby had mentioned something about that. Maybe her love language is gift giving? I should share that with him.

"Have you seen his hair recently, Ginny?" I ask, needing another conventionally attractive thing about Toby to talk about. Objectively, he really *is* good-looking. I mean, he works at a spa. It's kind of his job to look good. "Toby dyed it purple for the summer. It's grown out a bit, so now he styles it like Jungkook in the 'Butter' music video."

Nichole nods vigorously, tucking a silky strand of loose hair behind her ear. "I saw him post an update on Instagram! It looks really good on him. Ha! Now all I can see is scrawny Tobias as a K-pop star."

Ginny and I laugh. That's a step in the right direction, and yet my stomach twists. Also, why am I so sweaty? Is it because there are too many people in this kitchen?

"Totally agree," I add, fanning my face. What's something else Nichole would be interested in hearing about Toby?

"Well, he kind of *does* live a lavish lifestyle like a K-pop idol. His mom drives a Porsche, and the kitchen in his basement looks like it could be the set of a cooking show—"

"You've been to his house?" Nichole interrupts, eyes wide once more.

"Yeah," I say, smirking at my win. "He's my language teacher. Mandarin was my first language, and Toby's been helping me relearn it. Isn't that sweet?"

"Awwww," Nichole sighs, clutching her drink to her chest. "That *is* sweet. And my sister Lola absolutely adores him. Huh, maybe Tobias grew up more than I realized. It is strange that he's single, isn't it?"

Nichole says that more to herself than to me. Hearing this would make any wingwoman proud. So then why does the back of my mouth feel itchy right now? I clear my throat until the sensation subsides. Maybe it's not this conversation that's irritating me. It's the smell of alcohol and cologne in the air.

A song with heavy bass has been playing for most of this conversation. But as I turn away to cough, the music changes to one that I've been hearing a lot on the radio. It must be popular, because the people around me cheer and swarm the living room.

"You need to dance with me!" Ginny squeals, tugging Nichole onto the makeshift dance floor.

Before Nichole is swallowed up by the living room, she turns around and waves at me. "Tell Toby I say hi!"

I wave back and nod. Even though I know I should share this conversation with Toby, the knot in my throat tightens as if it doesn't want me to.

永恆的一刻

One Perpetual Moment

I've been so enveloped in my conversation with Nichole that I don't notice Toby's texts until I'm already headed up the stairs. My thighs burn as I climb, but the higher up I go, the quieter it gets.

I round the fourth-floor stairwell to find a quaint living room with a kitchenette against the wall. There are only a handful of people up here. A small quartet of friends sits around a TV watching *Avatar*—the blue aliens, not the airbender. They share giant bowls of popcorn and I can smell the butter as I enter the room.

Finally, a familiar flash of purple hair catches my eyes. Toby is in the corner of the room, next to the balcony's sliding glass doors. His back is to me and he's playing beer pong with three of his friends. There's a paddle in one hand and his cell phone in the other. He must be waiting for my response, but I wasn't sure he'd answer.

I cross the living area, careful not to block the TV for the people who chose to escape the chaos below. Finally, my hand meets Toby's shoulder. He turns carefully, slow with inebriation. But the moment he sees me, he's everything but slow.

"Catie! You're here!" Toby beams, pulling me into a tight hug.

I'm not expecting this. He's crushing me with his arms, and his breath smells like beer. Toby sways me side to side while I'm pressed against his cotton shirt. His body is extra warm like he just stepped out of a hot shower. When he pulls back, he smiles down at me with a goofy grin.

"Where's your sister?"

"She couldn't make it," I say without going into detail because I can't stop staring at the sheen over Toby's face. Despite his impeccable skin-care routine, it's done nothing to spare him from the wrath of the Asian flush. Blotches of red dot his forehead and line his neck. His cheeks are puffy like he's got cotton balls in his mouth, and I can't stop myself from giggling. "You're so drunk."

Toby jabs a finger across the Ping-Pong table. "You can blame those guys. I'm getting spanked."

Across the net is a cluster of red SOLO cups lined up like bowling pins. Two boys wave at me from the other side. One of them is tall and blond. The other is short with glasses.

"Hey," the guy with glasses calls to me, getting my attention. His dark hair is overgrown like Toby's, and he tucks the loose strands behind his ear. Maybe it's the fact that he's wearing a red polo with khakis, but he kind of looks like he's trying to sell me car insurance. "Are you Toby's *girlfriend*?"

My cheeks burn through my foundation as I slide my attention to Toby. *What did this guy just call me?*

Toby swipes at the air like he's brushing off the question. "Guys, stop that. No, this is Catie. She's got a boyfriend, but he lives in San Diego. We're just coworkers. Nothing more."

Nothing more.

And yet something about his words makes me want to correct him. Was I hoping he'd introduce us as more than just coworkers—friends, maybe? Or is it because he brought up my not-so-real boyfriend?

"What about you guys?" I fill my voice with playfulness. Now isn't the time to unpackage all of this anyway. I'm here to see if his friends are a good match for Mavis. "Which one of you is his *boyfriend*?"

The tall, quiet one rolls his head back and toots with laughter. Judging by the muscles exploding out of his tank top, he must be one of Toby's gym buddies. "Ha! Trust me, honey. There was a time when I tried."

Laughter surrounds me like these guys are all in on the same joke. They seem to have known each other for years and have a history I can't begin to fathom. Coming here is opening a window into Toby's past, and for the first time I'm able to see him from a perspective I'd never considered before.

"I'm Jeremy," he says when he finishes laughing. Then he slaps the back of a guy standing beside him. "This is Lucas, and that one next to you is Alex."

Alex—I remembered Toby telling me about them. A baggy

tank top dips low enough under their arms for me to catch surgical scars cut along their chest. Between the summer-tanned skin and the marijuana cap holding down a crown of curly hair, I can totally see Mavis cruising around a skate park back in San Diego with someone like them.

"Oh, so *you're* Alex. It's nice to finally meet you."

Alex raises a brow. "Finally? You mean Toby's been talking about me all this time and he's only introducing you now? For shame, Tobias. For shame."

Toby chuckles beside me. "Um, you didn't even want to grab ramen with me the other day, so don't even."

"Tobes is right," Lucas hollers, flashing his green metal braces. "Don't talk and let's keep playing. Show us what you've got, Catie the Coworker!"

Oh? I'm playing beer pong with a bunch of Toby's friends? I haven't done this since Francisca threw her Halloween party last year. I was an awful player then, which means I'm probably worse now. If Mavis had come, she'd easily crush these guys.

"Do you even know how to play?" Jeremy asks, bouncing a pong ball off his forearm before catching it midair.

I roll my eyes to let him know his intimidation tactic didn't work on me. If he's going to egg me on, I'm going to do the same. "I'm not exactly a pong *player*—I'm more of a pong *winner*."

Everyone throws their hands over their mouths and *oooohs*. Yeah, I can talk smack. Even if it's all a lie, which is something I'm really good at now, though it's nothing to be proud of.

Toby crouches down until his mouth is against my ear. "Are you sure you can win? Because I don't know if I can keep drinking for you and Alex."

He must be too drunk to realize his lips are only inches from my cheek. And I'm too sober to dwell on the way his breath somehow sends goose bumps down my legs. "Of course I can win. I've got a secret weapon."

Toby leans back and arches a brow. "What is it?"

"I'm sober."

Jeremy thumps his pecs as Toby and I break apart. "Hey! No conspiring! Show us what you've got!"

I grab the ball floating in a cup of water on my side of the table and shoot my shot. The ball arcs across the table and lands perfectly in one of the cups of beer. Alex cheers. Toby lets out a sigh of relief. And I stare at the floating ball in disbelief. Man, maybe I should smack-talk more often.

Jeremy and Lucas lose the first round. And the second round. They aren't even throwing in straight lines by the third. Between Alex and me, two sober players on one team seems to result in many victories.

Alex calls for a break when Jeremy grabs a cup of water. Toby excuses himself to the restroom, and I step onto the balcony for some fresh air. I lean against the railing, staring down at the party below.

Nighttime is weird. Hours must've gone by and yet there hasn't been any indication of it. The same shade of lavender haze hovers over the distant mountains as if this night is just one perpetual moment. But maybe I need this long stretch of time to digest the fact that I'll never see Ya-Fang again. And when dawn breaks, I'll have to do something about it or risk letting her death resemble Dad's. Like maybe I should look up my uncles. How many do I have? How old are they? They'll never replace Ya-Fang but at least it's *something*.

"Hey," Alex says, joining me at my side. "You having fun?"

I shrug. "It's a college party, so I think I'm supposed to say yes?"

Alex chuckles, bopping with the rhythm of the music down below. "You're funny. I see why Toby likes you."

I see why Toby likes you. The words play on repeat like my favorite song stuck in my head. Wait—what am I thinking? I shut the thought down the moment it appears. Toby doesn't like me the way he likes Nichole. I don't make him stumble over his words. I don't make him blush. Yet something pricks the space between my ribs. *Why does Nichole get to have that effect on him, but I don't?*

"I mean, we're . . ." I think about saying *friends* but push back on it. Toby has already labeled us so that's what I'll stick with. ". . . *coworkers*. I imagine you're supposed to like the people you work with."

Alex shakes their head. "You're not *just* coworkers. Come on, would you invite a fellow employee to a party like this?"

I peer back through the sliding glass door. People have moved from watching a movie to laughing on the couch. Jeremy is showing Lucas how to bounce the pong ball off his forearm. There's no business meeting, no PowerPoint presentations, and no inventory to discuss. If this were a job-related event, it most definitely wouldn't be happening on a night before a workday.

"I see your point, but we really are just work buddies," I emphasize. "Besides, Toby said you were interested in meeting me, and I wanted to meet you, too."

Alex shakes their head, coils bouncing. "He told me about your agreement. He teaches you Mandarin, and you help him land a date with Nichole. That doesn't sound like something *just coworkers* do."

I blink so fast, it's like I have a lash in my eye. I shouldn't be surprised Toby told Alex. They are best friends, after all. But still, now that someone outside our agreement knows, the reality of what I'm doing feels much more . . . well, *real*.

"Toby admires you for that, by the way," Alex continues, oblivious to my surprise. "And I can tell you're a great teacher. I don't think you understand the impact you've had on him these past few weeks. He's really changed, and I thank you for that."

I scrunch my brows because everyone keeps talking about the old Toby—the version of him I never saw. He was the dorky boy who played card games in high school—the kid who powered through to find his place in the teenage hierarchy. I'm missing out on so much of who Toby is.

"Do you think I'm doing the right thing by helping him date Nichole?" I'm not sure why I ask, but the question comes out of my mouth all the same.

Alex rests their hand on their chin while I ponder the answer I want. I want them to say I'm doing the right thing. That this lie is really worth it. That I'm taking Mandarin lessons and shouldn't feel guilty about the way I'm acquiring them.

"Yes," Alex finally replies.

My shoulders slump with relief.

"And no."

I stare at the side of their face, waiting for an explanation.

"I don't think you ever saw the version of Toby we grew up with," Alex says quietly. "He was a wreck after his brother died."

I nod. "Yeah, Toby told me about Ezra."

Alex cocks their head. "Yeah, he told me that he told you."

I push off the railing so that I can face Alex a little better. "You two seem really tight."

Alex nods. "Yeah, I lived with him for a while, actually. Did he tell you why I moved in?"

I shake my head, eager for more.

Alex twists a ring around their finger. "When I was in middle school, I told my parents to start calling me Alex instead of my dead name. They didn't. I told them to use they/them pronouns. They didn't. But I think the final straw happened when I was thirteen. My body was changing, and it made me so dysphoric that Toby bought me a binder. My parents discovered it in my closet and kicked me out. My dad was a Mormon bishop. Can't have a child running around church with short hair and a binder. Not if he wants to maintain appearances."

I twist my hands across my rib cage. I've heard of stories like this within the Mormon community, though they weren't as common in San Diego. But Utah Mormons are another level. Alex was just a young kid struggling to belong. A young kid who wanted to express love and be loved. A child with parents who cared more about what happened outside their home than inside. And yet they were powerless to change anything despite wanting change so desperately.

"I moved in with the Yoon-Hansons months before Ezra passed," Alex continues. "And even after, the Yoon-Hansons didn't want me going back to my house. It wasn't safe for me there, but it was always safe with Toby and his family. Toby was there for me when I needed him most, and all I can hope is that I was there for him when he needed me most."

Alex is still fidgeting with their ring. They don't need to go into details, but hearing this helps me fit all the pieces together. No one here knows Toby better than Alex. So when they say that Toby and I are more than coworkers, they must really believe that.

"That's why I think it's a great idea that you're helping him learn how to date," Alex concludes. "It's getting him out of his shell even more."

"I'm also kind of already playing matchmaker for him," I confess. "I ran into Nichole downstairs and hyped up Toby to her."

Alex turns toward me with a puzzled look in their dark, upturned eyes. "Really?"

I'm not sure why, but they seem more surprised than they should be. If I'm Toby's dating coach, doesn't it make sense for me to try to hook them up? That's been Toby's goal from the start. Nothing's changed—has it?

Alex pulls away and scoffs. "Well, if they do end up together, I'm not sure I see it lasting."

My breath hitches.

"Why?" I ask. This is something a best friend should reveal to the person who's trying to get Toby to date his dream girl. At least, that's what I tell myself.

Alex turns back toward the sliding patio doors. "You're the love expert, right? I'm sure you'll figure it out."

迷迭香

Rosemary

Even though I didn't have a sip of alcohol last night, my head is foggy. Ever since I left the party, I haven't stopped thinking about the *implications* of Alex's words. Does Toby see me as more than a coworker? As more than a friend? If that's true, then what does that mean for me?

I mean, Toby *is* kind of cute—sue me. But that's it. And he's kind. Besides, there's no way we could ever be together like *that* because he's in love with Nichole, for one. Secondly, he's my bosses' son—talk about awkward. And lastly, I'm moving back to San Diego this fall, so even if we got together, it would be short-lived.

Oh, and I'm already in a *relationship* with someone, apparently.

But as I move through another Monday at the spa, I can't stop biting my lip every time I hear his laugh over the whir of a blow-dryer. I can't stop glancing over to his station and hoping that he's looking up at me. Maybe the *idea* of him liking me is just a fun little fantasy. In another timeline—one where Dad is still here and we came to Utah under different circumstances—he'd shake Toby's hand. He'd invite Toby over for one of those "what are your intentions with my daughter" dinners. I feel that they would've gotten along, since they're both gentle people and great listeners.

I'm wiping down the keyboard when Toby rushes by, probably to get something out of the storage closet.

"Hey," I call to him even though I have no idea what to say. Maybe some part of me misses his company even though I just hung out with him yesterday. I know he's busy, but still. I just want to look at him for a moment longer before he disappears again.

Toby nearly trips when he stops to look at me. "What's up?"

Of course, I ruined his routine. Judging by the spatters of bleach on his apron, he's probably in the middle of foiling his client's hair. But I'm not about to tell him that the reason I called out to him is that I've been picturing him at a dinner table with my father.

"I've been thinking about our Mandarin lessons," I say instead. Because that's also true. Although it's been more at the back of my mind than Alex's words. But now that I've had a moment to process Ya-Fang's death, I know how to not let two years slide by all over again.

Toby arches a brow. "Oh. Is everything okay?"

"Yeah, yeah," I say, sensing the fact that Toby's still very much in the middle of things. "It's just—do you think I could start making my language lessons more specific? I, um . . . I recently found out that I have uncles in Taiwan, and, well, I've been thinking that I need to reach out to them so—"

"Catie!" Toby gasps, closing the distance between us until he's practically leaning over the reception desk. "That's amazing!

How—when—? You're going to have to tell me everything when we're not so busy, but yeah! I can plan a conversational lesson for you. Want to come back over to my place this Wednesday?"

My grin is almost as wide as Toby's. I know he's busy, but the fact that he cares so deeply despite our schedules is one of the reasons I like him so much.

As a friend.

"Wednesday sounds good," I say.

Toby pulls back and drums on the counter. "Sweet. And I'm serious. You have to tell me everything about your family."

With that, he rushes out of the foyer and back down the hall we once collided in.

♥

Toby's fallen so behind that I'm clocking out by the time he's toning his last client's hair. I wish there was something I could do to help him, but I don't even get a chance to wave goodbye to him before I'm out the door. That's fine. I'll get a chance to tell him about the genealogy office and Granny Eloise on Wednesday.

I drive to Aunt Joanna's place and park Mom's Subaru in the driveway. My head is so in the clouds that I don't realize Aunt Joanna's car is missing until I step inside the foyer. In fact, none of the Taylors are here—a reprieve from Uncle Nick's grating work phone calls. Instead, Maddie Sue greets me with a floppy tongue and a wagging tail as I walk into the kitchen.

The scent of rosemary chicken wafts in the air as I take a

seat at the dining table. Mom's stirring something on the stove and Mavis is seated beside me, scrolling through her phone.

"Where did the Taylors go?" I ask, sitting down beside Mavis. Maddie Sue crawls under the table as if she's ready to vacuum up any bits of dinner we might drop.

Mavis's words are squished by her hand resting against her cheek. "They went out. We have the whole house to ourselves, because apparently, Mom has some news."

I peer back to Mom at the stove. There's a bowl of steamed broccoli sitting on the island, and there's a pitcher of punch, too. Is Mom cooking to brace us for bad news? Or is she celebrating because something good finally happened?

"Did she get a job?" I mouth the words to Mavis, but all she does is shrug and keep scrolling.

I'm racking my brain. Is it someone's birthday? Did Mom inherit some money? If this were just an ordinary dinner, the Taylors wouldn't've gone out. So what's the big deal?

I'm tapping my foot as Mom brings the chicken over. As much as I want to tear into the buttery breast, I don't reach for anything. Mom sits down on the other side of the table and pulls in her chair. To look at her, I have to peer through the steam rising off the food.

"Is everything all right?" I ask, unable to contain myself.

"You don't have cancer, do you?" Mavis lifts her cheek off her hand. There's a giant palm print on her face. She's been here for a while, stewing in her own thoughts.

I don't blame her for asking. I'm pretty sure rosemary chicken was the dinner she made for us to cushion the blow of

Dad's diagnosis. The smell alone is taking me back to San Diego for all the wrong reasons.

"No." Mom shakes her head. "Of course not. Thank goodness."

"Then what's up with all this?" Mavis asks, gesturing to the food.

Mom nibbles on the corner of her lip. "Well, I don't know how to tell you girls . . ."

I wipe my palms on my knees. So it *is* bad news, isn't it? If not cancer, maybe Aunt Joanna and Uncle Nick have had enough of us and are kicking us out.

Mom clears her throat. "I got a job."

Mavis and I gasp in unison. My belly dips as if I'm on a roller coaster. This is one of those classic *psych* moments—right? Mom was just pretending like there's bad news when really, this is the best thing that could've happened. Now she can work on saving up money to go back home. *San Diego, here we come.*

The thought revives images of crashing ocean waves and soaring seagulls. Of weekends where we'd escape the heat under the shade of a tree and gossip. Of football games and pep rallies that made me scream so hard, my throat went raw. Our old apartment complex reappears in my mind. The smell of a chlorinated pool and the sting of construction in the air are the perfume of my childhood. *Home.* We are finally going home. Guess Jimmy and Francisca are going to have to add me back into their group chat.

"Does this mean we'll be back in time for senior year?" Mavis asks excitedly, leaning forward.

Mom's focus sinks to the table.

Wait. If this is good news, then why is she rubbing her hands together like that?

"That's what I wanted to talk to you girls about." Mom's voice quivers. "The job that I got will be paying more than I've ever made in San Diego. But it would keep me here. In Salt Lake City."

Mavis falls silent as I absorb the news. In an instant, it's like my memories have been wiped clean of the neon colors at the skate park. Of the Saturday night drag shows where we come home covered in confetti and draped in boas. No San Diego. No Del Rey High School. No Gucci Roasters with Jimmy and Francisca. We're staying in Salt Lake City, and I don't know when I'll ever see Dad's grave again.

"What?" Mavis recoils in her seat. "But you said that was the plan. We were supposed to go back. My whole life is there. My friends. My senior year—*our* senior year! And we're just supposed to start all over?"

Mom sucks in sharply. "That's why I wanted to break the news to you girls like this. I know we planned on going back—"

"I was counting on that!" Mavis exclaims, taking the words from my mouth. "Mom, I hate it here. I literally have no friends other than Catie. I can't get a job because it's like these Utah people can smell there's something wrong with me. I'm so sick of being the outcast. And I'm just supposed to *live* here? Start my senior year here where every day I'll be reminded that I don't belong?"

Mavis's face is flushed and her dark pupils burn. I'm

seeing my sister and remembering what Alex told me about what it means to be queer in Utah. How even in their own home, they were rejected like a bad transplant. Mavis already knows what it means to be pan and surrounded by Mormons. She got a taste of it in San Diego. But here, it's not just uncomfortable. It's dangerous.

"That was another thing I wanted to talk to you girls about." Mom avoids our eyes. "My new job will be at the University of Utah. I'll be one of their track-and-field coaches. And because I'll be faculty, you girls will be eligible for reduced tuition if you decide to go to college there."

My gaze lowers to the braided patterns in the tablecloth. How is this supposed to help me? Ever since Toby told me about the University of Taipei, I haven't even been planning to attend college in America, let alone in Utah.

"You lied to us." The betrayal in Mavis's voice causes tears to spring into Mom's eyes.

"I'm working with the resources I have." Mom's voice wobbles. "I don't have someone else to help me give you the life you deserve. But this is the best I can do for now."

Mavis blinks rapidly. Then, she kicks the table and storms out of the kitchen. As she disappears down the stairs, I catch her wiping her face.

I'm torn between following her and staying here because I know Mom's hurting, too. But telling her how I feel isn't going to help this situation, so I stare blankly at the tablecloth.

I'm not like my sister. I've made friends in Utah. I have a job. And even though Mom wants us to attend college here, I might be able to find a way to Taiwan. Toby will help me.

Toby.

Staying here means never saying goodbye to the greatest friend I've ever made. Staying here means . . . it means . . .

Maybe my daydreams can become real. I thought we had to be *just coworkers* because I couldn't bear the thought of never seeing him again. I've already said goodbye to so many people in my life, and I was bracing myself to add his name to that list. But living here in the city where his friends are, in the city where his parents live—it means never saying goodbye. Only see you later.

But it also means that my lies don't just disappear when I do. It means the longer I'm here in Utah, the more lies I'll inevitably tell. Unless, of course, I come clean and ruin everything.

"Catie?" Mom sniffs. "Are you okay?"

I meet Mom's gaze with a slight, genuine smile. One that no longer feels restrained by the persona I've created. I know this can't be an easy choice for her to make, but I hope my answer will give her some comfort.

"Yeah, I'm okay. And I think I know how to help Mavis."

冰淇淋

Ice Cream

I tell Mom to keep the dinner warm. If all goes well, Mavis and I will be back up here to eat as a family. But for now, I need to see how my sister is doing. I hurry after her, clinging to the railing as I race downstairs to the basement. It's dark and empty, just like the first time Aunt Joanna brought me down here. But I catch sight of the warm light spilling out from the bottom of Mavis's door.

I've gotten into the habit of walking into her room whenever I want, but this moment calls for a gentle knock. When she doesn't respond right away, I tap on her door again.

"Go away!" Mavis hollers with a stuffy voice. A part of me wants to respect her wishes. But another part knows she needs me.

I push the door open and poke my head inside. "Hey."

Mavis lies facedown with the blankets covering her body and a pillow over her head. Or that's what it looks like. I can't tell with the mess of sheets in the way.

I snake around the mounds of laundry before taking a seat on the corner of her mattress. Mavis sniffs but doesn't tell me to leave, so I sit there rubbing her back until she's ready to talk.

"Mom lied," Mavis croaks, voice hoarse from crying. "I don't think she ever wanted to go back."

I shake my head. There's no way that's true. I've seen in Mom's eyes how much she misses San Diego and how hard this decision was for her. We aren't the only ones who gave up our friends. Mom had several years' worth of clients that she'd racked up at the gym. But when Mavis is in pain, she can't think about anyone else's suffering.

"I'm so . . . ," Mavis says, removing the pillow from her face, ". . . tired of feeling alone. I just want to go *home*."

Mavis's shoulders shake and I stroke her back. "I know it sucks and I hate knowing you're lonely. But this city is huge, and there are so many other people and places you have yet to explore. Plus, I think I've finally found some friends you'll get along with."

Mavis rubs her eyes with the sleeve of her shirt. "Toby's friends?"

I nod. Despite her tears, she must remember our talk yesterday.

Mavis wipes her nose, then opens her mouth. She takes one long inhale before chuckling as if she hasn't just had her heart broken. It's a strained laugh, but a laugh nonetheless.

I arch my brow. "You okay?"

Mavis brushes the hair off her wet cheeks, then sits up. Her hair is a frizzy mess. When she looks at me, her nose is just as pink as her eyes. "Remember how Dad used to take us to the park with him for his Saturday jogs? He'd run the track while we played on the swings?"

I match her chuckle because I think I know where this is going. "How Dad saw me scratching your back that one time because those boys kicked mulch at you?"

"So he got us ice cream on the way home," Mavis finishes. Her eyes are pink, but she's also smiling. "All because he was so proud of you for being such a big sister."

I slide my arm over Mavis's shoulder and pull her into a side hug. We were twelve when we started the ice-cream-after-working-out tradition. Frosties, Blizzards, McFlurrys when the machine wasn't broken. Dad said it was our reward for being such great sisters to each other. But now that I look back on it, I remember he always got an ice cream for himself, too. Wait, was he *actually* doing it for us or for him? Either way, I wish he were here now. If only he could see me comforting Mavis without the promise of sweet treats.

Mavis exhales a long sigh. Her voice is extra nasally when she speaks. "I feel like all I've done this summer is cry."

I frown at my sister. "There's nothing wrong with crying."

"I know," Mavis says, tucking her hair behind her ears. For a long moment, she stares at the corner of the room as if she's seeing a ghost. Finally, she opens her mouth again. She releases a big breath as if she's letting go of everything within her. Then she straightens her shoulders. "Thanks. For the ice cream."

"Of course," I say, stroking her hair.

Who knew it would take coming to SLC to become sisters again? Because sisters get in trouble together, and they stand up for each other, and when one of them is sad, the other one steps in to help comfort. It's who we were before Dad died. Two girls who used to share the same bed while he read us nighttime stories. Two girls who stole each other's clothes, then ran to him when we got upset. But this time, we're learning how to do it in Dad's absence.

Mavis leans her head back on the wall. "Do you really think I'll make friends here?"

I roll my eyes at Mavis. "You're literally the coolest person I know. Well, you and Toby—which is why you need to meet him. And his friends. It'll be fun! We could go to the movies or something. Isn't there a film you want to see?"

Mavis sniffs. "They just released the fourth *Haunting* movie. You want to watch that?"

"Of course," I say. Another lie. I don't particularly want to watch another film in that franchise. It's a little too scary for me. The last one Mavis dragged me to was about a nun in a dark shroud who followed people even in their dreams. I had to sleep with the bathroom light on for an entire week and check for murderers behind the shower curtain before I peed. But if this is what my sister wants, then this is what she gets. "Why don't you look up showtimes and I'll see if Toby and his friends want to go?"

Mavis nods eagerly, then pulls out her phone. Her face is still puffy, but this is the most energy I've seen from her since coming down here. Maybe this is everything she needs right now. Even if it's just a pinprick of light in her darkness, at least it's better than nothing at all.

"There's a showing right after you get off work tomorrow," she says, rubbing her eyes.

Ugh, tomorrow? Watch a horror movie before bed? Obviously, I'm going to say yes. But Mavis owes me big-time.

I shoot a quick text to Toby. After all, he's the one who started the whole talk-to-each-other-outside-work-hours thing. I don't feel bad bugging him now. I can talk to him without the weight of San Diego looming over my shoulder. But then, if I'm staying in Utah, what does this mean for me? For us and my *lies*?

"Looks like it's official," I say after a quick back-and-forth with Toby. "I'm really excited for you to meet Alex. I have a feeling the two of you will hit it off."

Mavis rolls her eyes at me, though I can tell she's fighting a smile. "Yeah, yeah. If you say so. Hey, before I forget—I saw this app that made me think of you."

She plucks my phone out of my hands.

"Hey!"

"Hold on. I'm downloading it for you."

I give my sister a silent glower as she thumbs away at my phone. Moments later, she hands my device back. To my surprise, my screen saver has been changed. Instead of the familiar palm trees and San Diego sunset, I stare at some words written in English, Pinyin, and Hanzi.

Hello: Nǐ hǎo (你好).

I close out of my phone, then open it back up again. *Goodbye: Zàijiàn* (再見).

I close out of my phone, then open it again. *Thank you: Xièxie* (謝謝).

"Pretty cool, huh?" Mavis asks.

I close the home screen only to open it again. *Me: Wǒ* (我). Close. Open. *My: Wǒ de* (我的).

It's like Toby handing me his Taiwanese film all over again. I squeeze my sister tighter than I ever have.

"Xièxie," I tell her. "It means 'thank you.'"

Mavis sniffs into my sleeve. "Consider this my payment for your sacrifice. I know you hate horror movies."

I roll my eyes. I better not regret going to this film with her. If this movie gives me nightmares, she'll owe me a lot more than an awesome app.

未知的恐懼

Fear of the Unknown

The next day, Toby is stacked with clients. But he's able to wrap up his last balayage and clock out with me so that we can pick up Mavis. Along the way, I recount everything that's happened with my bio family search. Surprisingly, tears don't well up in my eyes when I talk about Ya-Fang's death. Maybe I really am moving on. Or maybe the guilt of losing her is being slowly replaced by the hope of meeting my uncles.

"Wow," Toby breathes, taking the last turn onto Aunt Joanna's street. Have I really been talking his ear off this entire time? "What happened to that picture Granny Eloise found? Have you had a chance to look at it again?"

I draw invisible circles on my knees. "Not yet. But this Sunday, I'll go back to the office and take a look."

Toby drums on the steering wheel as he pulls into Aunt Joanna's driveway. Mavis must've seen us through the front door because she's walking up the lawn right now. "Show me a picture of your uncles when you get a chance. I want to see which one of them looks the most like you."

Toby's too busy waving at Mavis to notice me biting my bottom lip. I can't stop this smile from lifting my cheeks no matter how hard I clench. I hadn't thought about it until he said something. I'm not an anomaly on this planet. There could be someone else out there walking around with a face like mine but twenty years older.

My thoughts are interrupted by Mavis jumping into the car. Toby starts driving straight to the movies. During the ride, Toby and Mavis connect over hair products and beauty trends while I watch from the passenger seat. The two sides of my Utah life are merging into one. I should be happy about Toby becoming Mavis's friend, and yet a thought tugs at the back of my mind. This is opening doors for her, but is it doing the same for me?

"Oh, my God! You have to tell me every embarrassing thing Catie has done at work," Mavis insists. She has her seat belt on, but she's leaning so far forward that she might as well be in the front with us.

I slap Mavis's knee playfully. "We are *not* doing that."

"I'm your sister." Mavis shrugs. "It's kind of my job to relish your embarrassment."

I give Toby a look. "Don't tell her anything."

Toby chuckles as he pulls into the parking lot at Sugarhouse Cinema. "There's nothing to tell. Honestly, your sister is kind of amazing. The most embarrassing thing to happen was probably when this guy came in and asked for her number or whatever. But she brought up her boyfriend, Jimmy—"

One microsecond stretches into a minute. In the span of time it takes for Toby to finish saying this word, Mavis's gaze slides to me and my spine stiffens. I send a telepathic message, willing her to stay silent, but I know she can't hear my thoughts.

"—and that shut him up," Toby continues, oblivious to Mavis's reaction. "Oh, and me spilling hair dye on her the first day we met. But that's probably more embarrassing for me than it was for her."

Toby laughs to himself. Mavis's eyes practically char mine as she waits for me to provide more information. But I don't. When the silence stretches even longer, Mavis must think that what Toby said is true. I haven't just been lying to him; I've been keeping secrets from her, too.

Toby finds a parking spot a couple of rows back just as another car parks right in front of Sugarhouse Cinemas. He climbs out of his seat and points. "Hey, that's Alex's car."

Toby shuts the driver's-side door and makes his way through the maze of cars. Mavis puts a hand on my seat belt as I move to unbuckle.

"Either you and Jimmy have been doing a long-distance thing without mentioning it to me and Francisca, or he's talking about another *Jimmy*." Mavis's tone is heavy. Before I can get a word out, Mavis plows on. "I cannot *believe* you wouldn't tell me this! You've had a boyfriend this entire time?"

"It's not like that at all," I blurt, stepping out of Toby's Mitsubishi. The evening sky is clear, which makes the neighboring mountain peaks shimmer with pinks and oranges. But with so many thoughts swirling through my head, I can't even appreciate the view.

Mavis hurries out of the car, slamming the door shut behind her. She's rubbing her temples and that spot between her brows at the same time. "Dude, what's really going on?"

From across the parking lot, Toby is giving high fives to

Jeremy and Lucas. He's chatting with them and hasn't noticed that we're not behind him yet. I don't have much time to fill Mavis in, but I rapidly try to explain the *real* reason why Toby is teaching me Mandarin. I ramble on about how I hadn't thought it was a big deal that Toby assumed I was a love expert. But then he inspired me to find my Taiwanese family—while all I've done is feed him lies I was supposed to walk away from.

We're dragging our feet while making our way over to the cinema's front doors. Mavis's gaze is lowered to her shoes. She's chewing on the inside of her cheek like she's still digesting my hurried explanation. How much time does she need before she says something?

"So, are you in love with him or something?" Mavis finally asks.

My shoe scrapes the asphalt, but I catch myself before stumbling. *This* is her takeaway? She's not asking me why I kept a secret for so long? Why I lied for so many weeks?

"Well—I mean—it's not like . . . So, the thing is . . ." Why am I stammering like Toby right now?

Wait.

Maybe Mavis sees a truth in this mess. There's a reason I feel so guilty. I care about Toby. I care about him more than a coworker should. I care about him more than a friend should.

Holy crap.

I've been *in love* with Toby Yoon-Hanson this whole time, and lying about it hasn't kept my feelings under control. But now that Mavis is saying it out loud, I can't keep pretending that the reason my throat itched when I talked to Nichole was that I didn't *want* to wingwoman them together. The reason my face burns at Toby's laugh is that I love watching him be happy. And each time I catch the smell of patchouli and ylang-ylang, I imagine his hands in my hair all over again.

As much as I wish our relationship was as simple as a crush, it's not. "It doesn't matter how I feel about Toby," I say, shaking my head as I find my voice. "I promised I'd help him land a date with Nichole and—"

"Hey, Mavis!" Toby's voice cuts across the parking lot. Mavis and I both snap our heads up to find him waving us over. "I want you to meet my friends."

Mavis gives me a look that says *we'll put a pin in this conversation.* I grind my teeth together even though there's so much more to say . . . like how Toby doesn't feel the same way about me. Like how I can't just come clean without also stopping my Mandarin lessons. Like how I could maybe even lose my job over this. I mean, I handle the Yoon-Hansons' money. What's the difference between a liar and a thief when they're both takers and keepers?

Mavis leads the way across the parking lot, but just before we get within earshot of Toby, she whispers, "The sooner you confess, the easier this will be."

I know she's right. Toby deserves the truth—that I've never been qualified to help him date Nichole and that all I wanted was an excuse to reconnect with my heritage. I'm so shallow, so selfish, so narrow-minded—why did my feelings have to get involved? If we really were just coworkers, the idea of coming clean wouldn't hurt this bad.

"Hey, Mavis," Toby says when we join his friendship circle. "This is Alex, Lucas, and Jeremy."

"Huh." Lucas's brown eyes slide back and forth between Mavis and me. "For sisters, you two look nothing alike."

Mavis swings an arm around my shoulder. "Yes, we do. We're identical twins, actually."

We've gotten enough comments about being adopted sisters that we've planned enough responses to them. I sink into Mavis's side, grateful to have someone like her to lean on. Literally. She might be able to pretend that nothing's wrong, but I'm having trouble looking Toby in the eyes right now.

Alex points at Mavis. "Do I know you from somewhere?"

Mavis's arm slides off me as she holds Alex's gaze. Then all at once they shout in unison: "The Pride Center!"

I scrunch my eyebrows. "What?"

"Alex was working at the Pride Center the day Mom took me," Mavis fills in. "They got me signed up for the Youth and Family Program."

"Are you coming to the Ultimate Frisbee event this Saturday?" Alex asks. "Since most of the volunteers will be out of town for Fourth of July, we could really use all the players we can get."

"You should come," Toby says, nudging my side. "The four of us have been going to the annual Ultimate Frisbee event since—what, sophomore year?"

Jeremy leans into the circle. "Just so you know, Ultimate Frisbee is a competitive sport in Utah. Be warned."

I chuckle at the idea of these four friends aggressively

fighting over a Frisbee. I don't know how to play, and I'm not sure how I feel about intertwining my life even more with Toby's, but Mavis needs her community, and at this point, I'd need a really big excuse to not go.

"Sure," Mavis agrees, and I nod along with her.

"Sweet," Alex says, pumping a fist. "And bring friends. The more the merrier."

The only other person I can think to bring is Rayleigh. But hell would freeze over before Aunt Joanna let her daughter play Frisbee with a bunch of queer kids.

Our little crew heads inside and shows our QR codes to the vendor in the ticket booth. Jeremy and Lucas fall in stride, chatting about how Lucas ran over dog poop while playing Ultimate Frisbee a few years back. Alex slides beside Mavis and asks her what other horror movies she likes. This opens up a can of worms I doubt Alex is ready for. Mavis knows *way* too much about the history of horror, but as I listen to their conversation, so does Alex.

Once we have our sodas and popcorn, we file into the theater. Mavis leads the way to the center of the middle row. Alex shimmies in behind her, talking about a subgenre of horror called . . . Lovecraftian?

I'm about to slide in behind them when Toby tugs on my elbow. The warmth of his hand and the tenderness of his touch is enough to get my attention. Toby meets my gaze with a quirk to his lips. He nods to a seat in the back of the theater, and I know exactly what he's saying.

Leave them and come sit with me.

I'm torn. Sitting alone with Toby in an empty theater? My

pulse climbs at the thought. Besides, the more time I spend with Toby now, the more he's going to wonder why I didn't tell him the truth sooner. Or what if I just ride this secret into my grave? That's still an option, right?

I tell myself I'm reluctant to follow Toby up the steps. But in reality, my fingertips buzz with a thrill more chilling than any horror film. Mavis and Alex don't seem to notice us disappear. Neither do Lucas and Jeremy. They've claimed the seats closest to the silver screen. Nobody looks back as Toby and I flop down in the darkest corner of the theater.

I meet Toby's eyes in the dim lighting. Being alone with him amplifies everything I've felt for the past weeks. A warmth starts deep in my core and rises to the apples in my cheeks. It's always been here—like drinking the richest hot chocolate on the coldest winter day. And now that I've defined the sensation, I can't just rip it out of my dictionary. If only I were an actual love expert. That way being in love for the first time wouldn't be synonymous with fear of the unknown.

What advice would Dad give me if he were here? I try to think back on the notes he left behind. He wrote a paragraph about how he thought he was running a fever the first time he asked a girl out. I guess I'm more like him than I realize. I pull my hair off my neck and drop it over one shoulder in an effort to cool myself off. *Act natural, Catie. Toby doesn't know you're shaking right now.*

"Do you like scary movies?" Toby whispers.

I can't hold back the smile that springs to my lips. Listening to him whisper only makes me lean in more. And leaning in only makes my smile grow wider despite my best efforts.

"I hate scary movies."

Toby's shoulders sag with relief. "Oh, thank goodness. Me too."

The theater lights darken. The movie is about to begin. Great. I'd rather listen to Toby, but instead, I instinctively curl into a ball on my seat. My heart hammers, and not in the way that Toby makes me feel. No, this is the heart-racing that also makes the shadows around me swirl like they're concealing monsters. I stretch the collar of my shirt over my mouth.

Toby chuckles. "The movie just started."

"I don't care," I whisper back. "I know there will be a jump scare."

I hate the sharp spike in music that never fails to make me shriek. I hate the terror of not knowing when it's coming and the humiliation of being scared by nothing but a loud noise. And the gore. Why do horror movies always make blood squirts look like that?

I pull the neck of my shirt over my eyes.

Toby laughs.

"It's not funny," I say into my shirt. Yes, I'm stretching it out, but I'll keep doing it for Mavis's sake. Even if it means sitting through an entire film like this.

"Wait, what if we make this fun?" Toby says. "You could turn this into one of your love language lessons."

I poke my head out of my collar, feeling like a prairie dog. In the faint lighting, the waves of Toby's purple hair fall around his face like a cresting ocean tide. Would it feel just as cool if I ran my fingers through it?

"I don't think you can make watching a horror movie fun," I insist. "Buuuut . . . this could be a good opportunity to work on . . ."

I rack my brain for the remaining love languages we still haven't gone over. Physical touch pops into my head, and I immediately think about holding his hand throughout this entire movie. No. I can't do that. He thinks we're just coworkers. Besides, my hypothetical boyfriend may be a *pretty chill guy*, but even I know hand-holding crosses a line. Words of affirmation is another one, though that doesn't exactly pair well with sitting quietly through the movies.

"Quality time," I finally settle. My improv skills kick into hyperdrive. "Instead of watching this like a movie, we watch it like a film critic. Point out every scary movie cliché that you see. And when you do, take a bite of popcorn."

Toby laughs as he inches his bucket of popcorn closer to me. "That's too easy. Oh, look. The lighting is dim even though it's the middle of the day. That'll be one handful of popcorn for me."

Toby pops a few kernels into his mouth. His jawline sharpens as he chews and my heart thrums again. It's a mix of thrill and fear—of wanting to explore the sensation of being in love, but not wanting it all to come crashing down. Because when I tell Toby the truth, he's never going to want to share popcorn with me again.

The roar of a chain saw makes me jump. I shriek and duck back into the safety of my shirt collar. Toby laughs beside me, and I don't have the courage to poke my head out to glower at him.

"Cliché jump scare," Toby asserts, scooping up another handful of popcorn. "Check."

From the safety of my burrow, I try to hold in my terror. What's worse? Chain saws and jump scares, or losing the people you love?

唇与舌

Lips and Tongues

Wednesdays at the salon are Toby's busiest days. That's his dad's day off. And since Toby is part of the Yoon-Hanson family, he's slammed with his father's regulars. But we cross paths while I'm taking out the trash—he catches me in the hallway coming out of the storage closet with that new finishing oil in his hands. It's supposed to make a client's hair smooth and glossy while smelling like vanilla and wintergreen.

"Hey," Toby says. He looks rejuvenated and glow-y even though we stayed out till midnight last night. Dang him and his perfect skin-care routine. "How did you sleep?"

I originally thought I'd have nightmares. But as soon as I got home, Mavis wanted to know every detail that led to Toby's and my *agreement*. She listened while flipping through Dad's edition of *The Five Love Languages*, gagging at the homophobic things Chapman wrote and applauding Dad for scratching them out. Like me, she hadn't realized he'd left this behind. But unlike me, she didn't have memories of him reading it before he met Mom. If he'd just had more time with us, he probably would've left behind his own sentimental gift for her, too.

And sometime during the night, Rayleigh joined the conversation. As the three of us lounged around my room talking about crushes, it almost reminded me of late nights in San Diego with Jimmy and Francisca. But there's one thing I still haven't told Mavis—one thing I still need to figure out on my own.

Yes, I could tell Toby the truth and he would hate me for lying to him. But there's another fear deep inside—one that no horror movie could ever top. What if I confess my feelings to him . . . and he doesn't feel the same way back? I mean, yeah, I know he's in love with Nichole. But after what Alex said, maybe he's not as infatuated with her as he used to be. Maybe someone else has captured his attention. But I'm not putting my heart out there for a *maybe*.

"Good." I condense all my thoughts into one word. Though the moment I speak, a yawn catches me.

Toby makes a doubtful face.

"Really. I swear I slept well last night. What about you?"

"I slept with my lamp on," Toby replies unapologetically.

I giggle, and Toby does, too. Why can't I just enjoy this rush without fearing it will end soon?

"Hey—real quick before you have to go." Toby nods to the trash bag in my hand. "So you're not going to believe this, but I woke up to a bunch of notifications saying that Nichole followed me on all my social media platforms."

The floor and walls seem to switch places at the name *Nichole*. I think I feel more scared than last night during the movie.

"We've been messaging back and forth, but it's hard to check my phone while I'm at work. She mentioned that she saw you at the party. You inspired her to want to get to know me better," Toby concludes sheepishly, fiddling with the finishing oil in his hand.

I shake my head to focus my thoughts. Wait. If she's DMing Toby, does that mean she mentioned what I blurted out about not having a boyfriend, too? No, right? Because if she had, Toby would've said something about that.

"Um, great. I'm so happy for you." My voice probably sounds layered in sarcasm. So, I force a smile as if this is exactly what I want for him. Good for Toby. Just so good.

"Thanks," Toby says. "We only chatted for a little bit, and then she left me on Read. What do you think that means?"

"Oh . . . I'm not sure." I need to get into teacher mode, but I'm still wrapping my head around the fact that Nichole followed Toby. Love Coach Catie is thrilled to hear Toby's getting closer to landing a date with Nichole. But *Catie* Catie regrets that Nichole even exists.

Toby cocks his head. "Oh. Well, if you don't know, then don't you think Jimmy would?"

Every muscle tenses as I attempt to keep a straight face. I need to tell the truth, but is 3:45 p.m. on a Wednesday really the best time? And if not now, then when? Either I tell him, or I pull another lie out of thin air.

But the silence lingers, and Toby clears his throat like he thinks I didn't hear him. My voice quivers when I speak. "I video call him every morning. I'll ask him tomorrow."

Why did I just say that? And why can't I just come out with it? If I really love him as much as I feel I do, then I owe him the truth. All of it. The part where I lied, and the part where I fell in love.

But what if coming clean only makes Toby's life more complicated? He'll be the boy chasing Nichole, and I'll be the coworker making everything more difficult for him by getting in his way. And since he's clearly still got his eyes set on Nichole, telling him the truth will only end in disaster.

"Cool, thanks," Toby says. I wait for him to scoot around me and get back to work. Instead, he hands me the bottle of finishing oil. "I'll trade you. Take this back to my station and I'll take the trash out?"

I can't stop the smile pinching the edges of my lips. I'll take staying in the AC over crossing hot asphalt and smelling stinky garbage any day of the week. And yet something twists inside me like there's a snake slithering between my ribs.

"Thanks," I say, handing the bag over. His finishing oil is so much lighter than a thirty-gallon bag of used foil.

"Of course," Toby says, taking a step back. "I'm so excited to teach you how to talk to your family in Mandarin. I've already got a lesson planned out."

There aren't any cars in the driveway when Toby pulls into his garage. Mrs. Yoon-Hanson is closing shop at the salon, but I'd imagined his father was home since this is his day off.

"Where's your dad?" I ask, climbing out of his car.

Toby holds the basement door open for me. "Some of his college friends talked him into entering a golf tournament this fall. He's been practicing his swing on his time off and he's surprisingly good. As long as he's playing Wii Sports."

I can't hold back my laugh even as a different, scarier

thought bubbles to the surface. Did Toby know that his father wasn't going to be home? Is it okay that I'm here when his parents aren't?

Toby climbs the stairs. I follow him up to the foyer, where he slides out of his shoes and sets them on a bamboo rack. The sight hazily reminds me of our apartment in Taiwan. Dad and Ya-Fang taught me to respect the home by taking my shoes off whenever I entered. But that's a habit I no longer practice with Mom and Mavis.

Out of respect, I slip my own shoes off and set them beside Toby's. "Wow, so this is what the rest of your house looks like?"

Large windows and white walls create a luxurious minimalistic aura. Giant paper fans and Korean scrolls roll down the walls. I can see how Mrs. Yoon-Hanson's heritage has impacted their interior décor, but there are also Mr. Yoon-Hanson's influences, too. Moody photographs of jazz musicians marching down cobblestone streets are mounted between the scrolls. The one of a trombonist wearing a Mardi Gras mask catches my attention. Even though the mask covers the musician's eyes, something about the shape of his nose and cheeks resembles Toby's. Could that be Mr. Yoon-Hanson when he was his son's age?

Toby stretches, his back bones crackling after a long day at work. "Yup. Come on, I'll show you my room."

I freeze at his words. Toby's going to show me his room even though we are all alone in this giant house? No Mom. No Dad. Just me and Toby. In his bedroom.

Before my nerves can set in, a ball of orange appears

around the corner. It seems we've woken the homeowner. Mr. Munch blinks up at Toby with those intense green eyes. He does a big stretch before following him past the kitchen and down a hall. His paws patter like morning rain across the wooden floor. My gaze is on his fluffy tail the entire time. At least we aren't *completely* alone.

"Sorry, it's a little messy," Toby says, opening a door and flipping on the light. His room is massive—twice the size of mine at Aunt Joanna's house. His back wall is lined with binders of collectible trading cards, Funko Pops, plushies, and manga propped up like they're meant to be a showcase at an art gallery. After what Nichole and Ginny said, I was wondering when I'd finally see this side of him firsthand.

"What do you mean *it's a little messy*?" I ask, stepping into his room tentatively. Even his carpet is vacuumed so that I leave footprints behind.

"My desk," Toby says, gesturing to the stained black wood that matches the sheets on his king-size bed.

Textbooks and loose sheets of paper litter the surface, but I'm not focusing on any of that stuff. Instead, my gaze is pulled out the massive wall-for-a-window overlooking his backyard. Patchy, sunburned grass sprawls out for an acre while a figure-eight-shaped pool sits right in the middle. The surface reflects the setting sky in shades of pastel watercolor.

Munch seems to be as amused by the view as I am. He races past Toby's legs, then hops up onto his desk. He tucks himself into the perfect loaf and stares out the window like he's surveying his territory.

I giggle. "Well, you could always blame the mess on Munch."

Munch is too busy guarding the land to notice me saying his name. And he especially doesn't notice Toby snatching up a book and beginning our lesson.

Mom, māma.

Dad, bàba.

It gets a little tricky when Toby explains there are different words for maternal grandparents and paternal grandparents— for big sisters and little sisters. And though my brain is fried with all these new titles, I push myself to absorb as much as I can.

After we've gotten the hang of immediate family members, Toby moves into explaining the structure of a question. If I'm going to ask my family things, I need to—well, know how to ask. Unlike English, where the question words start a sentence, Mandarin ends a sentence with a question. *Ma* is kind of like a spoken question mark. But I can't always default to *ma*. For instance, if I wanted to ask "what" something is, I'd have to end the sentence with *shénme*.

Hours tick by. We start at his desk, but since there's only one chair, Toby sits on the floor. As the lesson progresses, I join him on the ground and he leans against his bed. Once the floor space is littered with textbooks and scrap paper, I hop onto Toby's comforter and read over his shoulder. Eventually, we're shoulder-to-shoulder on his bed, writing words in Pinyin as Munch gently snores.

The scent of pencil shavings and rubber erasers burns my

nose as I try to write out foods I can ask for. If I ever have the honor of seeing my family in person, talking over tea would be ideal.

"Nǐ . . . yǒu . . . chá . . . ma . . . ?" Why does my tongue feel like lead when I ask, "Do you have tea?"

Toby must hear the strain in my voice because eventually he says, "We can take a break."

"No, I'm fine," I insist, pinching my brows with my fingers. "It's just this Pinyin is giving me a headache. Like the whole point of it is so that English speakers can know how to pronounce Chinese characters, right? But it doesn't even make sense. Explain to me how yǒu looks like 'you' but it's pronounced 'yo.'"

"If the Pinyin is too confusing, then we can just have our lessons audibly," Toby suggests. "That way it's more about mimicking the sound and less about the spelling. I just wanted to introduce you to Pinyin because it has the tones written into it. There's also bopomofo. It's like the Taiwanese alphabet but instead of using English letters like Pinyin, it uses Taiwanese characters to symbolize sounds. But I didn't want to start with that since it can be trickier for beginners who aren't familiar with bopomofo."

I roll onto my back and watch Toby's ceiling fan spin around and around. Dang. I guess technically I *am* a beginner all over again. But one day, I won't be. One day, I'll be able to speak and write in Mandarin. I'll have those conversations with my family. And they'll tell me how I remind them of my parents while I think of how much this language reminds me of Toby.

Toby flops onto his back, too. His body sinks into the mattress while gravity tilts me toward him. Our fingers are a breath apart. The fan's cool air must be drying my eyes out because they feel heavy with sleep. What time is it, anyway?

I force myself out of my haze by asking a question. "Have I ever told you that I used to have a lisp?"

Toby faces me. "What? Really?"

I shrug, eyes sticky with glaze. "Yeah, I think I was in first grade when I started learning English. Supposedly, I would speak with my tongue between my teeth when making the *S* sound. I don't remember hearing a difference, but I guess everybody else did. My mom eventually made me go to speech therapy for it. But now that I'm learning Mandarin again, I want to say that the reason I had a lisp was that I spoke Mandarin when I came to America. I didn't realize that I wasn't able to make the sounds native English speakers use until I went to speech therapy."

"Hmm," Toby says thoughtfully.

"Do you think that's strange?" His face feels so close to mine. I catch a whiff of vanilla and wintergreen. Did he use some of the salon's finishing oil in his own hair?

"Not at all. I think it's interesting," Toby says, his voice soft. "I learned in my language development class that it's easier for someone like you to relearn their first language because the muscles in your tongue, throat, and lips developed while you were speaking it."

I nod along. "I guess that makes sense. I'm working out old muscles to re-create those sounds. Maybe that's why my mouth feels so numb."

Toby's gaze slides down to my lips. At first, I think nothing of it—we *are* talking about lips and tongues, aren't we? And then it dawns on me. Toby and I are on his bed. His parents aren't home. His face is inches from mine. My gaze follows his own lips—up close, they're a muted pink, almost tan. I notice a freckle on his bottom lip and the sharpness of his cupid's bow.

Toby swallows, and the knot in his throat dips. Or at least, I think it does. The pillow of his pout is so tempting that I can't hold myself back anymore. I'm supposed to be learning how to communicate with my uncles, and yet all I can think about is how warm Toby's breath is on my cheek. All I can do is picture myself closing the distance between us. The fact that we are both alone on his bed in this big empty house can't be an accident. Maybe there is no *maybe*. No *what-if*. But if I'm going to kiss him, I have to do it the right way.

"Hey, Toby," I whisper. "There's something I have to tell you."

説實話 ○ ○ ○

The Truth Is

Toby tilts his chin upward. My eyes are only half open, and with the current of the ceiling fan, I want to close them tighter. There's a thought in the back of my mind that this isn't a good idea. Once I tell him the truth, our relationship won't ever be the same.

"What's up?" Toby's voice is as delicate as rising steam.

My fingers brush his arm and Toby doesn't pull back. I've been dreading this confession for so long because I've been so scared of rejection. But the fact that we're here like this alone . . . It's like Toby's giving me a chance to be perfectly honest with him. Like he wants me to tell him something he already knows because it's something we've both been feeling.

I gulp and will myself to speak. "The truth is, I haven't been—"

Toby shoots up in bed. I spin around to face his bedroom door just as a knock sounds. Though it's a gentle tap, it cracks the air like thunder. Someone else is here and Toby must've heard them coming.

The door opens and a familiar head pops in. "Hey, your mother says it's time for—" Mr. Yoon-Hanson freezes.

My face must be burning a shade of magenta brighter than the one Toby spilled on me. It doesn't dawn on me just how compromising this looks until I'm processing the wideness in Mr. Yoon-Hanson's eyes, the stiffness of his half-parted lips, and the way his deep tan fades to paper white.

"We were practicing Mandarin!" Toby exclaims, rolling off his bed. "T-t-tell Umma—I didn't know you guys were . . ."

Mr. Yoon-Hanson's gaze darts back and forth between Toby and me. Toby and me. And Munch. Then he shuts the door, and I want to disappear inside my shirt again.

Toby stares out the window like he's trying to get as far away from me and this situation as he can. "Um—let's . . . uh . . ."

"Clean up," I blurt. I don't wait for Toby's permission to leap off his bed and gather the loose scraps of paper littering his room.

We move around wordlessly, avoiding eye contact. Toby collects his books and piles them on his desk. I stack my notes together and resist the urge to slam my palms against my forehead. *Ugh. You're better than this, Catie. Why can't you just control yourself?*

Looking back on it, I should've known what I was doing when I first lay on his bed. It's bad enough that his dad caught us together. But there's no way Toby knew what I was thinking—right? My ears burn at the thought. Unless . . . What if he didn't need to hear what I wanted to *say* to know what I wanted to *do*? Was that the real reason why he sat up so quickly?

And now that the warm bed and draft of the ceiling fan aren't hypnotizing me anymore, I realize maybe I've been wrong about all this. After all, he just *excitedly* told me that he's been DMing Nichole in his spare time. Perhaps Mr. Yoon-Hanson's embarrassment saved me from *my own*.

Toby hands a jumble of paper to me, and this time, I make sure my fingertips don't brush against his. When we finish cleaning his room, he hurries me back through the house. It's clearly time for me to go home.

We reach the foyer. Toby is sliding his shoes back on when a pair of footsteps patter our way from the kitchen.

"Hey, Toby," Mrs. Yoon-Hanson calls.

I stop with my toes dipped inside my shoe. Great—now both his parents have spotted us together. Toby and I spin around slowly. My face is so hot that if I stay in his house a moment longer, I'll become the tomato version of Violet Beau-regarde.

Mrs. Yoon-Hanson's eyes widen when she sees me. Even from the opposite corner of the house, I can't mistake the look of absolute surprise on her face. "Oh, Catie . . . I didn't realize—"

"Toby's been teaching me Mandarin!" Apparently, it's my turn to blurt those words.

"Oh," Mrs. Yoon-Hanson says. Her attention snaps to her son, and now she's speaking to him in Korean. I don't need to understand a word to know they are talking about me. Between the way Toby mumbles with his face in his hands and Mrs. Yoon-Hanson's rapid-fire words, Toby is probably in trouble for having me over.

"Umma . . ." Toby groans, dragging a hand down his face. "Please don't."

Mrs. Yoon-Hanson finally declares something before

turning her attention back to me. "I'm so sorry, Catie. I didn't realize you'd be over for language lessons. If I'd known, I would've cooked something. But tonight, we are having take-out. You are, of course, more than welcome to stay for dinner."

"Or," Toby offers, not meeting my eyes, "I can just drop you off at home."

Though I haven't had dinner yet, the last thing I want is to sit across the table from Toby's parents after all of this. In fact, I'm not sure I want Toby to drive me home. Alone. Just him and me. In a car. With the thoughts of his parents burning into the back of my mind. No thanks. I can take an Uber. Or walk. Anything to get away from my bosses ASAP.

"Um, my . . . aunt is actually cooking us dinner," I lie as naturally as if I'm talking about the weather. "Thank you so much for the offer, but I've really gotta go."

I give Mrs. Yoon-Hanson a pleasant wave before hurrying through the garage door. Toby says nothing as we pass his parents' cars, both now parked in the garage. I can't actually afford an Uber, so I reluctantly let him take me home. We stay silent as he drives down the hills of his neighborhood. Even-tually, the houses morph from mansions to family homes. Pretty soon, Aunt Joanna's house will appear. It's only then that Toby breaks the silence.

"Hey, Catie?" His voice is just shy of a whisper.

The crown of my head prickles because I'm pretty sure I know what he's going to say. "Yeah?"

Toby uses his turn signal even though he doesn't need it for another two blocks. Finally, he says, "So, uh. What were you about to tell me?"

Am I sweating? Am I freezing? I can't tell anymore. All I know is that whatever just happened shouldn't have happened. It was a mistake to think I could tell him the truth. I was wrong about him bringing me over like this. I just wanted to kiss him so badly that I was making myself see things that weren't really there. Besides, I'm not about to drop an earth-shattering confession on Toby after all of *that*.

"I don't want to talk about it," I say. It's quick. It's easy. And best of all, it's the truth.

Toby finally comes to a stop sign and takes the turn. He cruises through the neighborhoods. The houses gradually shrink in size. I swear we pass a home that's been draped in one of those fumigation tarps like the ones in the valley down below. But it's so dark out that I can't see it clearly through the trees.

"But *I* want to talk about it," Toby insists. There's a layer of uncertainty in his voice as if he regrets opening his mouth. But instead of staying quiet, he pushes on. "Were you about to—?"

"No!" I blurt. Wait—what was he going to ask? Why am I jumping to conclusions? "I mean . . . were you?"

Toby's nose scrunches. What are we even talking about right now? Was he asking me if I was going to *kiss him*? I should've just let him finish. *Ugh. What is wrong with me?*

Toby shakes his head. "No. I wasn't."

A weight of disappointment plummets down my stomach. Even though I'm not sure exactly what he's responding to, I know his answer isn't the one I secretly want to hear. For the rest of the car ride, I sit there wordlessly, letting the silence intensify and wishing I was going home to Dad. What would he say about all this? Why can't he be here to give me advice like a real love coach instead of leaving me to skim through the pages of his book, looking for answers? Why can't he be home to give me a hug after all this?

Finally, Aunt Joanna's house appears in the distance. Toby parks in the driveway, and I unbuckle my seat belt. But before I reach for the door handle, Toby stops me.

"Wait." Toby leans across my lap and pops open the glove box. He fishes around for a moment before pulling out a notebook.

"Uh, what are you doing?" I ask, my hand still reaching for the door handle.

Toby doesn't answer. Instead, he pulls a pen from his cup holder. He flips through pages of what looks like workout routines and grocery lists before finding a blank sheet. Then he starts writing.

I lean over and squint down at the striped lines glowing blue in the faint lighting. Toby's pen scratches the paper, carving out squares and dashes, sloping lines and crossing Ts. Hanzi.

"What are you writing?" I ask, my brows pinched together.

Toby doesn't answer. He finishes his script, then rips out the sheet before handing it to me. I take the paper hesitantly and peer down at his writing.

我撒了謊。其實，我好想吻你。 雖然你有男朋友，我還是愛上了你。 某天，我希望我能勇敢地用英語告訴你。

We haven't covered these characters yet. We haven't even

started having full conversations in Mandarin. How am I supposed to know what any of it says? It's not like I can just copy and paste this into Google Translate, either. I know as much about typing in Hanzi as I do about cutting and coloring hair. I could try using my phone's AI feature to translate images for me. But the last time I did this in Spanish class, my phone wasn't sophisticated enough to read handwriting. There's no way it'll read Toby's words now.

"Is this my homework?" I glance back up at Toby, only to find him staring at me with a tight expression. "Do you want me to translate this into English?"

Toby loosens his jaw. "Something like that."

I purse my lips as I try to make sense of what he's really saying. Why isn't he just telling me? This has been one of the longest and weirdest nights of the summer. The more I try to read Toby's mind, the stronger the migraine grows inside my own.

Slowly, I push open the car door. What if this note is a reminder that we can only be coworkers? Knowing him, he's too gentle of a person to tell me he needs space. Coworkers is all we will ever be, even if I'll never stop daydreaming about becoming something more.

明顯的

Obvious

When I enter Aunt Joanna's house, I immediately head toward the kitchen, hoping that the leftovers in the fridge are still warm. Even though Toby's headlights are no longer shining into the foyer, I can't shake the feeling of his skin under my fingertips . . . and his parents hovering over us. Even an hour-long shower isn't going to wash away *that* cringe.

As I pass Rayleigh's bedroom door, I hear her giggling with what sounds like Mavis. Since when have they been tight like this? Though I suppose it makes sense. They're stuck at home while I'm at work. Not to mention that ever since last Sunday, things have turned for the better between them.

I'm not really one for knocking, so I push the door open. The giggling cuts off like I've entered a conversation I'm not supposed to be overhearing. Rayleigh's eyes are wide as she lies on her bed. Mavis has the same shocked expression, but she's cross-legged on the carpet. The moment they realize who's on the other side of the door, their shoulders slump with relief.

Rayleigh waves me inside and hisses, "Shut the door."

I do as I'm told despite the hunger gnawing at my stomach.

Mavis pats the carpet beside her, so I flop down crisscross applesauce. Her eyes shine with eagerness. "You'll never guess what I'm doing Friday."

A curious smile works its way over my lips. "Did you get a job?"

Mavis shakes her head. "No. Come on, Catie. It's Fourth of July weekend. Who works?"

I thunk my forehead. Right. The salon will be closed from Friday to Monday for the holiday. I was the one who blocked out everyone's schedule, but because of everything that's happened, I completely forgot.

"No—Alex is taking me to a bonfire!" Mavis squeals.

A cry of joy lodges in my throat as my head cocks reflexively. "Wait. Are you two—like—*dating*?"

Mavis curls her lips sheepishly. "Well, no. We're *technically* just hanging out . . ."

But the way her voice trails off says otherwise. And she won't look at me—her gaze shifts to Maddie Sue's nose poking out from under Rayleigh's bed. My sister is totally crushing on Alex right now. Based on their effortless conversation at the movies, it's not hard to see how this happened. Now I understand why Rayleigh and Mavis were so worried when I opened the door. This is a conversation Aunt Joanna wouldn't approve of.

"Just hanging out?" Rayleigh parrots, giggling as she reaches down to shove Mavis in the shoulder. "It's totally a date. Alex is picking you up and everything."

I plaster on a smile. This is more than Mavis could have asked for. And yet, all I can think about is how much I wish I could have a do-over with Toby.

Mavis paws Rayleigh's hand away. "I'm serious. It's just a friendly get-together. Are you sure you don't want to come?"

Rayleigh rests her cheek against her arm. "I mean—I want to. I wish I had more friends outside of church, you know? But it's *clearly* just meant to be you two."

Mavis bites her lip, holding back a smirk. "You should come to Ultimate Frisbee with us then. Alex is hosting a day at the park for some of the kids at the Pride Center this Saturday. I guess I never really told you about it because . . ."

She doesn't have to finish. We all know what's left unsaid.

"I still think you should come," I say, even though there's no way Aunt Joanna would allow her daughter to play Frisbee with a bunch of queer kids. In fact, she might not even want Mavis and me there if she catches wind of exactly what we're up to. But Mavis has been making friends this summer. Why can't Rayleigh? "Alex will be there, and you could meet Toby, too. Besides, you just said you want to make friends outside of church. I can't think of a better way!"

Rayleigh rubs her lips together thoughtfully. "Mom doesn't have to know *who* I'm with. Just where I'll be. And it would be nice to finally put faces to the names of the people you keep talking about. I know you said Toby has purple hair, but I still want to see it. Speaking of Toby—how did your language lesson go?"

My spine stiffens like I've just been caught with a hand in a cookie jar. Talks of Frisbees and new friends made me briefly forget the sting of embarrassment. But the moment it's brought back up, I'm slamming my palms against my face. Again.

"What happened?" Mavis asks.

I roll onto my side, collapsing to the ground like my bones have turned to noodles. I tell them everything. About the big empty house and the big empty bed and the big empty silence and the way our fingers brushed, our lips *so* close before I finally admitted to Toby that there's something I have to tell him. The way his *dad* waltzed through the door. The more I speak, the smaller the elephant on my chest shrinks. I'm laughing as I conclude my story because in hindsight, it *is* kind of funny how it all went down.

"So . . . ," Mavis asks once I've brought them up to speed, "when are you planning to tell him now?"

I shut my eyes as if it will block out the question from my mind. But there's no sense in delaying the inevitable. "I think after everything that's happened, the only thing I can do is wait until Toby lands a date with Nichole."

The idea had come to me halfway through recounting these events. Toby's getting closer than ever to his inevitable date with her, and I'd be the worst friend if I confessed my feelings now. Over the past weeks, Toby has transformed from a boy who stumbles over his words to a boy who can DM the love of his life. If he knew I'd made up all my relationship advice, it would be like taking the training wheels off his bike—even though he's technically been pedaling on his own this entire time. Only after they get together can I finally confess the truth about my lack of experience, because at that point, it won't matter. And even after that, I'll keep the part where I fell in love just to myself. Some secrets are meant to stay secret.

Mavis crosses her arms. "What are you talking about?"

I tilt my head. Isn't it obvious? "You know—I'll just finish taking him out on practice dates, because once he's dating

Nichole, he'll get what he bargained for. It's the only way I can break the news to him without damaging our friendship."

"Are you dense, Catie?" Mavis says, now waving her arms wildly in the air. "What are you talking about?"

My gaze dances between Rayleigh and Mavis. Why are they looking at me like that?

"What?" Apparently, I really am dense.

Mavis combs her fingers through her hair. "Dude—just tell Toby you love him, because *he's clearly in love with you.*"

Clearly? I shake my head. "Didn't I just tell you about that awkward car ride? I'm pretty sure we were talking about kissing even though neither of us said that. Either way, he still said no."

"That's because he thinks you have a *boyfriend*, you dolt," Rayleigh says, pulling up a Mormon swear I've never heard before. "Come on. He has to say no to repress the feelings he has for you. It's *soooo* obvious, Catie. You're the only one in your way."

It's like Rayleigh's shot an arrow through me. I don't want to believe it's true, but it's everything I've been feeling without wanting to believe it. I noticed it when Toby cleaned his car for me on our second practice date. When he asked me to meet his friends. When he laughed beside me through an entire horror movie. Maybe my sister and my cousin are right. Toby's in love with me, and he has been for a while now. I *wasn't* seeing things through rose-tinted glasses when he brought me over to his house.

"Alex has been telling me all the things Toby says about you when you're not around," Mavis continues. "He thinks you're beautiful, dork. He's impressed by how hard of a worker you are. Plus his parents adore you, so you've already got their stamp of approval. Come on, Catie. Are you really going to wait until he's with another girl to come clean? Or are you going to just tell him now?"

I press a hand over my chest to calm the thunder inside me. "So what should I do—tell him about my fake boyfriend at work tomorrow? Should I ask him on a real date?"

Mavis and Rayleigh look at each other, then back at me.

"Maybe don't tell him at work," Mavis says thoughtfully. "It's not the right vibe. Plus I'm sure it's going to be a lot for him to digest."

"Tell him at Frisbee this Saturday!" Rayleigh adds.

I giggle at the suggestion as I let my thoughts soar into the clouds. I'm still pretending, but this time, the daydreams really are right around the corner.

It's another busy day at the salon. Everyone is trying to get their hair and nails done before Independence Day. I'm so focused on answering the phone, checking people in, and cashing them out that I don't even have time to think about Toby.

On top of my stacked schedule, Mr. Yoon-Hanson has me unpackaging the boxes of products that've been delivered. After I've rearranged the schedule to fit in a last-minute facial appointment, I scoop up the shipment of vivid hair color and hurry to the supply closet. The salon phone is tucked into the pocket of my solid black romper, just in case someone calls.

I'm halfway through organizing the vivids in rainbow

order when the door swings open behind me. I spin around and my nose almost bumps into a familiar chest. Toby. He stands in the doorway, frozen, like he isn't expecting me. Judging by the loose strand of purple hair falling over his brow, it's been a hectic day for him, too.

"Sorry—I just need to grab . . ." Toby's voice trails off. He reaches over my shoulder for the goji berry conditioner that's usually kept at the shampoo bowl. As he leans in, his cheek brushes mine for a microsecond. Between the familiarity of his voice and the tight space of this closet, I'm whirled back to our moment on his bed.

"Hi," I struggle to respond.

"Hey." Toby lingers in the doorway, passing the shampoo bottle between his hands. "You're going to the Frisbee thing this Saturday, right?"

I nod. I know this isn't the right time to tell him the truth. The salon is so busy today that I can't even hear the soothing flute notes tittering through the speaker. But as we stand there not even a foot apart, I'm also picturing myself coming clean just so I can skip to the good part.

Toby takes a half step back. "But what are you doing tomorrow? Do you have another practice date planned?"

I've been so focused on my confession that I've completely forgotten about the fact that Love Coach Catie is supposed to be planning something every weekend.

"Oh—I . . . uh," I stammer. "I actually don't have anything planned. Besides, we kind of already did practice date number three, remember?"

Truth. And it tastes so sweet.

Toby blinks. I catch the corner of his mouth dip down. "Yeah, but that was kind of a rushed lesson. I was hoping you had a real lesson planned. I—you're really good at putting those practice dates together."

It's dark in this hallway, but does he look nervous right now? That, coupled with the fact that I caught him stumbling on his words, only makes me wonder what he was about to say.

"You could always plan something yourself," I say. "Think of it like a pop quiz. Show me what you've learned."

Toby rubs his nose. "I don't know if I can plan a whole new love language lesson. But maybe I can plan something that combines the ones we've gone over. I'll pit them against one another in a tiebreaker—see which one comes out on top."

I nod. "It's a deal. Maybe we can do that Monday since the salon will still be closed?"

Toby glances down the hall like someone's calling to him or maybe he's just remembered his client is waiting for him at the shampoo bowl. When he looks back at me, the corners of his eyes pinch as he smiles. "Monday sounds great."

I crinkle my toes as I watch him walk away. Mavis and Rayleigh were right. It is obvious.

結舌

Tongue-Tied

I'm doing my makeup in the back of Mom's car while Mavis drives us to the park. Rayleigh sits in the passenger seat listening to my sister talk about how amazing the bonfire was—how clear the air smells in the mountains and how many people were in attendance. I'm coating my lashes with mascara, but my hand is shaking. Today is the day I tell Toby the truth. *And* how I feel. But Mavis can't drive straight, and I don't want to jab my eye out.

We pull up to Applewood Park to see that Toby and his friends have already laid out a perimeter. Orange cones dot a flat plain of grass that rises into the neighboring hills. An equally orange water cooler sits atop a nearby picnic table. Alex is practicing their throw while Lucas and Jeremy chase after the Frisbee like golden retrievers. They aren't the only ones here. Pre-teens, teenagers, and even parents have arrived. Some of them are sitting in lawn chairs. Others are running around with red and blue bandanas atop their heads. They've already divided into teams, and considering that we're some of the last to arrive, I'm not sure if the three of us can fit on the same one.

Mavis parks under a leafy aspen tree and cuts the engine. "You ready, Catie?"

I cap my mascara and unbuckle my seat belt. "I still need to put sunscreen on."

Mavis reaches behind her seat to slap my knee. "You ready to tell Toby you love him?"

I rub my glossy lips together. "It's the only thing I can think about."

Truth.

I climb out and lather my arms with sunscreen while Mavis leads Rayleigh straight to Alex. They give Mavis a tight hug before greeting Rayleigh with a high five. Toby joins the trio, offering red and blue bandanas. He's wearing that goofy smile while giving Rayleigh a hug for the first time. These are my family and my friends. When they huddle together, they look like they could be featured on a magazine cover.

I finish rubbing sunscreen down my shins and am about to make my way across the grass. But when I look up, Toby is the only one still standing there. Except he's not alone. A tall girl with long brown hair and a panting Doberman are beside him. Even under the girl's baseball cap, I know who she is. *Nichole.*

A stone drops so far down my body, my freshly sunscreened knees wobble.

Did Toby invite her here? Alex had wanted there to be a huge turnout. And then it dawns on me—they've been DMing each other. Of course he invited her here.

I can hardly breathe—let alone stand here. Do I pretend that I'm not seeing them clearly engaged in a conversation? Do I just ignore that feeling like I'm going to vomit? I don't know what they're talking about. But by the looks of things, Nichole has a lot to say and all Toby can do is listen before slowly shaking his head.

He told her *no*.

No to what?

Did she ask him out in person?

My palms are still greasy from the sunscreen as I lean against Mom's car. If there wasn't another vehicle beside me, Toby would probably spot me watching him through the windows of the neighboring van. Finally, Nichole tugs on the leash. Her long hair bounces as she leads her Doberman back to the sidewalk and disappears into the park.

I push myself off Mom's van. Maybe I'm panicking over nothing. There's no way both Mavis *and* Rayleigh are wrong about Toby liking me. He can't still be into Nichole after all the dates and touches and almost kisses we've shared. But there's only one way to find out what Nichole really said.

I ease myself out from behind the car. I'm halfway across the field before Toby spots me.

"Hey," I say, waving. This is what I'm supposed to do, right? Act like nothing is wrong? When Toby doesn't reply immediately, I nod down at the bandanas in his hands. "What color are you going to play as?"

"Do you *really* have a boyfriend?" Toby asks.

Ice water slinks down my spine even though the late morning sun is making my hairline blister with sweat. I peer up at Toby, his expression unreadable.

"Wh-what?" I sputter. This isn't how the conversation was supposed to go. I was supposed to be the one to tell him—in my own words, at my own pace, and in a way that didn't leave any room for misunderstanding. And yet there's only one question on my mind: *How does he know?*

Nichole.

The way she spoke to him like she was giving a speech. The way he stiffened at her words, then shook his head. He wasn't rejecting her. He was shaking his head with disbelief.

"Nichole was walking her dog through here," Toby fills in when I remain silent. "We were catching up, and somehow you became the topic of our conversation. She said you told her you're single. That you don't have a boyfriend and you never did. Is that true?"

Someone's blowing a whistle. Kids' laughter whips through the air as they race through the park. A breeze slices through my hair as I stare at Toby, unable to do or say anything.

This isn't how it was supposed to go. I was supposed to tell him the truth. I planned this. I got him to agree to take me on a date. And now everything's ruined.

My mouth opens but nothing comes out. The sun catches the depth of Toby's dark eyes, and I can't mistake the realization behind them.

Toby leans back and massages the lines forming between his brows. "This whole time—you've just been lying to me? Is it because you wanted to use me for Mandarin lessons?"

I've heard his voice say different things and speak different languages. And yet all this time, I've never heard something so strained. So broken. So hoarse. It's as if it's easier for him to talk about Ezra than it is for him to say this right now. I did this. *I* did this.

"No. So . . . I-I don't really know how to say this," I stammer, thinking fast. I was giggling with Mavis and Rayleigh about him just a few nights ago. And now—this is where I am? "I've been trying to, um, to tell you—I guess. For a while. But I should've told you sooner. I just . . ."

I'm rambling. I haven't even said anything important yet, and already my throat is closing up. *What's wrong with me?*

Toby blinks and peers at something over my head. I'm not sure if something has pulled his attention away or he just can't look me in the eyes right now. "So Nichole's right? You *did* lie to me?"

"—No," I cut him off, finding my voice again. "Well, yes. That's the thing. I don't exactly have a boyfriend. I just— The guy I showed you a picture of—? He's just a friend from San Diego. But—well, I . . ."

I want to say more but my voice feels like sand falling down an hourglass. Why does this keep happening? I've thought about this conversation time and time again. But maybe I'd been so lovestruck at the idea of confessing my feelings that I skipped over the painful parts. And now that I'm here, it's like my body is betraying me.

Toby's gaze slides my way. There's a puzzle folded between his brows. "You broke up?"

I shake my head again and clear my throat. "No. I never had a boyfriend. I've never even dated anyone before. I'm not a love expert. I-I only made you think I was because . . ."

I try to keep speaking, but I physically can't. I need to finish this sentence. I *need* to explain it all so that Toby understands perfectly.

"Because you wanted free language lessons?" Toby finishes for me. "So you *did* use me."

I'm shaking my head so hard that my hair bounces. "Well,

originally, sure. But it didn't end up that way. It was never supposed to—"

This time, it's not my voice that cuts me off. It's the flood of tears suddenly springing from my eyes. Because if I say another word, they will run down my cheeks and I won't be able to stop them. And then everyone on the whole field will watch me sob.

Toby digests my words like they've sucker-punched him in the gut. "No? Yes? What are you saying? You can't even get your story straight. How am I supposed to trust anything at all? I genuinely believed your boyfriend was a gamer. I honestly thought you video called him every morning. I was actually kind of jealous of how healthy your relationship seemed. And—he's not even real?"

I force my jaw to move again. "I never meant to lie to you."

"But you did, Catie. You *did*," Toby snaps. "You didn't lie to me just once. You've been lying to me since I met you. God—I trusted you with so much more than relationship advice. I trusted you with my family's business. I even trusted you with—"

Toby's voice runs dry the same way mine does. I know what word makes him choke up like that. *Ezra.* He trusted me with the most cherished part of himself. And I still lied to him. I know what I did was wrong. But I never realized this is just how pathetic I really am.

"I thought that at the very least we were friends," Toby says, his voice cracking.

"We . . ." *Are!* I scream the word in my mind like I'm a child playing Red Light, Green Light all over again. But nothing comes to my tongue, neither in English nor in Mandarin.

Toby shakes his head and glances away. In his eyes, I see

myself—see the heartbreak I felt when San Diego was ripped away from me. When I stood beside Dad's coffin. When I read Ya-Fang's obituary. For someone who's never been in love before, I've known heartbreak since long before this moment.

"Toby." It's his name, but right now it leaves my tongue like a plea.

Toby sniffs like he's done listening to me. "Well, I suppose you should know that despite you lying to me about everything... Nichole asked me out."

I blink. A hot tear finally rolls down my cheek, but Toby isn't looking at me.

"We've been messaging each other for the past few days now," Toby says stiffly. "I guess seeing me here made her want to ask me out in person. You don't have to keep up our agreement anymore. You can stop using me now."

I don't need a mirror to know that my face has lost all its color. I'm such a fool. I've been projecting what I wanted onto our relationship, when in reality, every time Toby looked at my lips, he pictured himself kissing Nichole instead.

I'm so sick with humiliation, I need to lie down. I need to hide. I need to get out of here. I turn toward the restrooms at the end of the parking lot. I don't remember walking away but instantly, my world is a blur of salty tears. The swirls of leafy trees and black asphalt swim in puddles.

This holiday weekend was supposed to be the start of something new. And I guess in all the wrong ways, it is.

只不過顆棋子

Just a Pawn

I'm in bed scrolling through my social media. My blanket is over my head and all the lights are off. If it weren't for the light of my phone shining into my face, this entire bedroom would be pitch-black. My hair is still wet from the shower I had after coming home, and my fingers are still pruned from standing there too long. But sobbing as water whirlpools between my feet isn't going to make me feel better. Neither is doom scrolling, but at least I'm cocooned in a warm blanket away from the world.

I swipe through some of the stories Mavis has posted on social media. There's a picture of her pulling up to Café Rio. She's in the back seat of Alex's car. If it weren't for their curly hair poking out from under their cap, I wouldn't know who it was. She and Rayleigh must've gone out to eat after playing Ultimate. Meanwhile, I'm the sister who took the car keys and came straight home.

I swipe. It's a picture of Rayleigh sipping a fountain drink. She's making a silly face, which tells me she's enjoying herself. I should stop scrolling but I can't. Even though I need to quit thinking how my friendship, my *anything that could have happened* with Toby is over, I can't stop wondering what he did after I walked away. He's not in any of Mavis's stories, so I can assume he didn't go out to eat with them after. But if he's not with Alex, then did he go home? Was it unbearable for him to smile around friends because deep down he was hurting, too?

I click on Toby's profile. I'm not expecting to see an update, but when I peer at my feed, there's a carousel of pictures and he's on the first one.

There he is smiling with his overgrown purple hair and a blue bandana around his head. He's sandwiched between Alex and Jeremy while Lucas holds the camera out to cram everyone into the shot, all of them wearing the same happy grins.

So Toby did play Frisbee after our fight. As if me walking away with a face full of tears was as inconvenient to him as swatting away a fly. I suppose I shouldn't blame him. I was the one who lied and used him. Besides, Toby got what he wanted. And I got what I deserve.

I scroll down to the comments even though I know I shouldn't.

TOBIAS YOON-HANSON: That was fun we gotta do it again soon

JEREMY MCGUIRE: Hell Yeah! Before fall semester 🏈

LUCAS MONTGOMERY: Yeah but nothing will ever beat Spring Break senior year 😂 🏈 🙈 💀 🙀

JEREMY MCGUIRE: Screw you Lucas Montgomery I thought we wouldn't talk about that

---

NICHOLE YUNG: Lookin good ❤️

My gaze lingers on Nichole's comment. Two words. One emoji. And one like from Tobias Yoon-Hanson.

I curl into a ball as if it will ease the sting rising behind my eyes again. It doesn't. So I log off my phone and sink into my pillows. How have I gone from being a dating coach—someone who's supposed to be an expert on love—to someone who has no one to love at all?

A knock sounds at my door. Are Mavis and Rayleigh back from their lunch? Are they wondering why I left early, or were they having so much fun that they didn't even notice me missing?

"Catie? Are you awake?" Mom's voice is muffled through the wood.

Oh. I clear my throat so I don't sound like a frog when I speak. "Yeah. I'm up. Is it time for dinner?"

A glance to the light seeping in from the window tells me it's too early for that.

"No," Mom confirms. "We're having a family meeting with everyone."

I sit up slowly and rub the puffiness from my eyes. A family meeting with everyone including the Taylors? Since when did we have those? And if it's with everyone, that must mean Mavis and Rayleigh just got back from lunch with Alex.

For the first time all day, my thoughts drift away from Toby. Because right now, all I can think about are the photos Mavis posted on social media. Social media that Aunt Joanna sees. She must've noticed something she doesn't like—her daughter being happy with people who aren't Mormon.

Great.

"Give me a minute," I call out.

I rub my eyes one last time and attempt to calm down. Mom's shadow moves away from under my door. When I finally summon the energy to push it open, I can see into Mavis's empty room. She's not here, which means she must've been told about the meeting the moment she came home.

I shuffle upstairs, plotting what I'm going to say when Aunt Joanna inevitably calls us out for taking her daughter to a queer event. Should I defend Rayleigh? Or should I pretend to be oblivious? Either way, I hope no one will mention my puffy eyes.

Mom is already seated at the kitchen table when I get there. Uncle Nick sits at the head, Aunt Joanna beside him. I nestle between Rayleigh and Mavis. My sister's jaw is tight. Rayleigh nervously rolls a curl around her finger. They must all be thinking the same thing I am.

"What's all this about?" Rayleigh asks, breaking the silence.

Aunt Joanna looks to her husband. Then she looks to my mom. No one says a word, and I'm thumping my foot waiting for someone to make a sound.

"Do you want to go first? Or should I?" Aunt Joanna asks, nodding to Mom.

"I'll start," Mom says, then clears her throat. "As you all know, I recently got a job at the U of U . . ."

I lean my elbows against the edge of the table. Okay, this isn't the conversation I'm expecting, but it's going to circle around to the Frisbee thing, right?

Mom's gaze pans down the bench from Mavis, to me, to Rayleigh. She swallows hard as if she doesn't quite know how to find her voice. Here it comes. Bad news. The clock across the room grows louder with each tick. Can someone say something already—?

"Mom found an apartment!" Mavis blurts.

My jaw drops as my neck whips over to my sister—*she knew?* I must be too stunned to speak, or maybe Rayleigh's gasp drowns out my own. Whatever the case, I need a moment to process the fact that—holy crap! *We have a home now?*

"I thought I was going to tell everyone." Mom pouts from across the table.

"You were taking too long," Mavis says, her cheeks blooming with excitement.

"When did this happen?" I ask, still trying to process all my emotions.

"Well, the other day, Mom was showing me some of her favorite places in town and we just randomly decided it would be nice to see what apartments are available," Mavis says with a sneaky smile. "I mean, since we'll be living in Utah for a while and things just kind of lined up! You have to see the apartment, Catie! The pool? The lobby? It's way fancier than anything we ever had in San Diego!"

"It's newly renovated," Mom supplies. "It's a four-bed, two-bath apartment right next to the U of U campus. And since I'm faculty, I get a little bit of a discount on the rent. But because it's so close to the campus, it's designed to be a lot like student housing. So it's fully furnished. It comes with beds, a living room TV, and we have a patio view of the mountains."

"I want to see it!" Rayleigh exclaims, shaking in her seat like she's wagging her tail. "Can I take pictures by the pool, too?"

"Absolutely not," Uncle Nick answers, mustache quivering.

For a moment, I've forgotten they are here. As much as I want to see the new apartment, this can't be all the news. Why would the Taylors be a part of this "family meeting" if they don't have something to add?

"Unfortunately, the apartment won't be open for another week, which brings me to this point . . ." Mom's voice trails off as she meets Aunt Joanna's eyes.

I shift my attention, too. Of course there's a bitter bite to this sweet news. It wouldn't be a proper family meeting without one.

The room dips into silence. Aunt Joanna presses her thin lips together. She takes a deep breath as if what she's about to say will make her cry. Oh, no. Here it comes.

"We . . . well, I'm sure you've seen that some of the houses in our neighborhood are being fumigated for pests . . ." Aunt Joanna's voice trails off.

My mind races, thinking about the heat records this summer in Salt Lake Valley, and the fumigation tents Toby and I passed on our first drive together weeks ago. I hadn't realized it meant the Taylor home would fall victim to the infestations as well.

"On top of the spiders in our garage, and the ticks on our lawn . . . I recently discovered a termite infestation in our attic." Aunt Joanna's voice wobbles. "If we don't fumigate the house now, they could tear a hole in our roof."

The kitchen grows silent. The Taylor home seemed like the *Titanic* when I first walked in—something too masterful to succumb to anything. And yet a part of me thinks that maybe if Aunt Joanna hadn't hovered over Rayleigh so much, she would've noticed her house falling apart sooner.

"Does that mean we need to move out?" Rayleigh asks quietly.

Aunt Joanna sniffles. She tries to speak, but the idea of losing her home must be too overwhelming.

"We'll be moving in with the Brightons from church," Uncle Nick says. For once, his voice is a tender pitch I never thought he was capable of having. "They only have room for our family. Which means . . ."

"I've booked a hotel that will carry us over until we can move into the apartment," Mom fills in. "But we'll need to be out of here no later than tomorrow night. I believe the pest guys are coming in on Monday to fumigate everything."

A lump thickens in the back of my throat. Not again. All of this—moving out, losing friends, convincing myself that I can be happy by living a lie—I'm having to do it all over again. And once more, I'm just a pawn being moved by a player I can't see.

"Aw, man," Rayleigh groans. "I don't even like the Brightons."

"Then you should move into the hotel with us," Mavis suggests. "It's only for a week anyways. Plus, we still have plenty of summer vacation left. Girls' trip—woot, woot!"

Aunt Joanna sniffles. "Rayleigh, you can't impose yourself like that on your aunt Andrea."

"Why not?" Rayleigh asks. "She lived with us for a little bit. Why can't I live with them, too?"

A week in a hotel suite with four girls is probably going to feel like a crowd. And yet the thought of Rayleigh joining us makes me happier than I thought it would.

"What about Maddie Sue?" Aunt Joanna insists. "You can't bring her to the hotel."

"You and Dad can take care of her for a week, can't you?" Rayleigh says.

"It's just for a week," I add as the prospect of a mini vacation with Rayleigh plays in my mind. It's one of the few things lifting my spirits right now. "Mom, please?"

"Pleeeease?" Mavis clasps her hands in front of her.

"Pleeeease?" Rayleigh echoes.

Considering that our voices are harmonizing right now, Mom's answer is immediate. "Of course you can stay with us, Rayleigh. We're family."

反省

Reflections

Loading everything back into the car is relatively easy, considering that most of my boxes are still stacked in the corner of my room. Uncle Nick and Aunt Joanna have already gone to church, and for once, I'm kind of jealous. I'd rather be in the genealogy office with Granny Eloise than here stewing in my thoughts. Just because my language lessons are over doesn't mean I don't want to reconnect with my uncles anymore. Knowing that there's a picture of them waiting for me on Pan-Genea seems to be the only gas in my tank these days. I need to go back. I need to look at it. And I need to find a way to tell them that their niece is in America desperate for a connection.

I gather up my laundry, only for a slip of paper to fall out of my dirty pants pocket. Even before I pick it up, I know it's the note Toby wrote for me in Hanzi. Now it's crumpled and covered in pocket lint. I should throw it away, and yet, I can't part with this tiny token of our past. I stuff the note inside a random page in *The Five Love Languages*, then continue collecting my dirty clothes.

I should be happily packing my bags and moving out. And yet as I ball my dirty laundry into a garbage bag, I realize I'm as miserable as when I first moved into Aunt Joanna's house. At least back then, I had the hope of a new job to look forward to. Now I know that when I go into work on Tuesday, I'll see the friend I betrayed most. Beauty by Kimi Yoon was once the only place in Utah where I felt like I could embrace myself. Now the thought of stepping into the salon in a few days makes me brace for the worst.

Mavis and Rayleigh sing to the radio on our drive to the hotel. Eventually, we pull up to a three-star hotel located perfectly between Mom's workplace and mine. Rayleigh helps us lug the baggage inside. Before I know it, the sun has fallen behind the mountains and we've grown tired of watching cable TV.

Mom claims one of the beds in our suite while Mavis and I take the other. Rayleigh drifts off on the pull-out couch, and I lie awake, knowing that I should be going on a date tomorrow. But instead of spending his day off with me, Toby is probably spending it with Nichole. Only when I can hear the soft snoring of everyone else in the suite do I allow myself to cry until I'm asleep, too.

The next morning, my eyes are crusty, and my nose could use a tissue. Mavis and Rayleigh bring waffles up from the continental breakfast while Mom leaves for work. Since we're down to one car again, we're all stuck at the hotel until she comes back. Mavis suggests we spend our day of isolation swimming in the hotel's pool. Even though I'm not in the mood to do anything but cocoon in a hotel bed, she eventually talks me into relaxing in the hot tub.

"Did you sleep okay?" Mavis asks. The three of us are the only ones in the hotel's pool house. The jets in the hot tub bubble like I'm in a bowl of chlorinated soup. There's so much humidity in the air that it clings to the glass windows like fog.

I can't even see the parking lot from my seat by the tub's railing.

It takes me a moment to realize Mavis is talking to me. I look up from the prunes on my fingertips. "Hmm? Oh. Still tired, I guess."

Rayleigh slides around the lip of the tub until she's right next to me. She's taken her glasses off and braided her hair up so it doesn't get wet. "I guess I never asked you this because it's been a wild weekend, but how did things go with Toby? Are you guys dating now?"

I look down at the bubbles forming clouds on the surface of the water. Just the sound of his name reminds me of the coldness in his voice when he spoke to me at the park. Of the way that shadow crossed his face.

"He's dating Nichole now," I say at last. I turn my gaze to the foggy window, hoping it will center me as my world falls apart.

Surprisingly, Mavis and Rayleigh don't pry. It's like they know I'm dealing with a lot right now and the last thing I want to do is relive everything by speaking it out loud. Instead, Rayleigh slides an arm around my shoulder and Mavis swims around the tub to do the same thing. We stay like that until the tub gets too hot, so we climb out and dip our legs into the big pool.

The shock of going from hot water to room temperature feels like I've dunked half of my body in an ice bath. I kick my legs under the water, creating ripples on the surface that distort our reflections.

"What about you, Rayleigh?" I say when I find my voice

again. "How are you feeling about your house? And leaving your parents and Maddie Sue for the week?"

Rayleigh's reflection warps in the baby blue water. "Can I be honest with you?"

I lean back on my wrists and stop kicking my legs. Mavis peers around me to look at Rayleigh.

For a moment, Rayleigh says nothing. She picks at her nails while watching the ripples bounce from one end of the pool to the other. Then she takes a deep breath. "I miss Maddie Sue, but I don't really miss my parents. I've learned a lot about myself just by being with you guys this summer. I mean, Catie, seeing you dive into your past with Buddhism and watching Mavis light up around Alex . . . I realized I've finally had a chance to think about who I am without my parents force-feeding me my identity."

Mavis nods. "And what have you learned about yourself?"

Rayleigh scrunches her lips together as if she doesn't know what to say. Or maybe she still isn't sure *how* to say it. Finally, she utters, "I'm a lesbian."

I do a double take. Rayleigh? My Mormon cousin? *Is a lesbian?*

But the more I let the idea sink in, the more I can't unsee it. There's a reason Rayleigh looked like she belonged at the Ultimate event in the park. There's a reason why she understands Mavis in a way I don't. And now that I'm reflecting on the secrets Rayleigh kept this summer, I realize there's no way she was sneaking out of the house to see a non-Mormon boy. She was sneaking out to see a *girl*.

"I mean." Rayleigh's voice is hoarse, though I swear it

echoes around the tiled swimming area. "I've always known I'm lesbian. I just never had the courage to say it out loud. I've been making up excuses—calling myself a curious girl. A curious . . . sinner—"

Rayleigh's voice lodges in her throat. She swallows.

"The church has taught me to marry a man in the temple ever since I was a child. It's the hetero agenda, and I thought I could convince myself that it's something I want, too. It would make God happy. It would make my parents happy. But . . . I know *I'll* never be happy with a man. Not in the way I know I would be with . . . someone like *Trinity*."

So it *is* Trinity she's been texting—a girl who I should have realized is more than just Rayleigh's best friend. Even though the words are out in the air, my cousin can't seem to lift her gaze from the water.

"When you invited me to play at the park with all the kids from the Pride Center, it made me realize something," Rayleigh continues. "I want to keep the community I have in Utah. But I want to keep my queerness, too. And without my parents telling me what to do and who to be, maybe I can figure out for myself how to make room for both. I want to spend another week with you guys. I want to know who I am when no one is expecting things from me."

I break out into a wide smile. I'm so proud of Rayleigh. Who knew my little cousin would have all the confidence and self-awareness I want for myself? It turns out that she is the version of me I've wanted to be all along—someone who loves herself for being her. But where she succeeds, I've failed. Unless I try again.

Mavis reaches past me and squeezes Rayleigh's hand. "I think we can help you with that."

Rayleigh squeezes back before turning to me. "By the way, Catie, I still have those books if you want to keep reading them. Trinity's mom says I can keep them as long as I like. Well, as long as *you'd* like."

The pool water has finally stilled, and when I peer at the water, I see a shimmering reflection of myself. Of my sister and my cousin. Of three girls just trying to make sense of the changes in our lives. Now is the time to figure out who Utah Catie is without Toby. Without Mandarin lessons. Without lies.

Monday is over before I've had a chance to appreciate my four-day weekend. The next day, Mom drops me off at Moore Plaza before heading out to U of U. I trudge into work with my head down and clock in without saying hi to anyone. Clients roll in, and I go through the motions while I search for things about my job that I genuinely enjoy. Aside from the product knowledge I've gained, this spa kind of has me breaking my back. The Yoon-Hansons may need to hire another receptionist or give me a raise, because without Toby's company, it really feels like I'm doing the work of two people.

I've just finished calling to confirm tomorrow's appointments when Toby saunters up to the counter. It's like he timed it perfectly. Was he watching me this whole time? Because I know that despite my best efforts, I was watching him.

"Can we talk?" His brows are sloped at the corners. Even

though I can't see his hands, I know he's fidgeting with something on the other side of the front desk.

It's just three words, and yet all I can think is that no good conversation ever begins with *can we talk*. Even though Toby's looking at me like he's going to fire me even though he doesn't want to, my heart still swings for him. I'm a hive of hope and wonder. Has he forgiven me? Is he ready to listen to everything I have to say? Did he go on one date with Nichole and realize he's not as in love with her as he thought he was?

Against my better judgment, I nod.

Toby sighs as if he isn't sure where to begin. Finally, he says, "Are you trying to sabotage me?"

I recoil because this isn't anywhere near where I thought this conversation was going.

At my reaction, Toby fills in the blanks. "Some of my clients are saying that you were rude to them when they checked in. Is that because of . . . this past weekend?"

I can't move my lips. Me? *Rude?* Sure, I didn't have that usual pep in my voice when I greeted them. But I didn't think I was being *rude*. I've been in my own head about everything that's happened. But now I see it's bleeding out in ways I never intended.

I'm not sure if Toby's looking down at his palms or if he's playing with his scissors just to not look me in the eyes. "Look, can we both just be professional about this? Whatever happened, happened and it's over now. But I really can't have the first person my clients see greeting them with an attitude."

He's not saying it, but I'm hearing it. Our friendship is over, and he didn't come up here to remedy that. We're strictly coworkers. If anything, he's not a fellow employee to me anymore. He's my boss.

My mouth opens and closes as I search for the right words. Do I tell him that I'm living in a hotel right now or is that too personal to share? Should I try to back up and explain that I'm not intentionally sabotaging his clients by giving them attitude? Would he even listen to me if I said anything? Or is he really done trusting me?

Staring at him reignites every ounce of pain I've suffocated. I pull my gaze away before Toby can see the hurt still lingering in my eyes. I cast my focus to the front door just as someone pulls it open. It's her.

Nichole struts inside and swipes her manicured nails through her brown hair. Her upturned eyes flash when she sees Toby. "Hey, you!"

"Hi." Toby gives her a half smile.

It's one thing to hear about them dating. But it's something else entirely to see it play out before me. Nichole wraps Toby in a long hug. There's no way she's doing this maliciously, but the way my ribs concave with my heart feels like she's flaunting him on purpose.

My cheeks prickle and I can only imagine they are green with nausea. Or envy. I ground my feet in place to keep from running to the bathroom and locking myself away. I have a job to do. Toby just reminded me of that.

"You ready for lunch?" Nichole asks, arms still draped over Toby.

I can't believe it. They're going on a date? *Right now?* Even though I fabricated fake dating advice for Toby, a part of me wonders if he's planned something I concocted. Is he going to share his family's japchae with her? Is he going to tell her the secret ingredient that he never told me?

"Just give me twenty more minutes," Toby answers, voice so low it's practically a whisper. "I'm almost done with Mrs. Stevens's hair."

"That's fine." Nichole pulls back and rocks on her heels. "Hey, can I soak my feet in the spa while I wait?"

Toby nods before turning back to the client in his chair. As he vanishes, Nichole looks my way. She gives me a giant smile and waves. A little giggle seeps through her pearly teeth. Even though no words are spoken, I understand what she's saying. *Thanks for hooking us up!*

I return her wave but can't muster a smile. She's so bright— the star of Toby's childhood. The ultimate girl next door. The teenage dream. She's everything I'm not, and in a way, I made sure of that. If only I could go back in time and talk some sense to my old self. That way my world wouldn't be crumbling right before my eyes.

Nichole glides out of the foyer, and I'm left alone behind the receptionist counter. The thought of spending my summer watching them together is literal hell. I can't just stand here willing the clock to run down every day. So when no one is looking, I pull up a Word document and hurriedly type out a two weeks' notice.

Thank you for allowing me to be the receptionist here at Beauty by Kimi Yoon. Unfortunately, this is my official two weeks' notice. I cannot work here anymore because honestly, I'm in love with Toby and it sucks to watch him be with another girl.

Ugh. Okay, so obviously I can't print this out, but it feels good to get it off my chest. Once I've started typing, I can't stop.

I never planned on falling in love. Toby was just supposed to be a coworker. But then he offered me Mandarin lessons and I couldn't refuse. Not only did he make me fall in love with a language, but I fell in love with the idea of seeing my family again. Of being whole. No one has ever made me feel that way except for Toby.

The thing is, I kind of had to convince him to give me language lessons by telling him I was a love expert when I'm not. I never should've lied and I regret it every day. If I could go back in time and talk some sense into my old self, I would tell him the truth. Because in hindsight, I know Toby would've helped me reconnect with my family even if I wasn't a dating co—

A throat clears and I yank my gaze up from the computer screen. A client stands on the other side of the counter. I didn't see her walk in. In fact, I didn't notice that a whole line of clients have been waiting for me to finish whatever it is I'm doing on the computer. Wow. I really *am* off my game today.

I force a customer service smile and pull up the schedule. "Hi, yes. Mrs. Collins? I've got you checked in for your leg wax. You're esthetician will be with you in a moment."

I finish checking in the patrons all while knowing I need to delete that letter before anyone sees it. It simmers in the back of my mind even as I cash out the last client in line.

"I'm so sorry to bother you, dear." Mrs. Collins returns to the counter after her wax. That didn't take long at all considering that I've just cleared the line and was about to delete my letter. "But do you mind showing me the bathroom?"

I smile and point to a hallway past the whirlpool footbaths. "Just down that way and to the left."

Mrs. Collins furrows her brow. "Where?"

I roll my eyes internally, but I know that this spa can be a bit of a labyrinth, especially for new clients. And with Toby's words fresh on my mind, I walk her to the restrooms.

On my way there, I see Nichole seated in a massage chair with her feet soaking in a hot bath. But when I return, I see that she's gone, and the tub has been drained. By the time I've returned to the reception desk, Toby's gone gone, too, and so is his client. I try not to think about his lunch date as I delete my poorly written two weeks' notice.

歸來

Homecoming

The sunset is so orange that the air tastes like Dreamsicles. It bleeds with the gold hues seeping through store windows as Moore Plaza closes down. I'm about to sit under a streetlamp to wait for Mom when she pulls up to the curb. As much as I need a moment to mope, I'm relieved to see her here.

I climb into the passenger seat. My favorite song plays over the radio as Mom asks, "How was work?"

She's probably fishing for small talk and not genuinely curious. But writing out that two weeks' notice got me going, and now I can't stop. "I'm going to quit my job."

Mom pulls out of the parking lot as her gaze pans my way. "Why? I thought you loved working there."

She accelerates onto the highway while I spew everything that's festered in my stomach. Originally, I'd only wanted to share the pieces about Toby. But the full story doesn't make sense unless I mention Granny Eloise, too. I know Mom's probably hurt to hear that I was trying to find my bio mom. In another life, I'd never even have the option of telling her this. But as the thick rope of my lies loosens around my ribs, I realize this conversation is also two years overdue.

The skin around my nose is dry from rubbing it with the drive-through napkins Mom keeps in her glove compartment.

My eyes are swollen and puffy. I rip off my strip lashes and set them beside the wet teardrops drying on my jeans. And before I know it, Mom's pulling into the hotel parking lot.

She hasn't said a word this entire time. Even though we need to go inside, Mom sits in the driver's seat with the engine on. Maybe she's not saying anything because she's trying to figure out what our dynamic is now. She's still my mom, but I imagine it can't be easy sharing that title with another woman she's never met before.

Finally, she clears her throat. "That's a lot for you to go through."

I sniffle and glance her way. Doesn't she have anything to say about my family history search? I'm trying to focus on her expression—to read what I can't hear in her voice. But she's looking out the windshield like she's lost in thought, and all I can do is rub my stuffy nose and wait for her to continue.

"I've wanted to cook Taiwanese food for you, but I've been too scared it won't taste good." Her voice is just loud enough to not be muffled by the air-conditioning. "I've thought about enrolling you in Chinese school, but I wasn't sure if that's even close enough to Taiwan. I wasn't even sure that was something you wanted. But at the very least, I should've asked how you felt instead of waiting for you to come to me about it. Because if I had, you might not be so desperate for belonging that you lost yourself along the way. I feel like I've failed you as a mother. And I wish I could take that back."

It's been a long time since I've cried like this. It's the kind of sobbing that physically hurts—the kind that leaves my vocal cords raw and clenches all my muscles at once. The last time I did this was at Dad's bedside while an IV dripped into veins of stagnant blood. And yet here I am, biting back this wave because I never realized how validating it was to hear her admit she could've done more. After all, she already helped Mavis with her bio dad search. It's long past time for her to help me with my bio family search, too.

"They have some language programs at the U of U," Mom continues, pulling up classes on her phone. "If you want to go to college in Taiwan, I'll help you get there. You don't need Toby to teach you Mandarin. I'll find someone better."

I blot my eyes with my napkin. The paper comes away wet and smudged with blue eye shadow and black liner. I nod slowly. "Thanks, Mom. For trying."

Mom sinks back into her seat as a weary smile lifts across her face. Instead of reaching for the keys and turning off the car, she continues. "I know it seems hard right now with all that's going on. And I know you want to give up. But don't lose sight of what you love. This job makes you happy, and I don't think you should let it go just because you made a mistake. Take your time and think about it first, okay?"

Think about it. Meditate on it. It's not just time to start telling the truth, it's time to start living it, too. Holding on to the past is only going to prevent me from stepping into my future. And my future is about belonging somewhere I've always wanted to be but never realizing I've had it all along.

I wipe my eyes one last time. "You're right. I do need to think about this. And I know exactly how I'm going to do it."

We must first believe in ourselves before we can become our best selves. I think I've finally figured out what Dad's mantra is really all about. Except, Dad worded it wrong. Sort of. To believe implies I need to imagine the version of me I want to be, and not trust in who I am inherently. And I know who I am. I suppose I always have.

I'm a wonderer. I will never stop questioning where I come from, who my parents are, and what would've happened if I'd told Toby the truth. It seemed like a burden to question so many things all at once. But because these questions are a part of me, it also means that no matter where I go—California, Utah, or Taiwan—they'll never be forgotten.

Which is why I've come to a Mormon church building on a random Tuesday night. Toby may have only had me dip my toes into Mandarin lessons, but that's not going to stop me from finally reaching out to the family members I have—the ones who can answer what Dad couldn't.

The genealogy office hasn't been opened yet. To pass the time, I read from the book Rayleigh let me borrow and dive headfirst into the cessation of attachments—Nirodha. When I first read about it, I thought that Ya-Fang had let go of me because of her beliefs. But the more I study, the more I realize it's not really about rejecting, it's about accepting what is. Just like Dad's mantra.

I'm about to finish reading this chapter when the jingle of a heavy key chain pulls my attention away from the book. A church worker in a gray suit unlocks the genealogy office. He spots me sitting in the foyer and smiles. "You're here early."

I shut the book and cross the foyer. "Actually, this is long overdue."

The gentleman props the door open for me, and I step inside the office. It's still hot in this cramped room, so I turn on the fans, then take a seat at Granny Eloise's chair. This is the computer with PanGenea downloaded onto it. And in no time, I have the window pulled up.

I scroll to Ya-Fang's profile and look at the picture I walked away from when Granny Eloise first discovered it. It looks as if it was taken in the early eighties. A mother and father sit in the middle of a couch as four children scatter around them. They all wear traditional silk clothing—clothing I can't name to save my life. Banners of Chinese lettering drop behind them, and I wish I understood what they said. But there's one thing I'm fairly certain of in this picture. Ya-Fang is the girl with pigtails on her mother's lap. These are my grandparents. And the boys standing around them with shaved heads are my uncles.

Uncles.

Three of them. And it looks like Ya-Fang was the oldest. She was a big sister, just like me. There's no way to directly message the librarians who upload this information into PanGenea. But what if there's a way around it? Instead of waiting for someone to contact me, I upload my own bio. Even though Ya-Fang is dead, at least one of her brothers must be alive. One of my three uncles might be uploading this information on her behalf.

I click on the plus icon between the picture of my biologi-cal mother and father and start filling out the information that's not already there. Then, in the overview, I leave a message.

My name is Catie Carlson and I'm trying to reconnect with my Taiwanese family. When I was five years old, my parents, Roderick and Ya-Fang Carlson, divorced and I was brought to America. I've lost ties to my Taiwanese heritage. I've forgotten my first language. But I need closure on what really happened in Taipei, Taiwan. What was the real reason for my parents' divorce? In addition, I'd love to know more about who my parents were before I was born. Any information will be much appreciated. In turn, I can provide more information on my father following this separation. My email is listed below.

I read and reread my letter before uploading it onto Pan-Genea. The moment I hit Enter, a notification pops up on my screen. *We appreciate your submission. A PanGenea librarian will verify this information before allowing it to be accessed by other users. Thank you for your patience.*

I groan. Seriously? There's a chance this won't even be made public? How the heck are my uncles supposed to see this, then? Before my frustration can rise to a boiling point, I exhale deeply. Something tells me everything will be okay.

Even though I'm alone in this small room, the hot air from the computers makes me feel like people are crowding around me. I imagine Dad's hand on my shoulder. He's squeezing it as if to say *good job, kiddo!* I can hear his deep voice and feel the scratch of his stubble against my cheek as he kisses it. And Ya-Fang, too. She's stroking my hair, astonished that someone who looks so much like her has grown into someone like me. We're a family again. And I know they'll be watching as I take my time coming home to them.

附口袋粉紅休閒裙

A Pink Sundress with Pockets

The week is a blur of work, hotel, and checking my emails. I try not to think about Toby during my free time. When I catch myself eavesdropping on the conversations he has with his clients, I read a passage from the book Rayleigh lent me. And I check my email. Still nothing, but I'm not sure what to expect. How often does a genealogy librarian add to their index?

Eventually, Friday rolls around. I've survived an entire week of not talking to Toby about anything other than work-related things. And I haven't gotten any more complaints about my customer service. Mom was right. There's no point in writing out a two weeks' notice. I *do* like this job, even if it's a lot of work. This is somewhere that makes me feel I belong, with or without Toby.

It's midday at the salon and I'm shelving products. Cardboard boxes are piled in the corner, waiting to be crushed. The angle of the high sun shines directly into my eyes, and I squint at the conditioner labels. Between the blow-dryers, I can hardly hear the music strumming through the speakers.

"Catie?" A voice cuts through the noise.

I spin around and find myself facing Toby. Even though I don't want to, I can't help but take in his all-black uniform, the way the herbal scent of shampoo clings to his skin. And . . . he isn't wearing his apron. Strange. Maybe the strings broke, or he hasn't had a chance to wash it yet.

"Hi," I say, swallowing hard. "Did you need something?"

"Nah." Toby shakes his head. "I was just letting you know that I'm heading out for the rest of the day. I'm blocked off for the afternoon to set up for an event."

"Right!" I exclaim, awkwardly thunking my forehead. I've been so focused on keeping my distance that I never asked why his schedule was blocked. My gut twists. Is he going on another date with Nichole? Things must be going well for him, and if he's happy, I'm happy. Even though I'll never stop wanting his happiness to be with me.

"Have fun," I say as sincerely as I can.

"I'll see you later, okay?" Toby says as he moves toward the door.

Later? As in tomorrow? Because I don't work Saturdays. But before I can say anything, Toby is gone.

I finally clock out of work. Between the daily grind wearing on me and needing a distraction from Toby's second date with Nichole, I really don't want to go back to the hotel. So, I pull my phone from my pocket and text Mavis.

> **ME:** I know this is the most Utah thing in the world, but do you and Rayleigh want to get soda with me tonight?

I stare at my phone waiting for a response. Mavis looks at my message but leaves me on Read. Maybe she's asking Rayleigh for her input. I wait for the three dots to appear as I sit at my usual spot under the streetlamp. Eventually, Mom's car pulls into the parking lot, but Mavis still hasn't answered. Whatever. We can figure it out when I get back to the hotel.

I buckle up beside Mom as she tells me about the Mandarin tutors she's found at U of U. Some of them are returned missionaries who want to stay fluent in the languages they've learned. Others are foreign exchange students looking to make some extra cash for the summer. Mom even coaches a hurdler from Taiwan who speaks Mandarin, Cantonese, and Hokkien. She gives me her number and I save it in my phone. My thumbs hover over the screen as I contemplate introducing myself to this potential tutor. But my fingers refuse to type, because all I can wonder is if I'm going to like her teaching style or just miss Toby's.

We pull up to the hotel and I slide my cell back inside my pocket. I can text this tutor later. For now, I'm celebrating the end of the workweek and my last night at this hotel.

Mom pushes the door open to our room. She immediately flops down in her twin bed before pulling out a book and turning the reading lamp on. Meanwhile, Mavis and Rayleigh are sprawled out on the couch. They stop talking the moment they spot me. Rayleigh coughs in a way that seems practiced, not like she has a cold. Mavis has a mischievous quirk to her lips as if she's mid-gossip when I walk in.

"Did you want to go out?" I ask as Mavis adjusts herself

on the couch. I'm just now realizing she's wearing a black sundress over her swimsuit. In fact, Rayleigh is dressed for the pool, too, but she's got an oversize tee and shorts over her attire.

"We decided to go swimming again," Mavis says, leaning her elbow against the couch's armrest.

I wrinkle my nose. I don't particularly feel like going to the pool, but I'm itching to leave this hotel room. "Sure. I'll come."

Mavis jumps to her feet. "Wear your pink sundress!"

My brows pinch. "Why? We didn't change into sundresses the last time we went to the pool."

Mavis casually waves a hand in the air. "Cuz it's cute and comfy. Come on—I already pulled it out for you." Mavis points to the kitchen table. Sure enough, it's neatly pressed on the table next to my washed two-piece.

I cross the laminate floor and lift the dress up. I haven't seen this thing since last summer. I like to say it's one-of-a-kind because I found it at a thrift shop. The top is haltered, and this shade of peachy pink complements my skin perfectly. The ruffles along the waist hug my figure better than anything else in my closet. Plus it has pockets. Deep ones.

"Where did you find it?" I ask.

Mavis shrugs as she stuffs her toes into blue plastic flip-flops. "In one of the boxes. Now hurry up! Rayleigh and I are ready to go."

I roll my eyes and do as I'm told. Moments later, I'm standing in front of the bathroom mirror admiring the way the dress falls just above my thighs, making my full legs look longer.

"Ready?" When I turn toward the couch again, I find Mavis and Rayleigh hovered around Mavis's phone. A flash of irritation rises in me. My sister is the one who told me to hurry up, but she's the one dawdling.

"Can you text Alex later?" I ask, arms crossed.

Mavis looks up from her phone. "I'm not texting Alex. I was actually ordering food for you. The delivery guy dropped it off in the lobby. You should go get it."

"What? I thought we were going to the pool."

"We are," Mavis insists. "But don't you want to eat first?"

I narrow my eyes. There's something she isn't telling me. And judging by the way Rayleigh's face contorts, it's clear she's in on it, too. "Why are you guys being weird?"

Mavis scoffs and tosses her phone into her purse. "Look, do you want your food or not? It's getting cold."

I study Mavis's face, but she just looks impatient. When my stomach rumbles, I decide it's not worth digging into. "Fine. I'll be right back. And this food better be good."

I slip into a pair of sandals, then patter down the hall. Did she really order me food? Or is this a prank? And isn't there a rule about not swimming for thirty minutes after you eat or something? Maybe Alex ordered it for her, but she doesn't want to go downstairs to get it. That's such a Mavis thing to do. And if that turns out to be the case, I'm just going to eat it at the breakfast bar down here, then bring up the empty box for her.

The elevator dings, then opens up to the lobby. The modern aesthetic seemed classy when I first arrived. But now, the shapes and colors feel like an elementary school class-room. Stiff yellow couches line the lobby walls in an L shape.

Paintings in primary colors dot the walls by the front desk. If it weren't for the dusty chandelier hanging above the rotating doors, I would've assumed this place used to be a day care.

I strut up to the receptionist at the front desk, the ruffles on my dress swishing with every step. "Hey, I'm here to pick up some food."

The employee tilts his head. He looks like a college kid back for the summer. "I'm not sure about food, but some guy just left something for a girl named . . . Catty?"

"It's Catie, and that's me," I confirm, and then the employee hands me a small white box. A pink ribbon secures the lid in place. When Mavis said she'd gotten me food, I imagined pizza, or a giant bowl of phở. But perhaps she's gotten me some cookies instead. This box is small enough for maybe half a dozen macarons.

Slowly, I untie the ribbon. But when I flip the lid open, there isn't a collection of cookies to greet me. What lies inside is completely inedible because it's a small magenta *bow tie*.

I blink down at the folded cloth. Maybe this package is for someone else and my food hasn't been delivered yet. But then I catch sight of a handwritten note tucked under the bow tie. It's the same color as the dye Toby spilled on me when we first met.

Dear Catie,
You are hereby invited to a tie-breaker date. (Get it? Tie?) Please adorn your bow tie, then proceed outside. Your chariot awaits.
Sincerely, Toby

I pull out the card and read it. Twice.

Slowly the pieces fall into place. Before everything fell apart, Toby had said he was going to take me on a tiebreaker date. But I never imagined it would be a *tie*-breaker.

I look at my name on the note again, then to the magenta bow tie. I feel like I can't breathe again.

Oh. My. God.

I shake my head to myself as I pull it out of the box. No. No. No. This doesn't make sense. He barely speaks to me at work. He's happy with Nichole. But as I stand here gaping at the box, the ribbon, the note, and the bow tie, I'm wondering if he actually went on a date with her at all. Or did something else happen between them?

My fingers trace the silky fabric folded into perfect triangles. Toby left work early. Is this what he was *setting up* while I was at the salon? I have too many questions and no one to ask them. At least not right now, because apparently, I have a chariot awaiting me.

With shaking fingers, I wrap the bow tie around my neck. The vibrant color blends with the warm hues in my sundress. *Mavis.* She was in on it the entire time.

A giggle sounds from across the lobby. My gaze darts to the noise just as I catch a flash of shadows slipping behind a corner near the fire escape. My sister and Rayleigh. Have they been watching me this entire time?

"You guys!" I exclaim, marching toward them. They must've sprinted down here the moment I left the room. "What are you doing?"

I turn the corner. Mavis is smirking as Rayleigh fans her flushed face.

"How long have you guys known about this?" I ask, holding up the now empty box.

Rayleigh jabs a thumb to Mavis. "I didn't do anything. Mavis has been plotting this since you left for work this morning."

Mavis jabs an elbow into Rayleigh's ribs. "Shh! Don't spoil it."

"What's going on?" I ask again, sternly this time.

Mavis zips her lips and throws away an invisible key. "It's a secret."

I roll my eyes. Secrets are the worst. Especially ones that catch me so off guard that I can't take the time to appreciate how well crafted they are.

"Is Toby here?" I ask, glancing out the lobby doors. A car waits just outside, but it isn't Toby's Mitsubishi.

"I guess you'll have to go out there and see," Mavis sings slyly.

I tug on the bow tie until it lies on my collarbones like a necklace. It isn't on tight, and yet, I still am finding it difficult to catch my breath.

My sister grabs my shoulders and shoves me outside. "Come on! You're taking too long."

The breezy summer air greets me outside the hotel. I peer inside the car, expecting to find Toby in the driver's seat. But instead, Alex is the one gesturing for me to jump in. Mavis nudges me into the back seat as she slides into the front. Rayleigh nestles herself beside me, clearly giddy with excitement.

"Wait," I cut in. "Whose idea was this?"

"Whose do you think?" Alex asks. "I'm just here to give you a ride. There are more surprises to come."

I still haven't wrapped my mind around the gift Toby left me. So much time and energy must've gone into thinking up this surprise tiebreaker date. But I wasn't expecting to be on Toby's mind at all now that he's got Nichole. *And* I thought he hated me. What exactly is the dynamic of our relationship now? It seems like Toby wants to let go of the past and forgive me, but what if I'm projecting my wants all over again?

"Are you ready, Catie?" Alex asks, spinning around to face the windshield.

I press my fingers against the bow tie just to make sure it's really there. "Ready as I'll ever be."

對決

Tiebreaker

Alex drives us up the slopes of Salt Lake City, following the route to Toby's house. As much as I try to pry information from Alex and Mavis, no one says a word about what Toby has planned. I can't even get anything out of Rayleigh, because she confidently claims she knows as much as I do. Finally, we stop in Toby's driveway. I stare up at the house I've already visited twice, yet I feel like a stranger.

"Toby's in the backyard," Alex says, cutting the engine.

I climb out of the car and swallow the knot in my throat. My sandals patter along the concrete as I follow the pathway around Toby's house. Through his giant glass windows, I can see that no one is inside except Munch potato-ing on the coffee table.

Soft music plays in the distance. I round the corner of his home and step onto the patio. An outdoor speaker is set up by his back door. A guitar ballad floats through the air while crickets harmonize with the leaves rustling in the summer breeze. I look up and see magenta lights strung from the back door all the way across the glittering pool. They swoop above a patio table adorned with a white tablecloth. In the center of the table, candles flicker, flanked by two chairs. One chair is empty. In the other sits Toby.

Toby stands the moment he sees me. He's wearing formal slacks and a white button-up. His overgrown lavender hair is swept over his forehead and creates a perfect effortless wave. And, of course, dangling around his collar is a magenta tie.

My body buzzes as if my blood has been replaced with cola. Every nerve tells me to tread across the patio slowly. I'm still not sure what's going on even though it's becoming more apparent. I just don't know that I'm ready to accept the signs.

"Hey," Toby says, and I spot a dent in his lip where he's chewed it too hard.

I suck in a long breath. "Is . . . is this all for me?"

Toby looks around as if double-checking that everything is perfect. "Yes."

I shake my head in disbelief. "But why?"

Toby tugs on his tie as if he needs to loosen it for this conversation. "I saw what you left on the computer. Your two weeks' notice."

My eyes widen against my will, my thoughts swirling. How did he see it when I deleted it? Unless—he must have checked his own client out while I was showing Mrs. Collins to the restroom. While opening up all of the tabs, he must have seen my letter. My ramblings. I want to double over with embarrassment.

"For the record, people don't usually, um, confess their feelings in a two weeks' notice. Usually, they just say 'thanks for the opportunity, but I'm peacing out.'" Toby smiles like he's trying to defuse the tension, but it does nothing to wash away my humiliation.

"I-I wasn't planning on—you know—turning it in," I stammer. "Just had to get my thoughts on paper. I really am sorry for everything. For lying and . . . for hurting you."

"No, I got that." Toby grins before biting his lip again. "But I'm glad you wrote it out. I needed to know how you really felt about me because . . . well, I started thinking about what would happen if you really did leave the salon. And . . . I don't want you to go."

I want to be touched by that sentiment, but I can't be. "What do you mean? I thought you were with Nichole."

Toby slides his hands into his pockets sheepishly. "I went on one lunch date with her and realized . . . she's not who I want. She may've been my first crush. But you?" He looks at me with such intensity, I have to take a step back. "Catie, you're my first love language."

I can't believe this is happening. How long have I wanted Toby to think of me the way I think of him? And now it's here and all I can do is bask in the sunlight of it.

"You're not mad that I . . . you know . . . lied?" I say.

Toby's shoulders tense as he shakes his head. "What you did wasn't right. But I know you're sorry." He hesitates. "Besides, I'd rather laugh with you than be mad at you. And I've missed going on practice dates with you."

I grin, tucking a strand of hair behind my ear. "Well, thank you for putting this date together. I mean, *tiebreaker.*" I gesture to the lights, the tablecloth, and the music. "It's perfect."

"What can I say," Toby says, dimples popping. "I learned from the best. But . . . I was kind of hoping this wouldn't be a practice date. I think I've graduated to taking you out on a real one."

It's as if he's dropped a Mentos in my cola and now all the bubbles are building up in my brain. Am I about to pass out? Is this the literal definition of swooning?

"Catie?" Toby's voice catches me before I can lose my balance. "Um, is that okay? Do you . . . I mean, I guess I should've asked you if you wanted to make this official instead of . . . *crap*. Did I mess up?"

I shake my head to clear my thoughts. "No! I mean, yes! I mean—I love it. And yes, I want this to be real, too. No more practice dating?"

"No more practice dating." Toby gestures across the table, and I take a seat. Between the music and the way Salt Lake City glimmers like a backdrop behind him, Utah suddenly seems like the pinnacle of romance.

"I hope you're hungry, because I made some appe-*tie*-zers," Toby says, nodding down to the dishes.

I snort at his pun. Before me, a ball-shaped cover hides the entrée underneath. I pull off the cover and gape down at a perfect roll of sushi. Avocado slices blanket pillows of rice. Toasted sesame seeds dust the surface as dollops of eel sauce roll down the sides. My stomach rumbles again as my head fizzes with disbelief. Is there anything Toby can't cook?

"So cooking for me is clearly an act of service, but is this your idea of gift giving?" I tug on the bow-tie ribbon around my neck.

"I guess it kind of is, isn't it?" Toby smiles. "If I'm being honest, I saw it when I was at the mall with Nichole, and it made me think of you. I'm sorry for being too dense to see that I've had a crush on you since our first practice date. But I guess it took being with the wrong girl to make me realize I'd rather be with the one I love."

My lips quiver. Did he just say . . . ? The moon reflecting in Toby's saucer-sized eyes tells me that he's realized what he's said, too. I swear, even the guitar music scratches.

"*Love?*" I repeat.

Toby's Adam's apple slowly bobs. "Yeah. I love you, Catie. Wǒ ài nǐ."

Those are the words written in Dad's copy of *The Five Love Languages*. It seems so long ago since the last time someone told me that I was loved in my first language. And yet having that book fall down on my bed must've been his way of ensuring someone says it to me all over again.

"Wǒ yě ài nǐ," I reply. *I love you, too.* A phrase I didn't realize I'd be saying when I woke up this morning. But I'm grateful for the paths that led me to these words. "I like hearing you tell me how much you love me."

Toby chuckles. "Good, because I like telling you how much I love you. And since we're both coming clean, I think you should know that ever since our first practice date, I've wanted to tell you that." Toby glances away timidly before adding, "And I've wanted to kiss you."

He's so adorable that I can't help but giggle. "If you wanted to kiss me, then why didn't you?"

Toby rolls his eyes like I should already know the answer.

"You told me you had a boyfriend! Besides, I've never had a girlfriend before. What if I'm a bad kisser?"

Okay, that's a valid point. Great. New fear unlocked. Is this what first love is all about? Passion and awkwardness because neither of us really knows what we're doing? Too bad we don't have a *real* dating coach.

"Okay, be honest with me," I start. "When we were in your room studying Mandarin, did you want to—?"

"Oh, big-time," Toby says the words before I can finish my question. This time around, I know that he knows what I was going to ask.

"Toby!" I exclaim, half laughing and half relieved. "I freaking knew it! Ugh, you have no idea how many times I've played that night out in my head. You should've just kissed me then."

"But I wanted *you* to kiss *me*," Toby says. "I mean, look at you! You're gorgeous, you're hilarious—and you made up all those dates with no prior experience? How am I supposed to compete with that? Anybody would be lucky to be your boyfriend. That's why I had to write my feelings out in Mandarin. I couldn't find the courage any other way."

Of course. The note. That paper. The one I almost threw away but decided to stuff inside the pages of *The Five Love Languages*. "What did it say?"

Toby's eyes twinkle with the moon's blue light. "Wǒ sāle huǎng. I lied. Qíshí, wǒ hǎo xiǎng wěn nǐ. Actually, I really want to kiss you. Suīrán nǐ yǒu nán péngyǒu, wǒ háishì ài shàngle nǐ. Even though you have a boyfriend, I still fell in love with you. Mǒu tiān, wǒ xīwàng wǒ néng yǒnggǎn de yòng yīngyǔ gàosù nǐ. One day, I hope I can be brave enough to tell you in English. And I guess, I am now."

I've never heard poetry that makes me speechless. I can't believe I sat with this note all this time and never knew what it said.

"I'm sorry, too," Toby admits. "But I'm not sorry I fell for you. And I'm not sorry that I still want to kiss you now."

I find my voice somewhere tucked between my heart and my soul. "Then kiss me."

Toby stands up and walks around the table, closing the distance between us. He offers his hand and I take it, rising to my feet. The warmth of his skin comforts me as it has so many times before. He pulls me into him until I'm pressed against his chest. Toby's free hand cups my jaw and he cranes my face up until he's all I can see.

Toby's breath beats against my lips as I inch closer, rising to my tiptoes. This moment has occupied my fantasies for weeks now. I've pictured his touch on my hips, his breath on my tongue, and his heart in my hands. But now that it's here—now that I know just how little I know—I don't want to ruin our first kiss.

Our lips meet in the middle. Toby and I are tense. My jaw is clenched. His lips are stiff. My palm is flat against his chest while his hand holds my jaw. I'm not sure if my lips are lower than his or if they're off-center. But I'll take this awkwardness over pulling away. There's no one I'd rather be a novice with than Toby.

We part for a breath but instead of saying anything, our

lips meet again. And again. Each time his lips catch mine, my brain gets a little hazier. And each time his tongue grazes my teeth, I find myself relaxing into him.

Toby pulls me in tighter as if he'll never get enough of this. His palm loosens and he slides his arms around my back, hugging me with a longing that matches my own. My hands cup his cheeks, keeping him in place because this moment is mine for the taking and I'm holding on to it forever.

I kiss him until my lips burn. I kiss him for all the missed opportunities—for all the times we should've been honest with each other. I kiss him until I realize he's really good at this now. But so am I. Then I pull away with only one thing on my mind.

"Wǒ ài nǐ, Toby."

Toby's lips meet my cheek. "Wǒ yě ài nǐ, Catie."

第一次又第一次

Firsts

Our new apartment is in complete disarray. Bubble wrap balls in the center of the living room like a plastic tumbleweed. Cardboard boxes are flattened and stacked in the corner next to the new living room couch. All the windows are open to let out the smell of fresh paint. Every time a breeze blows in, crumpled bits of packing paper spiral around the room.

Mom, Mavis, and Alex are in the kitchen. Mavis matches silverware and slides the pieces dutifully into the drawers. Alex sits on the laminate floor opening boxes with the toothy edge of a kitchen knife. Mom stacks plates in the cupboard by the fridge while pots and pans go in the drawer under the stove.

Rayleigh has stayed to help us unpack. Besides, our apartment has a spare bedroom. If she ever needs more time away from her parents, she can always move back in with us.

"Hey, Mom," I call, stepping out of my bare-bones bedroom. "Have you seen my makeup tote?"

Mom brushes a strand of hair from her eyes as she tries to shimmy the toaster out of the box. "I'm not sure. Go ask your boyfriend."

I grin to myself. *Boyfriend.* Is that ever going to stop sounding like a treat? I hurry out of the apartment and down the spiral stairwell just outside the building. From the second-floor landing, the apartment's pool glimmers in the midday sun. Mavis wasn't kidding when she said this is the fanciest backdrop she's ever seen. The brilliant water is so clear, it resembles the water I'd find on the shores of the Bahamas.

I'm just about to drop down to the first floor when I recognize a flash of lilac hair sticking up from behind a stack of boxes. At the very top is my makeup tote zipped up so that nothing tumbles out. Toby is trudging up the stairs and probably can't see me from the steps. "Do you need some help?"

"No, I've got it." Toby's reply is either muffled by the cardboard or strained by the weight of the boxes.

I laugh to myself. "Seriously, I can help."

"Hey, this is my act of service, babe," Toby insists.

Babe. My cheeks bloom at the way it rolls off Toby's tongue. It's as if speaking this word of affirmation is a reflex for him.

I give in to Toby's persistence with a sigh. "Well, then I suppose I should just say thank you and let you help me."

Toby meets me on the landing. He stops for a moment to catch his breath, then turns and gives me a quick kiss on the cheek. "Yes, you should."

The imprint of his lips on my skin sends my toes curling. I giggle as I follow my boyfriend up the stairwell and guide him into my room. Carefully, the two of us set the boxes down beside my freshly made bed. It's nothing fancy—just a wooden frame that's been painted dark cherry. A matching dresser stands in the corner. Half of the drawers are open so that I can figure out what clothes go where. It's not luxurious and it's nowhere near as big of a bedroom as the one in Aunt Joanna's house, but it's home.

Toby unpacks my stuffed animals and lines them up on

my bed. I fold my clothes into the dresser as Toby matches my loose socks. I line Dad's old books on my bookshelf and place Toby's note right next to it—framed a few days ago. I still can't read the Hanzi, but I've memorized what it says. I angle it toward my bed so it can be the first thing I see when I wake up and the last thing I see before I fall asleep.

The sun sets on the first night of our new home. Mom orders us some food. Sizzling pizza and red soda cups join the clutter of flattened boxes and bubble wrap. Mavis sits on a bar stool in the kitchen giggling with Alex about the plastic bowl of fruit they brought as a housewarming gift. The rest of us are huddled in the living room, chomping on pizza and watching reruns on our furnished TV.

Toby's arm wraps around me, and I sink into his chest. His fingers trace the shape of my hips. Ever since he discovered the thrill of physical touch, it's become one of his favorite love languages—though he still claims he loves them all equally. To be fair, the love languages are a bunch of outdated suggestions. The language of love can be expressed by anyone if they are honest with their feelings—both to those they love and to themselves.

Truth.

As I'm finishing the last of my pizza, my phone vibrates. I pull it out and read the newest notification on my screen. I blink. Then blink again. This can't be real. But when I blink for a *third* time, I see that the email really is there.

I sit up quickly, still gaping at my phone.

"You okay?" Toby asks, pulling his arm back.

I nod. "Yeah, just give me a sec."

I excuse myself to the patio. I slide the door shut behind me and for the first time all day, I'm alone. From the third floor, I have the perfect view of the distant Utah mountain range. A rose gold sunset dusts the peaks—a sight that's the complete opposite of San Diego's icy blue shores.

I lean against the railing, my fingers hovering over the email before I finally open it.

Dear Catie,

Hi! I think you're my niece!

My name is Linn Li Hua. I am the mother of two lovely parakeets and one daughter, Jasmine—all of whom talk way too much. During the day, I work as an event planner in Sacramento, California. In the night, I spend way too much time doing genealogy and wishing my parakeets weren't such sleepyheads so they could keep me company.

*I saw your bio on PanGenea and wanted to reach out. I believe I'm married to your mom's brother Wei. I saw that you have a story to share and I am eager to listen! Feel free to email me back, or you can friend me on Facebook here: **Linn Li Hua**.*

I look forward to hearing from you!

Most likely your auntie,

Li Hua

PS—I've attached some pictures so you'll know I'm not a random internet stalker. Take a look! I think you'll recognize some familiar faces. Okay, toot aloo!

I read the email over and over, memorizing every word. I realize I'm crying and blink away the wetness to ensure I'm not missing a sentence, a phrase. I really do have a biological family. Somewhere on this big blue rock, someone else shares my flesh and blood. I'm this much closer to understanding the story that wrote me. All the work—learning Mandarin, breaking my heart by digging into my past—it's going to be worth it just to meet the people who can tell me stories about my biological parents. Stories about *me*.

I rub my stuffy nose before tapping on the attachment in Auntie Li Hua's email. When it opens, I'm gifted with a collection of thirty-seven photos. The first one is of a familiar face—Ya-Fang. She's in a hospital gown and her stomach is almost as big as the smile on her face.

The next picture is of an infant with a blotchy pink face. Her eyes aren't open yet, but she's already got a full head of dark hair. She's in Ya-Fang's arms, but peering over her shoulder is someone else. My heart does a somersault when I recognize his youthful, healthy face. Dad. His cheeks are so round. His blond hair is so thick. His eyes are tired but also full of excitement—this is the day he met me. I'm looking at the first photograph ever taken of my biological family. Mine. Truly mine.

The sliding glass door scrapes against the wood as someone opens it. Toby joins me on the patio, his arms wrapping around my waist. His lips find the skin behind my ear. "Are you okay? You've been out here for a while."

My voice is hoarse from crying. If I try to answer, I'll inevitably break down again. So I show him the email.

Toby cups my hands as he reads my phone. I watch him swipe through all thirty-seven attachments, pinching and zooming in so that he can see the fine details in these old photos. Eventually, he stops on one. It's a picture of a teenage boy with his arm around a girl exactly his height. They have the same smile. The same cheeks. The same pointed chin as me.

"Holy crap," Toby breathes. "Is this your uncle Wei? He looks just like your māma."

I'm finally able to breathe and my eyes aren't leaking anymore. "He looks just like *me*."

"Whoa." Toby sounds more mind-blown than I am. "How did your auntie reach out to you?"

I clear my throat to make room for a response. "I posted my email on PanGenea. She just responded to my note."

"That's amazing. She seems like fun." Toby chuckles. "I think she loves her birds a little too much."

I giggle back. "Yeah, I can see that."

We stand like this—Toby wrapped around me like a blanket, and me staring at my phone until the screen turns to black.

"Sacramento isn't that far away," Toby muses. "If you save up enough money, you could go see them in person. Fly out for a week. You still have the second half of summer to enjoy. Maybe you should take some time off and go visit."

I don't need to shut my eyes to picture it. A straight flight from Salt Lake City to Sacramento. I'd get to return to my home state. I'd get to meet my uncle. He's older now, but would he still see his sister's face in my features?

"I could," I say.

But I don't need to leave right now. Not when we just settled into our new home. Toby is right: I have the entire second half of summer. Considering the fact that I started this summer off with no ties to my Taiwanese heritage, I think I deserve a chance to relish finding an auntie.

I square my shoulders. "I'll see how much money I have saved up by the end of the summer. If I have enough, I'll fly out to see her before school this fall."

Toby nods. "I can't think of a better way for you to end your summer."

I spin around and loop my arms over Toby's neck. In his embrace, I'm already home. And from somewhere between the stars above, I know my parents know that. They haven't been here in person to watch me find myself this summer. But they've been here all along—Dad teaching me to fall in love, and Ya-Fang reminding me that I can find peace in simply *being*. Both of them guiding me back to Toby as if to say they've given me their approval to date him.

Toby kisses me and I melt into the softness of his lips, inhaling his scent. Wintergreen and vanilla. Patchouli and sandalwood. Brown sugar and milk tea. His hands trace my spine down to my hips. I sink deeper into his arms, the broken pieces of my heart put back into place, little by little. Right now, there's no place I'd rather be than here with my first love language.

Author's Note

Though *First Love Language* is liberally inspired by my own life, it is, above all else, a work of fiction. Like Catie, I lost ties with my Taiwanese heritage when my biological parents divorced. I also watched my father die of colon cancer when I was a teenager. It wasn't until my late twenties that I realized how deeply these events shattered my self-identity. I was twenty-seven when I wrote the first draft of *First Love Language*. In it, I took Catie on the journey I wished I'd gone on when I was ten years younger.

In addition to Catie's family dynamics and identity crisis, I also struggled to learn English in elementary school. As a result, I sucked at reading. But the cool thing about this ✦ traumatizing experience ✦ is that if I'd never hated reading as deeply as I did when I was a child, I never would've become a writer. It turns out, reading isn't so bad when you get to *create* the words in books. And if I could make reading fun for me, then maybe some other reluctant reader would enjoy my words, too.

Writing *First Love Language* has been deeply therapeutic. Born from the experiences that shaped me most is a work of art dedicated to people like me. The ones living in a perpetual identity crisis. The ones who were told derogatorily to *speak English*. The children of divorce. The adoptees. The queer

Mormons. The kids who lost a parent when they were still too young to understand the concept of *gone*.

If you find yourself like Catie, walking around with an emptiness so large it could swallow galaxies, please know that you're not alone. The Tobys who are fluent in pain are right there with you.

Acknowledgments

I'd like to thank my champion of a literary agent, Ann Rose, for seeing something in my manuscript that no one else saw. After countless rounds of revisions, this manuscript is almost nothing like the original draft. But you saw its potential, and you believed in me enough to take me on as a client. I am forever grateful to you and to my fellow Rosebuds for their unconditional support.

To my fantastic editor, Elizabeth Lee, thank you for giving me a chance on *First Love Language*. Thank you for seeing its potential and for your remarkable insight. You've challenged me in all the best ways as an author, and you've helped me discover things about myself that I hadn't yet realized. This story is so dear to my heart, and there could never have been a better fit for *First Love Language* than you.

To Jenna and Cindy—thank you for being some of the first people to read this manuscript waaaay back before Ann even scooped it up. Thank you for your confidence and your reassurance that it was worthy of representation. Thank you for being there to watch me land an agent, find an editor, reveal the cover, and so much more. Y'all have been with me since the beginning, and I'm so grateful to have enthusiastic family members to share my milestones with.

To my dad—I wish you were here. I remember you being

there for me when I fell in love with writing. Do you remember when you stayed up till 4 a.m. typing up my storybook about orcas because it was due the next day? I do. I was in awe of you for doing it because you knew how hard reading and writing were for me at that time. Remember that letter you wrote me before you passed? You told me, "You don't have to be the smartest person on the planet; you just have to try your hardest." And I did just that. I tried for twelve years to become a traditionally published author. And now, I am. I wish you could be here to see how far I've come. Thanks for rooting for me even when I was held back in fourth grade for being so far behind everyone else my age.

To my mom. My *real* mom. I cannot believe I found you while editing this book. Like Catie, I have missed you every day of my life. You were at the forefront of my mind while I wrote *First Love Language*, and I still cannot believe that I manifested our reunification through these words. We have so much catching up to do. But for now, I'm still in awe that we have the same smile. Thank you for being my inspiration. See you soon in Taiwan.

To my Woolly Mammoth, my best friend, the love of my life, the father of my three pups, and my most favorite person in the whole wide everything. I love you, my guy. Remember how on our first date you were like, "So what do you do for funzies?" and I was like, "Oh, I'm a writer or whatever." Well, now I'm getting paid to *be* said writer or whatever. No for real, thanks for being my shoulder to cry on when I spent years answering rejection email after rejection email after rejection email after rejection email . . . Thanks for never giving up on our love and for fighting for this marriage . . . because now you get to be the inspiration for all the love interests I write. Yaaay!

To my writing buddy, my reading buddy, my dance buddy, my theater buddy, and my bestest childhood friend—Hunter Ian Perfection. Thanks for being my OG. Gawd, can you believe we were teenagers swapping books, critiquing each other's writing, and going to each other's place for school lunch—now we're adults with exciting freaking publishing news?!?! AND I'm writing these acknowledgments at a time when you're on the cusp of something freaking life-changing?!?! Duuuude. IDK what secret spell we cast all those years ago, but man, are things finally coming together for us! I cannot wait to see where your career takes you!!

To my Taiwanese friends and beta readers who helped me bring this story to life—Jo, Lisa, and Cindy—thank you for helping me feel like I was enough despite being cheated out of what is truly mine.

To my siblings Josh, Mike, Tory, Dru, Jess, Matt, Hannah, and Monah—y'all have known this was my dream ever since we were sharing seats in our infamous fifteen-passenger van and terrorizing our poor guinea pigs. I love that despite all the chaos and trauma bonding, y'all always believed I could do it. You treated it like it was a fact. Thank you for that.

To the incredible team at Penguin Workshop—thank you for your careful reads, your attention to detail, and all the effort you've poured into making this book sparkle. Special thank you to Babeth Lafon for capturing the moods of *First Love Language* in your cover illustration. To Mary Claire Cruz for the stunning design work. And to Zhui Ning Chang for your brilliant attention to Taiwanese language and history. The translations in the chapter headings would not have been an iconic addition to this story without you. Thank you for giving readers a chance to appreciate a truly beautiful language. I feel so lucky and honored to have been given a talented team to bring this story to life!

To Nicole Chung and Shannon Gibney, thank you for carving out a space for adoptees. I am honored to be featured in *When We Become Ours* because without that anthology, I never would've been connected to the countless adoptees that have felt seen through our words. And to all my blurbers, thank you for reading my story and supporting my work!

And to you, the reader. Thank you for taking the time to read *First Love Language*. While writing this, I tried to imagine who you would be. I wanted to be truly authentic with my storytelling because authenticity and vulnerability are aspects of our humanity that link us together. Thank you for giving me a space to be that for you. I hope you saw a piece of yourself in Catie's story.